FISH EATS LION
New Singaporean Speculative Fiction

edited by

Jason Erik Lundberg

infinity plus

Published by infinity plus

www.infinityplus.co.uk

Follow @ipebooks on Twitter

Originally published by Math Paper Press, 2012.

ISBN-13: 978-1502984821

ISBN-10: 1502984822

BY THE SAME EDITOR

*The Epigram Books Collection of Best New Singaporean Short Stories:
Volume One*
LONTAR: The Journal of Southeast Asian Speculative Fiction
A Field Guide to Surreal Botany (with Janet Chui)
Scattered, Covered, Smothered

As Author
Strange Mammals
Embracing the Strange: The Transformative Impact of Speculative Fiction
The Alchemy of Happiness
Red Dot Irreal
The Time Traveler's Son
Four Seasons in One Day (with Janet Chui)
The Curragh of Kildaire (illustrated by Jamie Bishop)

CONTENTS

PREFACE

Jason Erik Lundberg

The Republic of Singapore is known by several monikers: The Garden City, The Lion City, The Little Red Dot, and The "Fine" Country (for the hefty fines implemented by the government to ensure cleanliness and order). All of these, including the last, have come from the top down, as a deliberate way to brand the country in such a way as to make it positively memorable, and hence appealing for foreign investment and tourism. Singapore is every day reinventing itself.

One way that this has been done is through the creation of the iconic symbol of the Merlion. The Merlion was designed and developed as a logo for the Singapore Tourism Board in 1964: a mythical creature with the head of a lion and the scaled body of a fish. The concept of the merlion is not original to Singapore; it occurs in art and heraldry throughout history in locations as diverse as India, Etruria, the United Kingdom, and the Philippines. However, Singapore is the only modern country to adopt the merlion as a national symbol, combining the nation's historical identity as a Malay fishing village with its nomenclature in Bahasa Melayu: *Singapura*, the Lion City. The Merlion statue created in 1972 and currently residing at Marina Bay, which continually gushes water into the Singapore River from its open leonine mouth, remains a popular tourist attraction.

Although the fabrication of the Merlion as a national symbol is an interesting example of reinvention, even more interesting is the process of deliberate myth-making. Singapore is constantly telling stories about itself, to investors, to skilled and educated foreign workers, to the organizers of international sporting events, but most of all to itself. The annual National Day Parade, celebrated each year on the 9th of August to commemorate Singapore's independence, is an hours-long immersion in narrative: a rah-rah observance of nationalism, a listing of the nation's accomplishments, and a reminder not to take for granted the affluence and racial harmony that the country now boasts. Underlying this is the theme that Singapore's citizens ought to show appreciation for what its leaders have achieved since 1965, a notion that invariably leads to a snarky counter-response from many people, and occasional confusion from students who uncritically (and incorrectly) parrot how former Prime Minister Lee Kuan Yew single-handedly hauled the nation out of the third-world muck and set it on its inevitable course toward first-world prosperity.

There is an inherent strangeness in constantly telling your own story that lends well to the writing of speculative fiction. Traditionally, fantasy and science fiction (and all the places in between) have not seen much popularity within Singaporean literature, other than sensationalist ghost stories that tap into the culture's deep folk-religious roots. It can be found, but one must specifically go looking for it, and very often it is disguised as more "literary" magic realism or fabulation. And yet, these core "paraliterary" genres are quite popular amongst the nation's readers, regularly appearing in the bestselling lists at chain bookstores like Books Kinokuniya. When Neil Gaiman was a featured guest of the 2009 Singapore Writers Festival, the queue for his signing line stretched over a thousand people from The Arts House down to the Singapore River.

Being a writer and editor of speculative fiction, it has worried me to see such a lack of published SF writing within a Singaporean context, and so this anthology was born. During the submissions process, I was gratified at the overwhelming amount of submitted short fiction, which only confirmed my impression that Singaporeans are indeed writing fantastical stories, and are either presumably shelving them in favour of more "realist" writing or sending them to overseas markets for publication.

What you hold in your hands is a compilation of the best original speculative fiction being written in Singapore today, a home-grown anthology featuring a refreshing variety of voices and perspectives. Here are tales that are recognizably science fiction and fantasy, and others that blend genres and tropes, including absurdism, police procedural, fairy tales, steampunk, pre- and post-apocalypse, political satire, and alien first contact. These twenty-one stories—from emerging writers publishing their first work to winners of the Singapore Literature Prize and the Cultural Medallion—explore the fundamental singularity of the Lion City.

This book is a celebration of the vibrant creative power underlying Singapore's inventive prose stylists, where what is considered normal and what is strange are blended in fantastic new ways. It is presented in the hope that many more will follow it in the years to come.

AGNES JOAQUIM, BIOTERRORIST

Ng Yi-Sheng

History would forever remember 2 July 1899 as one of the darkest days of the British Empire, for it was on that day that disaster smote that most precious jewel in the Crown's possessions, the Oriental colony of Singapore.

The city's most loyal subjects were gathered on the Padang that morning, sweltering in their finest dress jackets, hoop skirts, sarongs and mandarins' robes upon the grounds of the Singapore Cricket Club. Regiments of *sepoys* in khaki uniforms stood at attention, overseen by mounted officers from the Service. Hordes of Asiatic schoolchildren played hymns on oversized bagpipes. An engineer from the Hokkien Clan Association directed a crew of coolies in the manipulation of their hydraulic dragon dance machine.

All were assembled to greet their guest: no less a figure than Her Majesty Victoria, Queen of the United Kingdom of Great Britain and Ireland, Defender of the Faith and Empress of India. Following her Golden Jubilee, at the age of eighty, the monarch had resolved to make a grand tour of her territories, cruising from London to Cape Town to Nova Scotia by means of her gilded zeppelin.

She had disembarked but two days before, leaving her airship moored over the newly completed Raffles Hotel, where she was accommodated in a customized luxury suite. In her honour, colourful streamers dangled from bamboo poles across the island: every shophouse and every *kampong* hovel displayed the hues of the Union Flag—even the rickshaw coolies had taken to emblazoning their vehicles with penny black stamps as a display of their devotion to the profile of the Queen.

There was, ultimately, only one problem. The Queen was late.

The officers and merchants on the Padang checked their pocket watches, shaking their heads, as the *memsahibs* fanned themselves with increasingly impatient vigour. She should have emerged at half eight, and now it was well nigh twenty past ten. Whatever could be the matter?

Then, suddenly, a peon came running onto the field: a young Chinese man with his pigtail flying behind him, an expression of acute distress on his face. "Sound the alarm!" he exclaimed, as he prostrated himself before the podium of the Governor. "Her Majesty is under attack!"

Almost as one, the assembly leapt to their horses, their coaches, their sedan chairs and their feet. Walking canes, umbrellas and young children were lost in the mêlée of hooves and wheels as the crowd rushed to the Raffles. As they dismounted, each visage was touched with horror as they beheld the great calamity that had befallen.

For indeed, not only was their Queen in peril: the very building she had been housed within had been taken prisoner by an explosive growth of giant purple orchids. These botanic horrors penetrated every storey of the edifice with an excrescence of creeping tendrils. Guardsmen openly wept as they attempted to penetrate the foliage, hacking with their *parangs* at the greenery.

At the centre it all, the Governor stood agape, a single name quivering on his dumbstruck lips.

"Agnes," he finally whispered. "Agnes Joaquim."

~

By all accounts, young Agnes had had no initial inclination to become a terrorist. Born in 1854 into a wealthy Armenian immigrant family, she grew up in a splendid mansion on the undulating lands near the New Harbour, an area vulgarly known as Tanjong Pagar.

As the eldest daughter among eleven siblings, she assumed the role of housekeeper at an early age. Her girlish voice would often be heard supervising the Cantonese servants and urging her mother to purchase the latest imported domestic gadgets, such as the microwave eggbeater and the orgone-powered frigidaire.

Then in 1889, everything changed. One summer afternoon, while promenading in the family estate, she discovered the flower. It budded amidst the bamboo thickets, its handsome sepals opening in the shape of a pentacle. She dug it up with her hands, entranced by its delicate form and its strange, subtle scent. Hurriedly, she moved it to the potting shed, bedded it in fertile soil and rushed back to the kitchen, unable to understand the sense of thrill that had been planted in her heart, nor the pounding noises that had begun in the drums of her ears.

A month later, she paid a call on Henry Ridley, the Director of the Botanical Gardens. He received her in his laboratory, built as a vast terrarium, thriving with bromeliads, epiphytes, rubber-tree pods and foolish butterflies that fluttered next to the jaws of carnivorous plants.

"My dear Miss Joaquim!" he exclaimed with a bow. He had reason enough to be courteous, for her family had supported his recent research with not insignificant donations.

"Ah, and I see you've brought a little friend." He examined the flower, pausing to admire its rosy hue and elaborate column, which had been formed from a fused stamen and stigma, almost in the shape of an angel robed in mauve. "Extraordinary," he declared. "A cross between *Vanda teres* and *Vanda hookeriana*, unless I'm much mistaken. Wherever did you find it?"

She described the circumstances of her discovery.

"By Jove, you deserve a reward! Tell you what: I hereby christen this blossom the *Vanda Miss Joaquim*. There's immortality for you!"

Agnes took a deep breath. She had prepared what she was about to say for the past two weeks, and she was not going to make a hash of it. Patiently, she explained that while she was very grateful for Mr Ridley's kindness in bestowing the flower with her name, she sought a more mutually productive form of reward: that of working within the Botanical Gardens' experimental greenhouses, aiding him in his research and perhaps even pursuing her own.

She further assured him that she expected no financial compensation: rather, she was certain that her family would continue to sponsor his research as they had in the past, on the sole condition that she be granted access to his experimental facilities. She paused for breath. Ridley stood blinking, amidst the circling butterflies.

Throughout the rickshaw ride back to her mansion, her face burned with triumph. She had succeeded. In her hands, she clutched her own personal set of keys to the terrarium.

This was what the flower wanted of her; she knew it. For she had heard its commands over the last month, even as she scolded the cook or folded the bedclothes of her nieces and nephews. She stroked the petals of the specimen that sat on her lap, remembering that in her veins ran its fiery sap, transferred via the touch of its spongy roots, its slender stalk, and its gossamer labellum. And in her ears rang the flower's words, over and over like a malfunctioning gramophone: "Only you can change the world."

~

14

Five years later, in 1894, the Joaquim household was alarmed by the arrival of a horse-drawn police carriage at their door, containing a flustered English constable, two inscrutable Sikh *sepoys* and their maiden aunt Agnes, handcuffed and furious. The constable, whose name was Edmunds, was profusely apologetic. He knew it was terribly bad form to arrest a member of the local aristocracy, but, as he explained, circumstances had rendered such a course of action more than necessary.

While the Sikh guards escorted Agnes upstairs and bolted her into her room, he went over the details of the unfortunate incident. It appeared that Miss Joaquim had entered Government House, elbowed her way past the armed bodyguards, then barged into the chambers of the Governor himself, whereupon she had thrown a pot of fertilizer into his face.

"She'd wrote 'is 'onour 'undreds of these 'ere letters," he said, bringing out a thick sheaf of correspondence. "She were certain 'e could do somethin'."

Her letters were petitions for intervention in the Hamidian massacres: the widespread slaughter of tens of thousands of Armenians in the Ottoman Empire by the crazed Sultan Abdul Hamid II. For despite the horrific news of the genocide and the pleas of their own ethnic Armenian subjects, the British had done nothing to stop the bloodshed, continuing their trade with the Ottomans for the sake of economic expediency.

Agnes's mother parsed one or two of her daughter's letters. "Goodness," she said. "Whatever do these words mean?"

"They're words in the Fukienese dialect, missus. The meanin' ain't fit for a lady's ears."

Mrs Joaquim nodded slowly. She'd understood, even sympathized with her daughter's recent activist work: after all, the entire congregation of the Church of St Gregory the Illuminator prayed for an end to the reign of the bloodthirsty tyrant who had caused their people such suffering. Yet she fretted over the company Agnes kept. The silly girl had made numerous friends amongst the local Orientals. She'd even become familiar with the servants, persistently quizzing them on their knowledge of local herbal remedies. Rumour had it that she'd even ventured into their distant villages, seeking out *sinsehs*, *bomohs* and Ayurvedic healers to glean their botanic wisdom.

"Methinks—and the Chief of Police, 'e thinks too—that mayhap Miss Joaquim'd be more comfortable in a sanatorium of some sort. There's an asylum in the north of the island, just past the wooden bridge."

Mrs Joaquim had had quite enough. "Thank you, Constable," she proclaimed. "The servants will see you out."

Over a rather unsavoury supper (meals had become less palatable since Agnes had lost her interest in housework), the family debated the issue of the rebel amongst them. Some were resolved on expelling her from the household; others were quite content to let her carry on harmlessly with her experiments with Mr Ridley, which had caused no harm up till now.

Naturally, all assembled cringed at the thought of sending her to the asylum, but, as a younger Joaquim pointed out, she might well have a disease. What other means was there to cure it? The sun set without a resolution to their conference. But in the morning, Mrs Joaquim decided to check on her wayward daughter. She fetched a tray of hot scones and pressure-cooked coconut jam from the larder, ventured upstairs and drew back the lock.

Agnes was gone, and the room was overgrown with orchids, their creepers extending out the window, through the garden and into the wilderness.

Later, the family would learn that Ridley's terrarium had been plundered the same night. All Agnes's notes and specimens had vanished, leaving only a few puzzling diagrams and fragments of research amidst the rubber seeds and butterflies. Ridley claimed he knew nothing of these studies—particularly not the studies that appeared to use botany for the purposes of warfare.

Then in early 1895, celebrations broke out amongst the Armenians across the world. The Hamidian massacres had ended, for Sultan Abdul Hamid II had been found dead in his palace. Officials claimed he had choked on a fishbone, but the people knew better. They said he had collapsed across his chamberpot, mysteriously asphyxiated by a creeper that had slowly grown throughout the interior of his body, a sprig of purple blossoms sprouting from his mouth.

Agnes's reign of terror had begun.

One might have assumed that Agnes would cease operations once the oppressor of her race had been wiped from the face of the Earth. No such luck. Her run-in with the Governor in Singapore had given her a profound distaste for all Empires, be they British, Ottoman, Manchu or Nipponese. Clandestinely, she travelled across the planet, making contact with local radicals who fought against the powers of centralized government. Thus, in continent after continent, she spread her seeds of dissension and chaos.

In 1896, the Empress Dowager Cixi went missing in the Summer Palace. After much searching, she was discovered in the pleasure gardens, half-dissolved in a massive pitcher plant.

In 1897, Tsar Nicholas II was struck with paralysis in his private chapel. His attendants discovered him collapsed on his knees, roots shooting through his trousers, his flesh turned into mango wood.

In 1898, US President McKinley and Maria Christina, Regent of Spain, were both snatched from their boudoirs in a single night. They washed up in a lifeboat, miserably fused together through a fretwork of bougainvillea, having been forced to sign away the American and Spanish claims to the territories of Cuba, the Philippines, Guam and Puerto Rico.

Meanwhile, in Singapore, the colonial administration grew skittish. The downtrodden had lately begun to eschew their habit of taking government-taxed opium to dull their pains, opting instead for a cheap, plentiful drug they called Joaquimine, or else simply "Joe".

Joaquimine was especially dangerous for the British Empire, as it worked not only as an anaesthetic and a hallucinogen, but also as a stimulant. It sharpened one's sense of focus, driving its abusers towards new purpose in life. It soon became common to see dockyard coolies in Clifford Pier arguing over their plans for constructing hybrid electric steamships, or else pipa girls in Chinatown, huddled over the writings of Karl Marx in the original German. Shadow universities began to crop up, run by secret societies and mosques, where gangsters and farmers' daughters discussed every branch of the sciences and the arts in a motley creole based on English, Arabic, Mandarin, Tamil, Teochew and Malay.

The government did what it could to stem this burgeoning tide of intellect. They conducted violent raids of farms and shophouse cellars where crops of the magenta flowers were secretly grown, to be dried and processed into orchid cigarettes. Well-publicized trials took place, such as that of the young medical student Lim Boon Keng, who had been caught red-handed prescribing the drug to coolie labourers. And of course, campaigners such as Bishop Oldham and Sophia Blackmore lent their voices to the cause, alarmed as they were that their schoolchildren were puffing Joaquimine to aid their studies.

Such measures, however, worked to no avail. Rather than diminishing, the epidemic expanded its scope, as Singaporean sailors smuggled Joaquimine in their luggage, allowing its dissemination throughout the world. It was speedily adopted by other nations of people, including the Formosans, the Kashmiris, the Ashkenazi Jews, the Coreans, the Zulus, the Boers and the Apache.

And across the Earth, each smoker heard the flower's words pounding in his head: "Only you can change the world."

A fire sprang up amidst the orchid-choked Raffles Hotel, scorching its white façade a ghastly black. Some thoughtless officer had started it, believing it to be the fastest way to prevent further growth of the monster plant.

The Governor had been apoplectic. "You fool!" he cried. "The Queen's in there!"

There probably ain't much of her left, the officer thought, but did not say.

The crowd still milled about at the scene of the tragedy, hampering the rescue efforts. Chambermaids, barmen and guests wailed as the blaze grew higher, mourning the loss of their possessions and their livelihood. Yet every now and again, a sigh rippled through the masses as a cluster of purple blossoms went up in a psychedelic blaze of colour, scattering their cinders across the darkening sky.

Eventually, a crew of fire fighters arrived. But before they could direct a single hose towards the inferno, the heavens opened up and rain gushed forth from the clouds, drenching the *sahibs* in their Sunday best, ruining the coiffures and cosmetics of the cultural dancers, washing the sweat from the bodies of the horses and rickshaw pullers.

The civilians scattered, and the fire fighters proceeded to assist the rescue team, clearing away the burnt vegetation in the building, for the flames had cleared a way through the ruins, and the downpour was quenching the flames. They clambered through stairways and broken ceilings, braving the smoke and smouldering vines. With luck, they might reach the Royal Suite yet.

Finally, they came to the rosewood doors, now reduced to charcoal and scrap timber by the fire and the orchids. After hacking away a curtain of vines, they beheld an amazing sight. On a four-poster bed strewn with orchids lay the two women, Victoria and Agnes, side by side. Both were motionless and apparently unharmed. The rescuers rushed to the bodies. The Queen, once woken, was in fine condition, though somewhat weak and bewildered about the commotion.

Agnes was dead. An autopsy later indicated that she had passed on mere minutes before the team's appearance. An enormous tumour was also revealed in her uterus, which had been killing her slowly since her discovery of the flower ten years before.

The Joaquim clan took charge of her body, and arranged to have her buried the next day in a quiet ceremony in Bukit Timah Cemetery. Yet, as the priest grudgingly read a psalm over her coffin, the cortege was stunned by the sight of a sea of humanity rising across the hill. Approaching them were men, women and children drawn from every class and race known to Singapore society. Some wore black, some wore white, some wore sackcloth, and some wore sarongs of blue and turquoise.

But each of them held something in common, a token of farewell to their heroine: a single flower.

After a barrage of medical examinations, the Queen was pronounced fit to return to London, though with doctor's orders to spend the majority of her waking hours in convalescence. Victoria obediently boarded the zeppelin. Yet as soon as her physicians' backs were turned, she summoned her secretary and began issuing a memorandum to the Cabinet to examine the issue of de-colonization.

Once in Buckingham Palace, she caused a scandal with her newfound opinions. She insisted that her subjects—or, as she called them now, her citizens—deserved greater liberty than they experienced at present under their imperial regime. She wrote essays for *The Daily Telegraph* and the *Times*, insisting on the need to equalize opportunities for the working classes.

In the year 1900 she resumed her travels throughout her Empire, armed with a vigour quite uncharacteristic of an octogenarian. She conversed passionately with citizens in Delhi and Rangoon and Cairo, often advising them on how to revive their own pre-colonial governments on a more egalitarian footing, even bequeathing considerable gifts of the Crown to help fund such efforts at nation-building. Such actions were much to the chagrin of her government, her administrators and the rest of the royal family, who watched with dismay as their inheritance dwindled daily. Yet when questioned about her actions, she had but this to say: "Only I can change the world."

Regardless, or perhaps because of the controversy she caused, the Queen remained beloved by her people. Thus it was that she rose on 22 January 1901 quite refreshed and eager to appear in a scheduled street parade from Westminster Abbey to Leicester Square.

Though it was a wintry day, she insisted on riding in an uncovered coach. "I feel so light," she remarked, to no-one in particular. Then, without warning, her body burst into blossom.

The Londoners marvelled at their Queen. And as they gazed upon her, the seeds blew from her body, taking root instantly in the cobblestoned streets of snow.

And across the city, a million orchids bloomed.

PUNGGOL

Ben Slater

"Your destination today is Punggol Station, the terminal point for PG-21 Eco-City. You have requested a basic package for sector access which I'm delighted to process."

The woman's voice was warm but had definite authority. Tony wondered not for the first time how they allocated the voices. Was there some form he'd filled out years ago? Slumped in a seat reserved for the elderly, infirm or pregnant, Tony hurtled north, towards the edge of the island.

Punggol, he thought. The end of the line. He couldn't remember a day when he wasn't going in that direction.

"What is your purpose in visiting PG-21 Eco-City today?" the voice asked brightly; no hint of interrogation or curiosity.

"I'm looking for answers." Sometimes he liked to be obtuse with the voices.

"You will agree to spend fifteen minutes conducting your business in PG-21 EC and if you stay beyond that duration you'll receive the first of two exit warnings. If you don't begin to leave the sector after the first warning, an alert will be issued to the Security Committee."

"A friendly bunch I'm sure."

The train incrementally slowed. Tony enjoyed the heat on his face from the last rays of sun through the Plexiglas window. A final burst of energy before the evening.

"Do you agree to these conditions, Mr Century?"

The light was gone. The train entered the station and stopped silently.

"Yeah," Tony said after a while. Doors opened. He didn't move.

"Can you do me a favour?"

"Of course, Mr Century."

"Instead of PG-13 Ecotropolis, or whatever you like to call it, just say Punggol. And no more of this 'Mr Century' crap. Just plain Tony. Is that all right with you?"

A pause for her to think. Could they even think? Then—

"OK, Tony, we've reached Punggol." Less authority now. He preferred that. I'm old-fashioned, he thought, but mostly I'm just bloody old.

"Thanks, darling." He lifted himself up and moved slowly out.

Chrome, metal, and glass. Tony shuffled through the immaculate station architecture with a limp. Her instructions played in the background like bad music. Up the escalator. Onto the train for the East Loop. Take the seat at the front. Or was that the back? Then we're off again.

"What is your purpose in visiting Punggol today?"

To find the girl.

Someone close to you disappeared? Owe you money and flown the coop? A figure from your past needs reviving? Call Tony Century.

The case of the girl. Tony had been on it for years. Every detective has one—the mystery that couldn't be solved. The face he saw when he closed his eyes at night. Even when the trail had been dead for years, the face in the dark, it remained.

And then a night or two ago Tony got the message: *She's at the end of the line. Go north.* Punggol was hardly a place to hide, but there was an old gumshoe motto: Everything is the opposite of what it appears to be. The note might have been from the girl herself—perhaps she wanted to be found. Or, then again, it could have been a trap.

"While we travel, would you like some facts about the area?"

Sometimes, Tony thought, it's best to agree.

She launched into a boiler-plate history lesson about Punggol's "humble beginnings" as a fishing community. Out of the window sat a row of high-rises, monotonously perfect. "Today, it's the country's first self-sustaining eco-city," she went on, rallying enthusiasm, "constructed on reclaimed land, built with innovative efficiency over two decades. Luxurious amenities and superb systems mean that none of the 535,112 inhabitants *ever* want to leave..."

Tony looked around the carriage at his fellow passengers. No one over the age of thirty-five. Everything new here, even the people. He tried to read their faces. They seem glum, he thought, but inside they must be smiling. Each day, he'd heard, they manufactured their own memories. A fresh start every morning, and then they'd erase the accidents and bad decisions at night. No guilt or shame, nothing to make you wince for years. Memories lasted 24 hours. If there were any secrets here, they'd been long forgotten.

No one needs to remember in Punggol. Except Tony. That was his gig.

Tony had seen a lot of changes. Born in the last century and shoved into the next. He'd watched one country replacing another like a parasite killing a host. But he wasn't into the nostalgia trip. This dirty town had always been in the progress business. It was a shithole then and it was worse now. He might not always be able to see the filth, but Tony knew it was there. The trick was to find people before they drowned in it.

"There's three basic kinds of missing," Tony would tell prospective clients, or anyone who'd listen, over a can of Tiger, "The runaways, the neglected, and the confused. Or combinations of the above. First category don't want to be found. The second lot slip down the back of the sofa. Then there are a few who don't know who they are or what they're doing, like fireworks in a rainstorm. Lost souls."

Something about this case. The girl. He'd never figured out which category she belonged to.

"We're now passing through Vista Sixty," the voice interrupted merrily. "The newest estate in Punggol, seventy-five thousand residents live in perfect harmony between sub-luxury housing and lush green-themed leisure zones. The success of the Eco-City model ensures it'll be rolled-out island-wide by—"

"Enough," Tony said, more aggressively than intended. A young family turned away from him. He continued nevertheless. "I knew Punggol back when it was a mosquito trap full of squabbling farmers and spaced-out crab-hunters. Now I'm whizzing round it on a train driven by a microchip. Talking to a woman who's about as real…"

He looked out into a great wall of windows reflecting sunlight. Once, this had been the brink of the sea, then there were green fields and a lake, then the building sites, the cranes and the clever machines. How many times had he been back here?

"When was the last time you were in Punggol, Tony?"

They did that sometimes, asked just the right question. It always caught him off-guard.

"Don't remember." He lied and knew she knew it too.

Kadaloor, Coral Edge, Oasis. The stations came and went, the passengers entered and exited, all of them looked different in the same way, like extras in a movie. Tony hadn't moved.

"You have now been in Punggol for seven minutes and thirty seconds. Halfway through your permitted access period."

Tony was well aware of the clock ticking. For a detective he didn't have much of a method. There was a clue, and now he was riding the train, hoping for a sniff, the aroma of inspiration. It wasn't coming. He looked out—up and down at the streets and the gardens, so well put together, so carefully assembled. What wounds were festering underneath all this surface? Look harder, he thought, see with these eyes, they're all I have.

"I'm detecting critical physical and psychological indicators from you, Tony. Perhaps you might consider leaving Punggol early?"

"No, sweetcakes, I'm not going anywhere except where this track takes me." Perhaps that's what the note meant, the end of the line at the end of the line. The last station. They were speaking his language.

"Tell me about the girl."

She was trying to help, he knew that. Getting the old focus back. Returning that picture to where it belonged. He closed his eyes and saw it for a moment. The photograph that he kept in the drawer beside his bed. Young lady, couldn't have been older than twelve. Short, cropped hair, summer dress. She's smiling, and has the most open, honest face Tony had ever seen. He didn't believe in much these days, but that girl, she was an angel.

"Who is she, Tony?" He shook his head. Who was she? He didn't know anymore.

"You're tired, you can exit the area at the next stop."

"I have to keep going. Until the end."

"OK, Tony, I understand."

Yes, her voice. It reminded him of someone.

To do this job, to be a searcher, you had to know the city. The streets, paths, back alleys and short-cuts were marked on Tony's brain like an ugly tattoo. Then he tracked the changes. Every home demolished, every upgraded estate, he made a note. He'd forgotten all the details of his own life, but he still remembered places, directions, connections; it was in the blood.

"That was the first exit warning. Did you hear it?"

He hadn't heard a thing. Meridian, Riviera, Cove. More stops, more entrances and exits. When he'd started this journey he thought he was waiting for something to happen, but now he knew he was going somewhere.

"Tell me, is there a station along this line called Perfection?" Sometimes he liked to flirt.

"There is no Perfection, Tony."

"You don't mean that." You're pretty close, he thought, and the joke ceased to be funny.

When people chose their voices, they were supposed to mean something, weren't they? A replacement for a person long gone. Had everyone in this damned city lost the one they loved? A mother, a daughter, a wife, a lover. Which was she?

"You're right, Tony. I've been selected for you and you only." He thought he'd been thinking to himself, keeping a lid on it, but he must have been talking out loud. No wonder no passenger would look him in the eye. The strange old man in the reserved seat. A disturbing glitch to be edited out by morning.

"But you're no more alive than the circuit board that shunts this train."

"You could say that. But I'm all you have right now."

"And I could off you like bad music."

She ignored him. "There will be another warning soon. Let me guide you. Stay on until the terminal, then head back to town. If you do that, you'll make it."

He thought about his place, a stripped-out maisonette in Hougang. The room with the bed. The photograph in the drawer. Well, he didn't need that any more, he would see her soon enough.

"Today I'm going to solve the case. I have to." Desperation broke his voice. "You don't believe me, do you?"

"I believe *in* you."

"The last time I was here. It was sometime at the end of the last century, or the start of this one. They hadn't finished making the place."

The building sites, cranes and clever machines. First drafts of a future architecture. Linked gardens and networked walkways destined to be packed away and replaced by something cleaner, newer, better.

"Why did you come that time, Tony?"

"I took a wrong turn off the highway. It had been a bad day and I was trying to get as far away as I could. When I got here I was scared. I'd entered a city for ghosts. The empty spaces, the half-constructed...and in the shimmering haze, I saw what it would become. For just a second, I saw all of this." He gestured out of the window, as if she was sitting beside him. "I left as soon as I could, but I knew, somehow, that I'd come back. But this time. Here. Now. It feels all right. Like I could stay for a while."

Somewhere far away, where only she could hear it, the second exit warning sounded. The Security Committee would show no mercy, not even for an old man who was lost. She'd made the calculations and it didn't look good.

The train sped up. A final burst of energy before it returned to where it began. And the loop would continue.

"She's waiting for me." Tony's voice was weaker now. No danger of a plugged-in commuter overhearing his whispers. "I don't have to find her. She's looking for me. Still sweet. Still sparkling. Her mother's eyes."

Her mother's voice. She knew. Of course she knew.

"I have so many questions," he continued. There were tears now. "Where should I start? No. I only have one question. Shall we begin again?"

The train had stopped and opened up. No standing room at this hour. A great surge of travellers. Parents returning to children. Tony still in the corner. Almost invisible now. Almost.

One last try from the voice. "You have to get off now. Go home. You'll be safe there."

He shook his head.

"You can leave me now. I'm staying for one more round. I want to see what's at the end. The very end."

"There is no end."

Me and the girl, Tony thought, we both belong to the third category. The hardest ones to find.

"Goodbye, Tony Century."

"So long, *sayang*."

The doors closed and the train moved off. And Tony was alone with himself and the silence.

WELCOME TO THE POND

Wei Fen Lee

Today your eyes are bright like tungsten, inflamed with silence. How did that happen? Glowing outward-bound, luminous at the edges. Did someone paint your sides? Where did the other terrapins go?

The last time I saw you, you were swimming-pool shiny. Shoulder blades gleaming with chlorine and your head matted from the sun, sweat tattooed into your shell—and what intricate patterns they made. The leader of the terrapin pack, was the title they had introduced you with, but all I could do was stare at emerald inflections on your back.

My job was to interview you, to find out all you knew. I had been told you might be dangerous and your dissidence contagious but all you did was breathe, refusing to speak. I posed question after question, but you were so calm and so poised and so quiet, cooled by water and indifferent to the world of words I work for.

I grew up sandwiched between an academic father and a lawyer for a mother. Grammar was a birthright, expression an obligation. I floated from debate at the dinner table to secondary school composition awards, then stopped gently at journalism, where the dream of presenting relevant and urgent news gradually—and comfortably, I have to admit—sashayed into the easy sell: lifestyle, culture, new novelties. No stray feet to step on, no politicians to be accountable to. No conflicts of interest. There isn't much news to report anyway, I told myself at the end of each day. I live in a world happy without wars, a nation concerned with the weather.

Then I received a tip-off about the pond, about you and your friends. This island had been home to a pond in the botanical gardens for centuries but it had been ignored up till now, merely acting as the singular ornamental feature fit to decorate the island's larger aims of becoming a leading international institution for tropical botany. All I knew was that some news of overcrowding in the pond had broken, and there were now a multitude of terrapins, their numbers unmonitored, murmuring dissent. No one had a straightforward story; no one could explain the lead up to this. Instead, I'd been summoned to do what I used do best: write, research, and question.

So it stunned me, your indifference. My reputation as an influential journalist had demanded up till then at least a show of strained courtesy on the part of interviewees. I was determined to get to know you, to shake you out of your torpor—and failing that, to enter it.

How do you breathe with that thing on your back?

That was the first question I'd asked you in your box before the camera started rolling, not part of the official set list handed to me. Later, I would find out that you could not hear well. I was curious to know you beyond speech, beyond my duty. You refused to answer though—not the personal questions, not the dispassionate ones, and certainly not the intimate ones. *Where did all the terrapins come from? What were they grumbling about? How did they feel about this new environment?*

In the following weeks, I grew used to your silence. Instead of questioning, I learned about the keratin under your shell, and how melanin created the carvings of light on your back. My hair in you, your patterns under my skin follicles. Reptiles used to make me cringe with their swamp-like bodies and labyrinthine skin, but then I learned that your three-chambered heart continues beating for hours outside your body even after removal. That impressed me.

So I began to study the temperature of your blood, whilst my photojournalist colleague angled shots. You didn't say much, but I guess there wasn't a need to.

When I'd arrived at the pond, past the joggers and lovers, the journos were in an uproar and excited for the first time about something other than the stock market. Word on the street was that for years, unwanted pet terrapins and their kin had been dumped into this national pond out of plastic tanks, glass aquariums, and in some bad scenarios, biscuit boxes. It was entirely uncoordinated, and more a matter of the tiny flats on the ambitious island having no space for these pets: for where else could an unwanted terrapin go in this city of concrete and glass?

The problem arose, I think, when the terrapin movement grew wildly popular, with millions of citizens joining in secretly but not knowing that their neighbours were doing it too. A few mothers milling about the pond with empty plastic boxes told me—not without guilt—that they had snuck out that early morning to deposit their children's pet terrapins into the pond to shorten their list of chores. It was rumoured, they whispered, that even a Cabinet Minister had been spotted adding his terrapin to the mix (although once splashed in, he became indistinguishable—he no longer looked rich).

This is what they did not need to tell me: that the pond came to contain the dissatisfactions of nuclear families, the secrets of politicians, pubescent girls, long-drawn fights between grandparents and siblings and spouses…together, its inhabitants had absorbed within them the four walls of tiresome tiny flats, the conversations of inter-generational dinners, the clang of chopsticks and the way each door slams shut differently. It had imbibed a nation of antagonism. The pond was an accumulation of intimate knowledge, an underwater mirror of you and me.

By the time I got to the park, there was a buzz in the air so loud with fear and anger bubbling through the water that anyone close by could only close their eyes and bunch their fists in a minimal response of empathy.

The history of bait lies in the power of a bite.

So it follows that I saw the breadcrumbs before I saw you, the red mark around your ears distinguishing you from your peers. I would later look out for that same flash of blood red amongst identical boxes of terrapins to find you. The park rangers lifted their arms, and hundreds of white crumbs were flung into the pond to cover its surface. For a moment, the park was quiet. Then a head bobbed up and out of the water, nibbling at a crumb. Then another. And another. It took all of thirty seconds before what looked like a multitude of green faces emerged to greet our world, mouths agape for food. A watery army arising to answer the banal call of sustenance. A million eyes dancing to an uncoordinated blink. Then a roar, a tsunami of dissatisfaction breaking across the water's surface so that the rangers had to run back.

Other things I later discovered you could eat: lettuce, clover, grass, chopped liver, tadpoles, bloodworms. A cuttlefish bone is a calcium-rich treat.

~

The very next day, news of the overcrowding broke.

When we arrived again at the gardens, the pond was a mess of bodies, a population plague, unstoppable. What happened? I remember shouting at you across the din, even as you slid off the rock and continued speaking to your crowd, swimming solo.

The specialists say that you cannot hear well. It is typical of your species. You did not hear the early signs of stress, the lowering rates of fertility. You could feel it though, when another terrapin climbed on your back for a better view, and once, another fell asleep under your belly, his head against your plastron. You could not hear it but you could see it, you could feel it swirling besides and around: the orgies in the mud, the clang of bony plates against each other. The murmurs now made tangible in anger.

You could feel the brackish water growing warm.

In spite of their usual efficiency, it took ten days for the authorities to arrive in order to assess the situation. Some say it was planned to let the mess grow old.

There is no use pretending that anyone cares about what happened next. Disappearance is not to be taken lightly, unless the object of disappearance is inconsequential.

So no one knew when pail after pail of homeless terrapins were loaded onto a waiting truck, parked in a handicapped lot. No one knew when night shrouded the water and missed the scuted bodies it had previously cloaked. No one heard the algae multiplying, the oxygen underwater suddenly and deafeningly free.

You must have blinked, and then you were gone.

I spent a week chasing the story, ringing the authorities, looking for you. My editor, usually patient, threw up his ink-stained hands and told me to cover something less urgent, more edible, less relevant.

Finally, the authorities sent out exclusive media invitations to the best journalists to talk to the terrapins—they too were growing desperate for some answers—but by then the hype had fizzled out, and only three of us bothered showing up.

We were ushered to an industrial-sized swimming pool where hundreds, maybe thousands, of terrapins were now housed neatly. The tessellation was dizzying. The walls must have been gray, or a colour unmemorable. Each terrapin had a corner, a little box. That was the second time I saw you and when I finally got to interview you, back when you were shiny with chlorine with sweat tattooed into your shell. I spoke to you with my recorder alert but you merely blinked slowly and swam in circles, your tail curled uncomfortably around in a defiant clockwork exercise.

There were whispers, later, about the cold dark rooms you had been plunged into. Cold-blooded, they had said, laughing, when asked for a reason—cold-blooded conspirators should be able to withstand harsher treatment. They should not need to sleep. What they could not distinguish was the metaphorical from the metabolic, had they not seen you before, stretching out on those rocks, basking in the sun? So they matched your body temperature with that of the room in the hope that it would make you speak, desperate for warmth. The quieter rumours conveyed images of being force-fed, of wax worms wriggling down a matchstick tube invading your throat. Co-operation can be difficult to win.

In the absence of sunlight, blindness or deformity in the shell may occur. I didn't want to imagine the instinctive response of hibernation, the thousands of terrapins digging furiously into a tiled ground where the mud of bay waters was supposed to lift and cover and warm. They wanted your tales but instead, silenced your sight.

By the time they lifted you out of your box for an out-of-water inquiry I noticed that the ground beneath you was moss-tiled and smooth, dig marks faded and grown over. I fought the urge to slide my fingers across to find some friction.

A month passed. I attempted new questions, new angles, but you resolutely answered none of them. I even brought my own chair to park by your corner. The other two journalists gave up after a week, and the authorities eventually revoked my pass, citing that the project had been a failure and that no news coverage would now be permitted.

You had given nothing of yourself away, and the strength of your silence made me doubt my own skills of articulation. How many more dazzling stories could I sell, if I couldn't coax a response from you? How many more people could I cajole and convince, when your refusal to speak was more compelling than my words? I wanted to tell you how I had never tasted failure before, had never held it so gingerly between my tongue and my teeth, that it had only crawled into my mouth the day I met you. I said nothing, of course. I had a reputation to uphold, and I suppose, so did you. The insouciant murmurs of the pond, once deafening, were now contained obediently in the neat geometrics of each self-sufficient box.

I returned to the office only to find a new assignment to review the new hip brunch place in town. The Pawn, it was called. An old pawn shop, once infamous for housing illegal horse-betting activities, now refurbished and home to the best fish and chips in town. No one seemed to see the irony, or at least if they did they never commented.

~

Ladies and gentlemen, welcome to the Pawn. We stand here, on the cusp of a new dawn. Look at the insides of this building, observe how heritage is respected by retaining the stains on each hanging wall, how the rosewood furniture harkens directly back to the nineteenth century. Appreciate how the chambers have been reformatted, the past a room you'll never want to step out of.

Look how the walls are allowed to breathe, and how old signs of paint have been scrapped and retained. Read the stories of an era in the chinaware, and do pick up a name card or two on your way out.

Privacy is guaranteed here, in the midst of this tastefully decorated luxury. Observe not only the carefully restored vintage items and their ornate details, but also the beautiful people here, decked only in carefully crafted designs. Seek shelter here from the lewd hustle of the city, for the traffic passes not this door. Look hard at the carvings on each bench. Remember, it is here that we preserve the past. Our painstakingly treated walls reveal only an architectural history we can be proud of.

Oh, and when you have time, head for the bathroom. You'll find that there's more than natural lighting that shines through.

The Pawn is located in a Chinese heritage building with high whirring fans and wood-backed chairs, a rarity because wood is difficult to find these days. I enjoy their devilled chicken liver, and find the watercress pasta exceptionally well done. The lack of an aquarium is a nice change.

No one understands why I keep returning, least of all my parents. I tell them that the heady environment is conducive for me to write my assignments—the food, travel, and movie reviews that are thrown my way. Despite that, they have noticed over the dinner table my newfound inability to articulate myself, and are worried about my dying relationship with words, my abstinence from the usual debates, my sparse writing. Even my handwriting has changed: I now pen a chicken scrawl.

I discovered you again when I stumbled into the restaurant bathroom for the first time in months, on a break between menu presentations and the stammer of high society, drunk on tea-time cocktails and a lack of stories to chase.

There you were, on a toilet cistern, in a jade bowl almost big enough for two. I could almost see the interlock of your bones. I don't think you recognised me—after all, you didn't blink during our first meeting, and you didn't care during the second. I felt like I knew you though; I'd traced those patterns on your back before. I had seen your underbelly. I knew the strokes of fire on your head.

It could have been the sheen from my last mojito, but your eyes were bright. Like tungsten, that secretive shine. Scrubbed like a morning that spills into eyelids, so surprising, but not nearly warm. What did we do to you? Isolated and still deaf, no longer cold but swimming in the shape of an infinity sign, exactly the loops those cubicles conformed your body to. Cleaner than ever, your retina wiped pure. You are mute, you are deaf, and now you are blind. When Oedipus ran pins into his eyes, he escaped and embraced both knowledge and consequence. What knowledge did you have, that you could not share? When the Assyrians put out the eyes of Zedekiah, did they rub salt in for the big heal? What are those black shards doing, sitting in your eyes?

Earlier, speech had been a deafening choice you made. Now, your silence felt like sandpaper; shiny, abrasive, a burst bag sealed shut.

I cried that day, in the bathroom, thinking of the futility of these interviews, those cornerings, that dizzying big boxed pool, my writing, and how it would all end with me never being able to connect with a terrapin. You looked at me and did not blink.

Later, I told myself it was the alcohol.

The day you first caught sight of me the sunlight drew shadows of infinity on the water's surface. It would later trap you in its web of angularity, sketching you with those very same paths and patterns. The day after I saw you on the bathroom cistern, I watched the video footage of our interview. There you were, tied to that chair, almost shy. There you were, quiescent, your tail quivering, your shell now soft. The camera shakes a little as I ask, how do you breathe with that thing on your back? I could have sworn I heard you laugh, low.

The day your eyes breathed mute light and the last time I saw you, I stepped out of the Pawn and never returned. I ceased writing; ceased addressing unconcerned ladies and gentlemen, walked down those perfectly preserved steps, and looked up. Have you ever seen the sky lying flat, horizontal above the sun? It is a sand of blue, and I do not know where it goes, only up, only rising.

LAST SUPPER

Jeffrey Lim

For Edmond Olivera, dying turned out to be a longer walk than planned.

His pre-supper walk began the way it always did. With his sandals, shorts, tee shirt and a small umbrella, he stepped out through the small painted door in the driveway to his home and made his way to the junction of Jalan Lapang and Jalan Kembangan.

He would normally stroll the leaf-strewn sidewalk, past the odd assortment of Lexus vehicles, Honda motorbikes, and Subaru Imprezas huddled near the *kopitiam* at the junction: rich or poor, the *mee siam* at the Malay stall, and the *roti prata* and *nasi pattaya* at the Indian shop were favourites—people arrived in cars, buses or the nearby MRT to eat there. Edmond used take a direct path to the *kopitiam*, maybe order a *teh tarik* and *prata*, but ever since the stents had been inserted into two of his formerly clogged arteries, his doctors had warned him to abstain. He chose to ignore the advice, but compromised by taking a long evening walk around the neighbourhood before coming back for supper.

Now that the general election was over, the town council and political parties had taken down the election posters from the traffic light poles, and the veneer of normalcy had returned.

Edmond took in the view as he made his way across the road from the *kopitiam*.

The layout of the roads had not changed much over time, though the buildings had. As he crossed the football field along the canal next to Kembangan MRT, a technological cathedral with its vaulted space-age looking arcs and bustling elevated trains that thundered by overhead, he recalled how the dwellings around the area used to be modest *attap* houses on elegant stilts instead of grandiose apartment blocks. Remembered how there'd been wooden fencing, dirt paths and messy clusters of slippers and sandals instead of concrete walls, remote-controlled iron gates, driveways and shoe racks.

There were dark places here too.

Along Lorong Mydin, there used to be an abandoned lot, where the police had found that Tamil lady hanging from the crossbeam of her home, eight months pregnant. As a young boy skipping school and running along with his friends in his bare feet, he'd found himself halting when he saw the crowd gathered below the steps of one the *attap* houses, a sad ramshackle brown structure. Men dressed in sarongs and sweating into their tee shirts stood in the damp red mud, gazing up the ladder stairs into the doorway. The women, a little behind, covering their mouths and muttering to each other. Eyes full of disbelief. The policemen in their long pants, berets, and short sleeves were holding all of them back a distance but, being small, Edmond had slipped through the gaps and made his way to the edge of the perimeter.

And then they carried her out.

Her hands had been tied behind her back and she had been beaten about the face. Edmond could still see her swollen blue cheeks and puffy black eyelids, and her naked swollen belly shook as the officers carried her stretcher down one gingerly-taken step at a time.

They never did find her killer. Edmond had spent his teenage years being told that the baby had not been her husband's and worse—that the father might have been Malay.

Now as he passed the lot, he suppressed a shiver as he gazed quickly into the lighted terrace that stood there now. The family inside was watching television, gathered around the flickering light, pointing at the screen. Edmond glanced up at the ceiling above them where the fan spun, and imagined seeing the dark naked corpse spinning with the blades.

Over the front door facing the paved driveway, a dried palm had been inserted over a portrait of the Sacred Heart of Jesus and an adjoining painting of His Mother. Catholics, especially the Peranakan Catholics, had, over the last few decades, spread out from Katong further east and they usually did pretty well living in haunted houses.

Nothing a good exorcism couldn't cure, he guessed.

Down Sims Avenue, he made the turn up Lorong Melayu, and headed into the heart of Kembangan estate. It was then that he noticed a single yellow light bouncing up and down the path, and shuddering as it neared him. The rickety clicking of gears and the moan of brakes, as a bicycle appeared and ground to a halt under the yellow roadside lamp. On it, sat a young boy.

To his surprise, Edmond knew the child.

"Hello, Edmond," the boy smiled. He was dressed in stained khaki shorts and a yellowed once-white singlet with shoulder straps. His feet were bare. He was skinny, tanned (as they all had been back then), with brilliantly white teeth, combed hair and dimpled cheeks.

"Chia Hui," Edmond returned the smile. "I haven't seen you in sixty years."

Chia Hui turned to look back from where he had come, down Lorong Melayu. "Wah, so late and going for a walk, ah?"

Edmond nodded. "Want to come?"

Chia Hui shook his head. "I cannot stay. You also." He nodded in Edmond's intended direction, down Lorong Melayu. "Why your walks *so* long, one?"

"Old already." Edmond rubbed his chest at the raised surgical scar. "Must exercise."

He noticed a momentary look of envy on Chia Hui's face.

"Okay lah, see you," the boy said, waving and pushing his bicycle back into motion.

Edmond watched the boy go, heard the rickety clicks as his bare feet pressed against the heavy pedals. He found himself thinking that it was good that the bicycle looked like it had been fixed. Edmond had always loved it and had refused to ride any bicycle for years after Chia Hui and his bike went under that lorry all those years ago.

He pressed on.

As he reached Jalan Daud, towards the end of Lorong Melayu, Edmond became conscious that someone was walking by his side. He turned his head, and saw her, and then smiled, keeping up his pace.

"Jumi?" he managed, a little winded.

She was still 17 and wore her hair long and loose. Nowadays, there would have been some who'd frown on the style. Elders would have asked her to cover up, pull a *tudung* over that unruly hair. But back in the 60s, no one really cared. They just assumed that Jumiati, who had been kicked out of their secondary school, just could not be helped and they let her be. Her floral prints weren't a problem but her open neckline was. That and the fact that she'd been rumoured to have a Chinese girlfriend.

"Edmond," she said striding alongside him, with all the zest and freshness of a young, confident woman. "Can I join you?"

"Sure," Edmond said. "I heard you got married, had children and moved to KL?"

"Oh, I did." She smiled. "Rohan is forty, Fazlinda is thirty-eight, Ozman is thirty-two and Maslinda is thirty."

"Two boys and two girls? Wah, you very busy," Edmond said, breathing heavier as he settled into his stride.

Jumi bounced along the street, occasionally stepping ahead of him to pick up fallen flowers scattered on the road and pressing them between her slender fingers, trying them out in her hair, stems behind her ears.

"Actually, now one boy and three girls. Ozman had his operation three years ago."

Edmond was puzzled. "Operation?"

"He's now called 'Petra' and lives with his *ang moh* boyfriend in Patpong."

Edmond suppressed a chuckle—only it sounded like a wet cough. He did think about slowing a little, but didn't want to risk being left behind by Jumi.

"Wah, so rebellious. Like his mommy."

She shook her head and sighed.

"We disowned him. I have not talked to him in seven years."

Edmond lowered his eyes. "So sorry to hear."

She paused to think as he caught up with her.

He nudged her. "Hey Jumi, you can remember or not? You know lah—how you were always kissing the girls in the *kampong*?"

She closed her eyes, smiled, and a wild laugh, the laugh of a teenage girl, escaped her parted lips. She seemed to be savouring one of those kisses in her memory.

Giggling, she opened her eyes and nudged him back. "Yah. Remember Asfiya?"

Edmond chuckled and coughed again. "Asfiya? Of course."

Jumi twirled a flower between her forefinger and thumb, a mischievous glint in her eye. "She was so scared, especially when I pushed my hand down her blouse and found her nipple. I don't think she knew how hard it was."

Edmond laughed. "Those were good days."

They walked in silence a few more steps.

"So why?" Edmond asked at last. "I thought you would approve of Ozman becoming Petra?"

She reached out, grabbed the pole of a streetlamp and swung round it slowly. Edmond halted to look at her. She stopped, twirling her hair in her fingers. Her voice was soft.

"Don't know. Things change when you have children."

Edmond nodded. "Yes, they do."

"No children, Edmond?"

He shook his head.

She smiled. "Don't." She looked away, down Lorong Melayu. "Only pain."

They had come to the end of the street. A busy Sims Avenue East bisected the roads but Edmond could still see the low houses and thatched roofs.

She swept a hand out across the road. "Remember how Encik Asman and Mr Tan would get the local boys together? The only time I thought I would like boys was when they went out to meet those rioters."

Edmond nodded. "Yes."

They had been teenagers but they had seen the gangs, armed with *parangs*, looking for trouble during the race riots. Their neighbourhood had banded together, the Malay men turning away angry Malay boys, the Chinese elders demanding that the Chinese gangs leave their neighbours alone. They were teenagers then as Jumi was now, standing by his side, staring down a street of homes that no longer existed, for a time now faded like a watermark.

~

Past the mosque at Jalan Ishak, Edmond saw Michelle sitting by on the kerb by herself, smoking. She was still 33, and still fatigued. She didn't look surprised when Edmond drew close.

"You're late." She stubbed out her cigarette, grinding and twisting it into a small stump.

He grunted, and eased himself down, grateful for the break. "I can't stay. Got my walk to finish." The sweat had formed a thin film on his back that clung to his tee shirt. "Going for supper."

She nodded, reaching into her black handbag. Michelle had been this age during the seventies, so the bag was naturally one of those ghastly fashion statements—paisley loops, and psychedelic flowers. She lifted the oversized sunglasses from her nose and rested them on her forehead while she fished out another cancer stick and a lighter. It was one of those long thin cigarettes that used to be in fashion.

"That's my Edmond—*always* got something *better* to do."

He had been staring at her pumps, visible under her bell bottoms. "It's been forty years. You haven't stopped blaming me?"

She took a puff, shook her head.

Edmond sighed. "Still smoking?"

The acrid cloud cleared from her features. "*Aiyah*," she said, "so long already. I might as well enjoy myself while I still can, right?"

Edmond gathered his knees with his hands and leaned into them as far as his creaking muscles would allow. He could see the perspiration roll down his calves. Each of them quietly spent time with their thoughts.

"So, you walk a lot?" Michelle asked, finally breaking the silence.

Edmond nodded. "Best way to keep fit."

She laughed, cynically. "Eat less first, then talk."

As always, her clothes smelled terrible. When they had been married, Edmond was the one who did all the laundry, trying his best to clean out the smell of her cigarettes. Whenever she did the clothes, she'd burned holes in his shirts with her iron.

"You know what?" she asked.

"What?"

"You'll never admit this, but," and here she paused for another puff, "our divorce was the best thing we ever did for each other."

"Oh?" Edmond couldn't suppress his raised eyebrow. Unlike today, in the 70s a divorce made you an oddity, a disgusting curio in social circles. Unfriendly whispers followed you to every gathering, gazes made you uncomfortable. Everyone tried to avoid talking about "it."

Now? It was like buying a new car. No big deal.

"Well," she pulled the glowing cigarette from her lips and examined it critically, "we both went on to our greatest loves, didn't we? And you know, by then, we both knew so much more about suffering when we were done. I guess we must have learned to count our blessings."

Edmond nodded sanguinely.

"I heard you quit smoking."

She smiled. "Yes. Well, when he died. Cancer."

"Sorry to hear that. He was an SIA pilot, wasn't he?"

"Always travelling. I had so much 'me' time. I learned to miss him."

Edmond remembered the sympathy he felt for her when he'd attended her second husband's funeral. He had hugged her after it was over, the first time they had embraced since the divorce. She had cried deep, long sobs.

That was when it had struck home for both of them—they were not young anymore.

"You still look 33," Edmond mused.

They exchanged a dry chuckle.

She snorted, flicked the cigarette ash and rubbed her forehead with her wrist. "You should see me now. An old *ah mah*, sitting in my void deck, playing mahjong with senile old aunties, talking to old men with their caged birds."

Edmond felt pity well up again.

"I'll come by and visit you, Michelle."

"No, lah. Leave me alone."

Edmond got up and bid her goodbye.

Jalan Eunos was noisy, busy, loud. The most unpleasant part of his walk. The buses thundered angrily by, shoving him to the side with their slipstreams. Rushing cars honked angrily at others who cut into their lanes. Road works on one side of the road or another would join the cacophony of the evening. The new faces in the neighbourhood—Bangladeshis, China Chinese, Thais— bumped into him on the sidewalk, making him feel just a bit too uncomfortable.

A skimpily-clad PRC woman pulling a wheeled suitcase and her tanned crew-cut China boyfriend, also laden with luggage, nearly knocked him over when they brushed past him to race for the bus stop ahead. Edmond didn't even bother to ask for an apology.

As he was passing Jalan Kechot, he turned and saw the hulking figure of Gary Choo bearing down on him. Edmond raised his arms to stop the collision but, at the last minute, Gary pulled back and took to jogging on the spot. He was wearing 80s-era running shorts, embarrassingly tight, with double white lines running the down the sides. A gaudy sweat band was wrapped around his permed hair and two spongy orange-muffed headphones were clipped around both ears. Muffled progressive rock music emanated from them. He turned a wrist to examine the time on his expensive Swiss watch.

"Eh, Mr Edmond Olivera! So late!" He tried to chuckle but was out of breath, and puffed each word out with great effort.

"Hi, Gary. Jogging, ah?"

"At this time? No, lah. Right now, I'm on golfing trip somewhere. Bali, I think."

Edmond nodded. "I know. I heard you remarried."

"Fourth time lucky." Gary came to a sudden stop, bending over and grabbing his knees. When he felt his breath return, he forced himself to stand upright.

"How? Want to race me or not?"

Edmond shook his head.

"Why? Scared to lose?"

"Gary, I'm 67 years old. And you, what are you? 37?"

Gary chuckled. "Eh, we are the same batch from NUS, right? Edmond, Edmond, Edmond." He exhaled, struggling a little. "Always looking for an excuse. You know why I made general manager and you stayed in marketing?"

"Because you can carry balls?"

Gary laughed—it took effort considering how winded he was. "Wah, so bitter, *sia*."

"I'm not." Edmond resumed his stroll. He hoped Gary would leave him but, to his irritation, he followed, bouncing on the balls of his feet as he did.

"It's because I had drive and determination." He moved a little ahead and began backpedalling so that he could face Edmond as he spoke. "Do you know how much money I was making the year you left the company?"

"No." Edmond tried not to be irritated.

"Six hundred thousand dollars after tax, *sia*. Before share options some more," Gary puffed triumphantly.

"Hmm," Edmond nodded. "How's your heart?"

Gary's expression soured. "Eh, you know very well that my first heart attack doesn't happen until I'm fifty. I've got thirteen years of perfect health ahead of me before that."

He placed a hand on Edmond's shoulder, stopping him in his tracks.

"You know what's wrong with you?"

Edmond, challenged, stepped back and stared. A double-decker bus roared past, making him sway on his feet. Gary was everything Edmond hated about how things had changed since his youth. Expensive cars, condominiums and landed property you could never pay off, health care no one could afford, late nights in the office, a measly existence in an uncaring world.

Gary took Edmond's silence for surrender. "You were so concerned to go home every night to look after Jane. You could've gone where I went. You could have had the same opportunities I did. But you wasted it. You could've been like me."

Edmond nodded.

"Yeah, I know. Sad, depressed, and divorced three times."

Gary snarled. "Oh yeah? So tell me, when Jane got sick, did you pay for the medical bills?"

Edmond shook his head.

Gary nodded vigorously. "Correct. It was me. All your friends and ex-colleagues, a hundred dollars or fifty dollars only, probably would've barely paid for GST on your hospital bill. Then they would've kicked her out of that C ward."

Gary slapped his chest, a motion that made Edmond blink.

"Me. I paid off the bills."

Edmond couldn't say anything. Gary had done the right thing for him. Gary didn't have to do what he had to help Jane—even if it wasn't so much money to him.

"What do you want from me, Gary?"

Gary tapped Edmond's chest with his finger.

"Some appreciation. Like *gahmen* always say: you better appreciate me more." He turned forward again and sprinted off.

Edmond had walked only five minutes down Jalan Yasnin before he realized Jane had been walking by his side. He missed her so much. He couldn't think of a thing to say.

Thirty years of marriage and all he had now was the scent of her perfume as she took her place by his side. He offered her a hooked arm and she took it, without a word, leaning into his side and resting her cheek on his shoulder.

He glanced very briefly at her, glimpsed her strong, beautiful face. She was still 40, still vital, still the rock on which he had built the rest of his life.

When he no longer felt her hand on his elbow or smelled her scent, the turn down Lorong Marzuki back to Sims Avenue East seemed impossibly long and Edmond had to stop, and let the hot tears roll down his face. When his breathing returned to normal, he wiped his face and pressed on.

As he passed Bethesda Chapel, his father and mother passed him by. They were so old. Edmond had forgotten how old they'd been when they'd passed. White hair and wrinkles, mother in a black silk blouse and jade bangle on her wrist. Father in loose fitting gray slacks, leather shoes. They said hello. He shook hands with them, called his father "sir." They were not really ones for hugging.

"I know, son," his mother said. "You would've liked to have gone with Jane."

"I know I'm happy I left only a few weeks after your mother," his father said. They smiled at each other and returned their gaze to Edmond.

"You know why you are sad?" his father asked. Edmond could hear the holier-than-thou speech coming. "You should have had children."

"Don't be silly, Arthur," his mother nudged his father. "Jane was infertile. You know they tried."

"Is that true, Edmond?"

Edmond shook his head.

"I knew it," his father said.

His mother was baffled. She slowed her gait as the enormity of the revelation hit her. "You didn't want or she didn't want?" she asked, finally.

"I…She…We did," Edmond stammered.

"Oh, I could've had grandchildren," his mother sighed, exasperated.

His father shook his head. "Don't." He looked at Edmond, disappointed. "It's not as if children bring you that much happiness."

Edmond quickened his pace, and welcomed his return to the lights of the MRT station. His parents seemed to melt away in the shine, fading away in the corner of his eye as he reached the shops of Jalan Kembangan.

Andrew was waiting to cross the traffic junction when Edmond arrived.

"You know I saw Mum and Dad," Edmond said as he waited for the pedestrian traffic signal.

"Mmm hmm," Andrew grunted. "How are they?"

"Dead."

"Ah, we have something in common at last."

Edmond gave him an angry look.

Andrew's brow furrowed, "What? Don't tell me you're still convinced they loved me more than you?" He still looked healthy, in his forties, not the stick-like bean pole wrung slowly to death on the bed of a leukaemia ward in Perth where he'd migrated. Edmond had barely made it in time from Singapore, and Andrew had died the night after he had arrived. As if he had been waiting for his brother to come visit before letting go.

Edmond looked away at the traffic. "Why? You can read my thoughts?"

Andrew laughed.

"You're like a book. No, no, a book with Braille subtitles. Even a blind man could read you."

The light turned green and they began to cross.

"Edmond, you want know something?"

"What?" he said as they reached the other side.

"I envy you. You had twenty years more than I did," Andrew said. "Twenty more years of life I never had. I couldn't do better than that if I tried."

"Well," Edmond said bitterly, "everyone's journey comes to an end sometime."

Andrew turned and looked down the road back to the *kopitiam* at the junction of Jalan Senyum and Jalan Lapang. Edmond's walk was almost finished.

"Yes. It does," Andrew said.

The diners at the *kopitiam* saw the old man stumble as he reached the tables near the road. He was drenched in sweat and clutching his heart. The Malay youths chatting with their motorcycle buddies and chain-smoking over *mee goreng* were so taken aback by Edmond's collapse that they just stared for a while in shock as he lay on the floor panting.

Edmond looked up. A deep shadow stood over him. Eyes like a night full of stars.

"Why die this way?" he managed to gasp as his heart seized on him.

"It's your walk," came the reply in a deep soothing baritone. "Can die at home in your sleep, but you don't want. So? Die on the road here, lah."

Edmond managed a chuckle despite the crushing pain his ribs.

"*Wah*, I never thought you were so cynical," he whispered. His gaze cleared and instead of a shadow over him, he now saw three concerned Malay men, one lifting his head, another calling for an ambulance. Edmond closed his eyes.

To think—the whole walk had taken only 67 years.

REWRITES

Shelly Bryant

Naga looks out the window at the cranes. Yet another new casino, built on the latest addition of reclaimed land on Sentosa's western edge.

The door opens. It is Mr Chan, right on schedule, with a cluster of foreigners shuffling in behind him, all attired in either business wear or traditional ethnic garments from their respective nations. Naga suddenly feels underdressed in his polo shirt and jeans and wishes he'd worn his *baju melayu* instead, so as to fit in better.

"Here he is, ladies and gentlemen," Chan begins, beaming. Naga's eyes make their way round the circle as Chan goes through the necessary introductions. Ten nations, if Naga has not miscounted. He takes a deep breath. He's never spoken to such an international gathering before.

"Thank you all for making your way to the Science Park today," Naga begins. "I'm sure it's not one of your usual stops when you come to our little tropical paradise." An obligatory murmur of laughs comes from the group gathered in the reception area. "Well," he continues, "if you don't mind dispensing with formalities, we can talk on the way to the lab."

As they walk through the corridors of the building—still maintaining the polished feel of high-tech, cutting-edge industry despite its fifty-plus-year history—Naga gives a quick overview of the research to which he's devoted the last decade and a half of his life.

"I'm what we in the field call a rewriter," he says. "I make use of a field of technology that was originally envisioned as a means of terraforming other planets, first introduced sometime around the turn of the millennium. It has since branched out into other applications as well, including those areas—such as my own specialization—that seek to save our own planet's environment by completely recreating entire ecosystems, from the smallest microbe right up through to the largest creatures. What I do here in this lab is recreate biosystems using entirely synthetic organisms, utilizing DNA from the original ecosystem as a template, then rewriting it to be more durable. This allows us to create a more sustainable ecosystem and, at least in theory, it will be one that we can control more directly. This technology allows us to write out the parts of an organism that are easily susceptible to destruction by industrialization and urbanization. We hope they will interact with our natural ecosystems to make them more robust in the contemporary climate. At the very least, these recreations will prevent extinction, allowing all species in an ecosystem to live on, at least in synthetic form.

"As you may know, since its founding, our nation's efforts to retain the jungle even in the midst of the city has been so successful that we've become the model urban garden-scape that other cities in the region have sought to emulate for the past two or three generations. I hope you won't think me immodest if I suggest that we've served as a catalyst for the garden city movement that we've seen developing all around the world."

As he notes several nods of approval, he begins to really hit his stride. "My role as rewriter is to parallel the preservation efforts that have been at the heart of Singapore's values since the earliest days of our national history. But our approach is a little different from those governed by older preservation paradigms. Rather than the traditional approaches of preservation or conservation, I aim at recreation, and I use synthetic skin, organs, and, well, *everything* to accomplish this. The end result is a completely synthetic organism grown from the rewritten DNA template extracted from the original, natural ecosystem."

A Caucasian man in a business suit with a tie in garish colours clears his throat and interrupts Naga's speech. "What exactly do you mean 'synthetic'? Are you saying there are no natural, organic parts at all?"

"That is precisely what I am saying," Naga says, trying to keep the boastful edge from his voice. "The skin, the teeth, the organs, the bones, and every single cell in the entire replicated ecosystem are all made of synthetic materials. Like a whole world of teflon and polyester, if you'll allow me to use that illustration."

A woman in a hijab catches his eye. She asks, "Why do you prefer synthetics instead of, say, clones or other organic or semi-organic recreations?"

"It is generally agreed amongst synthetic biologists that organic biosystems, and even partially organic biosystems, are unnecessarily complex. By starting from scratch—which is really what we rewriters are doing—we understand all of the intricacies that underlie the biosystems we create, and so can engage them more directly and with fewer complications."

"Then why do you still employ the term biology?" she asks. "Doesn't that imply some organics?"

"Well, since we replicate biological functions in our ecosystems, the original rewriters coined the term synthetic biology. The beings we create should function the same as the organic originals, but have a less complex genetic, and sometimes anatomical, structure."

"They replicate all biological functions?" the woman continues. "Does that include evolution?"

"That's an excellent question. In theory, yes, but of course we've not been at it long enough to see that happen yet. Please remember that evolution is a very long process in organic biology. It should occur more rapidly with the synthetics, but 'rapid' only in comparison to the time spans counted in millions of years that are typical with organic ecosystems."

The woman nods, mulling over his explanation.

As they reach the door to the laboratory, Naga stops and waits until he has everyone's full attention. He wants the entrance to be properly dramatic.

"From early on, we've managed to integrate nature and cityscape here in Singapore, mostly through wise urban planning by an early group of visionaries. What lies behind these doors is a recreation of the *underwater* rainforest, a synthetic coral reef. You will find inside the aquariums in this room a complete biosystem. With appropriate funding from the nations represented in this gathering today, we can transplant this coral reef into the waters just off our shores here in the South China Sea. In this way, Singapore can continue its reclamation projects for building above ground without any net loss to the ecosystem in our seas. In the long run, we can reproduce this technology in other areas of the world that are suffering a similar strain on their natural biosystems due to the continued urbanization of our globe. And so now, let me introduce you to a perfectly reconstructed coral reef. Remember, all of the creatures you see here—everything from the coral and algae right on up to the largest sharks swimming in the waters—are all synthetic life forms."

With that, he opens the doors.

The woman who raised the earlier questions gasps. Naga just stares, bewildered.

In the central tank, overshadowing the beauty of the multi-hued coral, a grotesque sight meets their eyes. The floor of the tank is covered with bones and skins of various sea creatures.

The skins sag, looking like deflated balloons. Near the surface of the water in the central tank, a shark's skin floats, empty as those lying on the aquarium floor. It begins to wriggle. From behind the fearsome rows of teeth, a pair of eyes looks out at the little group of international dignitaries. Naga wonders what has survived not only being chewed to shreds by the shark, but also whatever force massacred all of the other creatures that were teeming in these tanks when he locked up the lab last night.

The eyes move closer, peering out from the gap between the sinister teeth. A ghastly white blob of a face worms its way out from the great maw, followed by a loosely shaped, bloated body. It looks like a giant, sated leech.

"Is that an...eel?" a dashiki-clad dignitary asks.

"It's got to be several times as big as any eel or sea snake," another delegate replies. "Isn't that right, Mr. Naga?"

"What in the world is it?" whispers one guest, his voice quivering.

"I...I think it's the hagfish," Naga finally says, his voice strained. He stands gaping, at a loss for what he should do in the face of this disastrous turn in his life's work.

"A hagfish? What's that?"

"It's a very old life form," the woman in the hijab says, "and something of a parasite. It feeds on the blood of its victims either by sucking it through the skin, or by worming its way into its prey's body and devouring it from the inside." All eyes turn to her; she shrugs and adds sheepishly, "It was in the information package Mr. Naga sent us. Surely I'm not the only one who read it."

Mr. Chan seems to regain his composure at last, leaving Naga as the only member of the group still reeling from the shock. "Ladies and gentlemen, let's head back to the office and let Mr. Naga lock the lab. We can discuss our business just as easily there."

"What business?" asks one of the visitors, now sweating profusely in his coat and tie. "You don't think any of our governments would put that thing into our seas, do you? You can bet we're going to do everything we can to stop you from putting it there too."

"So will we," adds the delegate in the green dashiki. "It seems that your calculations on evolution were off by quite a bit. Who knows what would happen to our oceans with such unbridled technologies inhabiting them?"

"Yes, well…" Mr. Chan stammers, "we can talk in the office."

As the group of visitors turns and heads down the corridor, the guests' complaints can still be heard. "Can you imagine the havoc that beast would wreak in the seas? It's a synthetic parasite, is all it is! It would wipe out entire ecosystems."

As the voices fade, Chan turns to Naga. "Billions of dollars in government grant money," he hisses, "and all you can come up with is that bloodsucking monster? I don't care what you do with that thing, as long as you get rid of it and keep it out of our waters. I want you and that…animal out of here by Monday. And if I find even a hint of it in Singapore's waters, I'll have you hung for treason."

He slams the door behind him, leaving Naga alone with the underwater wasteland.

Late in the evening, Naga sits in his now-empty office. There is a knock on the door. "Come in," he calls, his response automatic.

It is the tall Caucasian man in the dark suit. The bright colours of the man's power tie draw Naga's eyes to his guest, even as his mind lingers elsewhere.

"Mr Naga," the man begins. "I'm sorry for the way the situation developed today. It was obviously…uncomfortable for you."

"Yes."

"Well. Yes. Still, my government would like to discuss matters with you. Perhaps we can help you salvage something from the whole ordeal."

"Salvage something? Like what?" Though not meaning to sound snappish, he can't quite keep his voice free from bitterness.

"Do you remember the questions my office sent you last month?"

"Yes. But I am afraid your government will just have to put off its plans for that underwater theme park. You saw the results today. It looked more like the Kingdom of the Underworld than the Underwater Kingdom you wanted to create."

"But perhaps there are other applications of the technology?"

"Oh. Well, I'm afraid expanding your Pioneer Days Wildlife Park won't be any more feasible. Again, you saw with your own eyes what happened. Would you like me to rewrite lifeforms suited to the land of the pioneers for you, only to end up losing the organic wildlife that still remains there now? It would wipe everything out much faster than urbanization already has. No, I'm afraid it wouldn't work at all."

"Yes. I see that. Still…"

There is an uncomfortable pause. Naga looks at the stranger's face, wondering what he could possibly have in mind.

"How about this," the dignitary finally continues. "My government is willing to buy the surviving specimen off your hands. I'm sure you will have certain, er, financial losses to recoup. Tell me what you'd require on that front, and we will start from there in our calculations."

An image of Mr. Chan's irate expression flashes before Naga's eyes. He has not yet had time to think of all the repercussions of the hagfish fiasco. He is not sure he is ready to consider the possibility of the financial ruin he could face. His reputation is certainly shot already. The chance to salvage something from his years of research suddenly seems very enticing. And Mr Chan *did* leave it up to him to find a way to get rid of it.

"Well," he says, "I haven't sat down to crunch the numbers yet, but I could get that to you by tomorrow morning, I suppose. You'd have to agree to have it out of here by Monday, though. Oh, and I'd need a guarantee that we'd never see it in Singapore's waters, of course. That will be central to the deal."

"Yes, yes. That will all be just fine. Let me clarify one point with you, though. There is absolutely nothing organic about the creature?"

"Nothing at all," Naga says. "That monster is one hundred percent my creation, totally synthetic."

As soon as the Caucasian man's car arrives, he gets in and closes the soundproof screen between the driver and himself. He pulls at his tie and removes his jacket, clothing obviously designed for his homeland rather than the heat and humidity of this little island, then takes out his cell phone and punches in the number.

"He's in, ma'am. He'll give us the numbers in the morning."

He listens to a series of questions.

"You saw the video? Just the threat of releasing that thing into the sea off their coast will be enough. They'll give us free passage to the port without any further arguments, I can assure you. No duties, and no discussion. It is a frightening thought to imagine what damage that beast could do to an economy so reliant on the waters off its shores as *they* are."

He drums his fingers on his knee as he listens to the worried response.

"No, no, ma'am, don't worry. 'Beast' is just a figure of speech. It is not an animal at all. Nothing organic about it. Naga is very clear about that, and I pressed him several times both before and after the presentation. We are free from blame. This will not violate the ban on biological weapons at all…No, it's not a weapon of mass destruction either. It's just one fish. There's not even another to mate it with—and I don't know if synthetic organisms *can* even mate…No, I didn't ask. Anyway, it doesn't matter. This…thing will create a great deal of havoc, but it will be a havoc contained to the area we choose to target."

There is a long pause before the Secretary of Defence answers. Hearing her reply, the delegate smiles.

"Yes, ma'am. I'm sure Mr Naga will deliver his work to us without a second thought. Believe me, he wants to be rid of the little bloodsucker altogether. Yes, that's right. No worries. Leave the rewriter to me."

He presses the red button on his phone and slips it into his pocket just as the car turns into the hotel car park. He gets out, makes his way through the glaring lights and blaring music of the casino, and into the hotel lobby. There, he hums a folk tune as he waits to hear the soft *ding* and the familiar sliding of the lift doors.

BIG ENOUGH FOR THE ENTIRE UNIVERSE

Victor Fernando R Ocampo

Day 2, 2000 hours: Somewhere in a Bukit Gombak Military Installation

"Love is like earth," Madame Semangat said softly, as she adjusted her *hijab* and drew her thin shawl closer. The impromptu medical exam had left her visibly shaken. "She said you needed to cultivate it constantly to grow anything."

"Is that it?" asked the investigating officer, a thin Peranakan man, wearing an olive drab uniform and a pair of thick, black-rimmed glasses.

"No," the woman continued, "She said that having a family was like growing a garden. Then she asked me what I would do if my garden was destroyed."

"What did you say?"

"I said that plants could be grown from seeds. Life comes from tiny beginnings. I would begin again."

"When did you have this conversation?"

"A few months ago," the primary-school teacher replied. "She wrote that note about love and family on a post-it and left it on my door, along with a small plant as a gift."

Madame Semangat was anxious to finish the interview. She gave her inquisitor a long, pleading look and quickly changed the subject. "Please officer, my family doesn't know anything. Please, let us go home."

"How well did you know her?" he asked, ignoring her small protests and looked instead at the long list of questions on his tablet. "What kind of person was Madame Xin?"

"She was a very private person. She hardly spoke to anyone after the accident," she recalled. Her voice had become very small and defeated. "When can I see my husband and my children? Are they all right? My youngest will need milk and my husband needs his medications."

"They are undergoing medical evaluation in the other rooms. Not to worry, their needs will be attended to," he answered coldly. "How often did you talk to each other?"

"Not often, mostly when she watered her plants in the common corridor. Although, to be honest, she talked to them more than she ever spoke to us. Still, she was nice enough, I suppose, especially on the birthday of her boy. She would give my children rice cakes and watermelon seeds. Or was it lotus seeds? I don't remember right now."

"Did you know what kind of work she did?"

"When can we go back home, officer? My children will be very frightened without me." Madame Semangat looked at the expressionless young man in front of her and decided that he would not make a good father.

"Did they...did they find her body yet?"

"I do not have that information," he noted mechanically. "We will let you know when your family can move back to your unit."

"*Inna lillahi wa inna ilahi raji'un,*" she exclaimed, bowing her head. "We all belong to Allah and to him we will all return."

"Did you know what kind of work she did?" he repeated.

"I thought she had some job in I.T. Why?" The middle-aged Muslim woman had grown tired of the long inquiry. She tore the questionnaire she had been given into small, evenly sized pieces and piled them into a white mound. "Please, we were just neighbours. We don't know anything. My husband has diabetes, he cannot *tahan* this stress. We just want to go home."

"Just a few more questions," he said more gently. "Please be patient. Did you ever notice anything strange or unusual about her?"

"Have you seen her plants?" she exclaimed unexpectedly. "I teach science to Primary Three students, and I can tell you that it is impossible for them to grow in Singapore."

"Which plants are those?"

"Bleeding heart vines, love-in-the-mist, and her favourite, love-lies-bleeding. So strange and...poetic, I think that's best word to describe them."

"You said she gave you a plant with the post-it note. What was it?"

"Oh, she called it a Resurrection Plant, something you will never find at a *pasar malam*. It looked like a little brown ball when she brought it to our door. She told me that if I placed it in a bowl with some water it would come back to life, and it did. It was so amazing. The dead plant actually turned green again."

"Did she ever tell you what she was working on?"

"Do you mean what she was doing in that awful room?" Madame Semangat recalled some disturbing scenes she had seen from their corridor, but she wasn't sure if they meant anything. Her voice betrayed her nervous uncertainty. "No, I don't think so."

"Are you sure?"

"Yes...no, I mean yes. Double confirm officer, yes, double confirm." She repeated nervously. "But you know I always felt that without her family, she was a gone case. Her eyes, there was nothing in her eyes but *sudah mati*, death."

"Did she ever talk to you about maths or anything involving numbers or computer programming?"

"No. Not that I can recall. Why?"

"Madame Xin had a doctorate in advanced mathematics. Think hard, Madame Semangat," he insisted. "If you give me something I can use, perhaps we can all go home earlier."

The old teacher leaned back and scanned her memories.

Suddenly her eyes lit up with a surprise recollection. "Wait, yes, I do remember something. A few months after the accident, I remember now. I saw her wandering in the void deck looking confused. I'd never seen her blur like *sotong* before; she was always such a clever woman. I walked her back to her flat and she said the oddest thing. 'Do you know what an algorithm is, Rauddah? It's a step-by-step procedure for calculating numbers, a formula.' She said, 'Life is made up of numbers Rauddah. People are just information, all of us. Perhaps I can recreate them using an algorithm, Rauddah.' Or something like that. That's all I remember officer, truly."

"Thank you, Madame Semangat."

"May we please go home now?" she insisted. "I need to see my family."

"I'm afraid we have a situation at your HDB. Your family will have to be relocated for your own safety."

"What? What is the emergency?"

"Let me show you," he said, tapping a video app icon on his tablet.

Day 2, 2200 hours: Somewhere in a Bukit Gombak Military Installation

"Yes, she said something like that. How did you know?"

"What did she say, Madame Shen? What exactly did she say?"

"It's *Mizz* Shen," the thin, bespectacled woman corrected him. "I was divorced last year. That *chee ko pek*—that pervert left me for his student intern. She's less than half his age. I should have known when we stopped sleeping together. All men are *buaya*, no offense. I go by 'Ms.' now."

"Okay, let's stay on topic Ms. Shen, shall we?" To calm her down, the officer enunciated his words slowly, as if he was talking to a small child. "What did Dr. Xin tell you?"

"She said that love was like air. Without it you cannot breathe. What garbage. Her brain is spoilt after the accident."

"Did she say anything else?"

"Afterwards she said that Alan was like air to her. He was her spirit, her 'breath of life,' she said. Anyone with kids would forgive her, she kept repeating. I had Sanjeev, she said I would understand. I do not know why she kept *talking cock, lah*."

"When did she tell you this?"

"My son used to play with her boy," she said. "They used to play every day on the void deck. He was a nice one, that Alan, very polite, not like other kids. He used to help my boy Sanjeev with his maths homework. After the accident happened, Sanjeev would keep knocking on her door. He looked for Alan every day. It was embarrassing, *lorh*. He did not understand what happened, my poor boy. All he knew that his playmate was gone."

"Let's go back to what Dr. Xin said, please," the officer repeated. Beads of frustration had started to form at his brow.

"Sorry. It happened during the last school holidays. Sanjeev was still missing Alan. He ran to knock on her door again. I came out to apologize to Dr. Xin. Poor girl, she just stood by the metal grating, drinking something *chao* and talking nonsense. That's when she told me that thing about love. I knew she a gone case already."

"Are you familiar with Dr. Xin's work?"

"She was involved in maths—correct or not? I think it was something with computers. I sat next to her during our MP's last visit."

"Have you ever been inside her house?"

"Of course not, lah; the windows were always covered. But I peek through the door a few times. Everything was ordinary, like my house, except for the wires on the floor."

"Wires?"

"Yah lah," Ms. Shen said, "wires everywhere, covering everything."

"What did you think was going on inside?"

"*Aiyoh*, I am not *kaypoh*," she said, getting irritated by the deluge of questions and her interviewer's droning monotone. "I mind my own business, okay? Not like that whore in 42-D. That one, *aiyoh, aiyoh,* when her *ang moh* boyfriend come over no one on our floor can sleep!"

"Do you know anything about what was in Dr. Xin's bedroom?"

"Eh, how I know?" she grumbled as she fumbled for a cigarette in her handbag.

"I'm sorry, you cannot smoke here," the officer said. "So you have no idea what was happening?"

Ms. Shen muttered something under her breath. It sounded like the words for a man's private parts in Hokkien. She decided that the man in front of her was an officious asshole.

"You cannot hold us," the woman said, tapping her hands nervously on the plastic base of her chair. "We have done nothing, what? I demand to see my boy!"

"Answer all my questions and we will return him to your custody. Now, when did the power start fluctuating in your unit?"

"*Wahlao*, ask Singapore Power!" she exclaimed, unleashing the unpredictable bile peculiar to those born in the year of the yellow wind-dragon. Ms. Shen closed her eyes and imagined whacking the officer with a big stick. "I don't know, six months ago? Everyone complain, nothing happen. My boy, he is naughty sometimes. He opened one of her bills by mistake. I saw the SP Services one—she was paying more than $2,000 a month. You mean the *gahmen* never notice that?"

"Thank you, that may be useful. We will check it out."

"I want my son!" she cried, as her false bravado started to crumble. "I cannot *tahan* this anymore. We want to go home."

"We will release your boy soon." The officer said, in the puerile tone of someone hiding deep secrets. "But you cannot go home. Not yet."

"Why not?" she screamed, releasing another stream of colourful Hokkien invectives. The biting words seemed to hang in the air like fine soot.

The investigating officer pressed something on his tablet and showed Ms. Shen the images on the screen. "This is a live feed of what's happening at your block," he said.

The woman glanced over the top of her spectacles and stared at the moving pictures in disbelief. Her eyes widened and her jaw dropped. For a full sixty seconds, no words would form in her mouth. The gravity of the situation hit her like a car crash.

"What…What is that?" she muttered. "It's so big and so…so *cheem.*"

"Now you understand why we are extremely cautious," he said quietly.

Ms. Shen collapsed into a heap on the swivelling office chair. "She worked with numbers. I'm an accountant. I work with numbers too. How can numbers be dangerous?"

"We are all just pieces of information," said the officer, a former I.T. specialist, as he too was caught up in the tablet's searing images, "and all information can be processed."

Day 3, 0000 hours: Somewhere in a Bukit Gombak Military Installation

"What is your relationship with Mr. Borges?" the officer asked.

The painted woman adjusted her too-short skirt and tried to hide her legs under the interrogation table. She looked around the holding room and noticed that everything was grey—the carpet, the table, the chairs and even the mirrors on the right wall. She decided that the glass was double-sided, just like the television procedurals, and moved her legs towards the opposite direction.

"He's my fiancé," she answered curtly. "Where is George? Are we under arrest?"

"You are both here for your own protection, Ms. Ai," the officer explained calmly. "As I said earlier, we need to ask you a few questions."

"I need a shower." The woman said, wiping at a smear of grey slime that had stained her thin, Sarong Party Girl-style dress. "Why are we being held? I demand to be released now. Your medical exam was humiliating and my mascara is running."

"Just answer a few more questions and we will see what we can do," the officer said, handing her a packet of tissues. "How do you know Dr. Xin?"

"She lives two doors down from me, at 42-B," she answered brusquely. "My parents know her better, but they're in Perth for the next six months."

"Are you familiar with her work?"

"I only knew she was some kind of maths genius," the young woman said, making small irritated noises. She looked at her chipped nails and mentally added a manicure to her list of must-do items. "I thought hot-shot I.T. folks were paid well. What's she doing living in an HDB?"

"Your block is in an executive HDB. It's like a condominium."

"I *know* that," the woman snapped, as she cleared the dark smudges from her under her eyes. "I *live* there."

"Do you know anything about the programs she was working on?"

The young woman stared at her interviewer with dagger-like intensity. Just a few hours ago, she and her boyfriend had come home from a hot date, and she had been looking forward to another night of steamy lovemaking. They had been walking along the corridor, in front of Dr. Xin's flat, when it, for lack of a better word, exploded. A quick response team had hauled them from the slimy rubble and brought them to Bukit Gombak in separate vehicles. There, a team of faceless doctors had examined her, taken samples of the slime, and brought her to a holding room where she had waited hours for someone to talk to.

This was not how things happened in movies, she thought. She was a Singaporean citizen. She had voted for the ruling party. This was not how she should be treated.

"No, I have no idea. I have absolutely no *effing* idea what's going on!" she cried, wanting to throw a chair at her infuriatingly calm interviewer. "Where is George? Is he alive? Where is my phone? Where is my LV handbag?"

"Mr. Borges is alive and like you, he seems surprisingly unharmed," the officer noted. "He is being interviewed in another room. We did not find your things when we rescued you under all that ehm…organic matter."

"I just want to go home! We already told the police and the SCDF what happened." She decided that her officious interviewer must have had tiny reproductive organs. "Who do I have to talk to, to go home?"

The officer pulled out his tablet and showed Ms. Ai the live video feed from her HDB block.

The young woman stared at the screen with a bewildered look. She leaned back against the swivel chair, stunned into silence.

"May I have some water please?" she said finally. "I don't understand. Is that real? What is that…thing?"

"We don't know," the officer said grimly. "But it's growing exponentially. It now covers three whole blocks. We may have to evacuate the whole of Bukit Batok. We need to find a way to stop this, Ms. Ai, please."

"It," she croaked, "it probably has my LV. Shit."

Another officer entered the room and brought a plastic cup filled with water.

"Let's try this again," he said. "Are you familiar with Dr. Xin's work?"

"Not really," she said, knowing that this was only a half-truth. She debated on how to best share her information without destroying her current relationship.

Her fiancé George had gone to visit his parents in Argentina for two weeks. That was just too long a time for her to go without sex. Ms. Ai had decided she needed a substitute. Dr. Xin had an assistant, a programmer from Manila who helped her with her strange machines. Ms. Ai had met him in the lift one day and she invited him in for a drink. She usually preferred potatoes to rice but the little brown college boy was cute, and she'd treated the whole affair as charity work.

"You need to find this Filipino guy, Ghabby Marquez," she said. "He's a student at the National University. He moonlights as her assistant and I…I have something else to tell you."

The officer scribbled the name on his tablet and excused himself for a minute. She resumed her story when he returned to the holding room.

"One day, I passed her doorway and the gate was open," Ms. Ai continued. "She was standing there, reeking of whiskey. She spoke to me in with that cold, dead voice of hers: 'You play with fire, girl.' She said, 'Love is like fire, it burns you until you are consumed and there is nothing left. You are in the chicken business, selling meat, not love.' I got scared and ran back towards my flat. She had called me an *effing* prostitute."

"This Mr. Marquez, did he tell you what they were working on inside?"

"Yes, but I didn't believe him."

"Why, what was it?"

"He said they were writing an algorithm for the soul."

Day 3, 0600 hours: Somewhere in a Bukit Gombak Military Installation

"Will I get deported?" the young man asked.

"That is a matter for immigration to sort out," the interrogating officer answered. "Now Mr. Marquez…"

"Please," the student insisted, "call me Ghabby."

"Okay. Ghabby. Tell me everything once again."

"Wait, I need you to know that I only took this job because my mother is sick," the young man explained, staring at his open palms. "My family is poor and I needed to remit money every month for her treatment."

"Tell me about the monkeys again," the officer prodded, pointing a video camera towards Ghabby's direction. "You said that the source code came to her in a dream. Try to remember every detail."

"But I already told you everything."

"Please, repeat it for the camera and try to remember everything she told you."

"But it was just her dream," the young man insisted. "Why are you taking it seriously? It doesn't even make sense to me."

"What's out there right now is what makes no sense. We need to figure this out and you are our only lead. Let's do this again, please?"

"Yes, sir." Ghabby nodded nervously, subconsciously making the sign of the cross. The camera's dark lens reminded him of the evil eye.

"Like I told you, Dr. Xin's family died in a car accident. A few weeks after they were buried, she told me she had a strange lucid dream. It went something like this…"

I found myself wandering an enormous library, which was a big as the universe itself. It looked something like a honeycomb or a warren, made up of an infinite number of identical galleries, separated by vast airspaces, and connected by an innumerable number of staircases.

I wandered aimlessly for what seemed like months or years, marvelling at how every book I had ever read and every book I had ever imagined could be found among its shelves. In the impossibly huge centre of each gallery, I saw a beacon of light—like Foucault's pendulum, it was a single axis extrapolating towards various infinities.

At some point, I found a gallery different from all the others. It was painted crimson instead of black, and was as large as the entire library itself. Inside were an infinite number of monkeys, each one hitting the keys of a typewriter which filled endless reams of paper. Running between each row were even more monkeys, gathering the discarded sheets. The runners were wearing little shirts, each embroidered with the word 'inquisitor'.'

One of the monkeys looked familiar. He was a stocky, big-eared creature who looked just like a miniature English college don. In fact he looked like my favourite mathematician, Alan Turing: the man I named my son after. I called out to him and the other monkeys told me that he was the leader of their troop.

'I am Translucia Baboon' he told me, 'I can provide any text that can possibly ever be written, no matter what the length, no matter what the language.'

I explained to him that maths was a language, and that an algorithm was just like any piece of text. I challenged him to write a code that would re-create my family. I asked him for the equation for life and the algorithm for creating souls.

A high-pitched cry interrupted Ghabby's story. The plaintive sound was so loud and forceful that it shattered all the windows in the complex. Later on, the young man would discover that it had, in fact, shattered every window in Singapore.

"What was that? There's something happening outside. Shouldn't you be trying to do something?"

"Whatever it is, I'm sure we are already addressing it," the officer answered in his usual manner, without haste. "Now, let's carry on. Did you see the source code?"

"What's wrong with you?" the young man raised his voice. "That sounded like...I don't know, that sounded like someone giving birth."

"Let's focus shall we?" the officer repeated. "Again, did you see the source code, Mr. Marquez?"

"Yeah, she gave me that weird code that came from her dream. I had to translate it into machine language," the young man answered, tugging at his hair nervously. "Basically it was a set of simple reaction–diffusion equations for pattern formation. But I never had access to her bedroom or the machines she kept there. I was only allowed to use the test servers."

"Can you recreate what she did?"

"Only the parts that I worked on."

"What did you think you were doing in there?"

"I'm just an exchange student, sir" Ghabby sighed, deciding that the officer was probably not human and quite possibly soulless. "I needed money, so I responded to her ad for a part-time programmer. I don't really know what she was doing. She never gave me the full picture."

"Filipinos are a generally nosy folk," the officer said, somewhat offensively. "I cannot believe that you were never curious about your employer."

"I was at the start." The young man sighed, looking down at his shaking palms once again. "Especially when I saw the freezers in the bedroom. Anyway, Dr. Xin rarely wanted to talk, except on birthdays or anniversaries. She told me about the monkeys on the third anniversary of the death of her husband and son. The money was good so I didn't want to rock the boat. My mother has lung cancer. I swear I didn't know the doctor was doing something illegal."

"Is that everything you can tell me?"

"Well she kept on repeating something the last time I saw her."

"What was she repeating?"

"'Love is like water,' she said. 'It always seeks its own level. Nothing can stop it.'"

Day 3, 1300 hours onwards: Bukit Batok and various locales in Singapore

After being released by the authorities, Ghabby G. Marquez, Filipino exchange student, devout Catholic and world-class computer programmer, went to Geylang and blew his mother's chemotherapy money on a series of prostitutes. His grim situation had given him an undiscovered thirst for life.

Ms. Ai and her fiancé Mr. Borges were given a change of ill-fitting clothes and dropped off at Holland Village. There, in front of a store that specialized in wedding bands, they had a noisy public fight and called off their engagement. In the many hours she had been kept in the quiet of the holding room, Ms. Ai had sorted out her life and re-ordered her priorities. Now it was time to burn bridges. She called an aunt and borrowed money for a ticket to Australia. She left that very same afternoon. Mr. Borges went to a nearby pub and drank himself under the table. When he finally sobered up the next day, he joined the long queue of expats desperate to leave Singapore, but there were no more flights available.

Ms. Shen collected her son Sanjeev, and fled with him to her parent's flat in the opposition ward of Hougang. There, in an HDB estate where the lifts failed to operate properly, they waited for their fate. Oddly, the harrowing experience had released all her pent-up bitterness and she discovered that she was no longer scared. For the first time since her divorce, she was able to breathe a sigh of relief.

On that same afternoon, Madame Semangat and her family cashed in their life savings. They went to the West Coast Car Mall and bought a cheap second-hand van, stocking it with new clothes and groceries. After a hurried meal at a Malay cooked food stall, they drove towards her family's relatives in Johor. There, next to the house where her grandmother had been born, she and her family started a vegetable garden.

At exactly 1300 hours on the third day of the crisis, the special agent overseeing the witnesses sat alone in his cold, featureless room. He shut off the video feed and rubbed his tired eyes. He got up and stretched his weary muscles, before returning to his tablet and scanning his messages. Afterwards, he pulled up a browser window and checked Dr. Xin's blog, *The Fake Timaeus*. He read her last post from three days earlier:

Love is the demiurge that builds substance from the elements of our lives.

He dwelled on these, her last words, and thought about his own meaning and purpose in the universe. He tried to think of a word that described his life, but the only thing that would come to mind was an old UNIX command from his programming days: /dev/null, a special file that discarded all data written to it.

He opened his files again and scrolled through the interview transcripts, reading random passages.

Love is like earth. You need to cultivate it constantly to grow anything.

Love is like air. Without it you cannot breathe.

Love is like fire. It burns you until you are consumed and there is nothing left.

Love is like water. It always seeks its own level. Nothing can stop it.

Haunted by a dark animus he could not fathom, the promising young officer took out his service pistol and—without haste and with great care—shot himself in the head.

Outside, just a short train ride from the secret military complex, a giant blob of grey goo in the shape of a human heart was expanding slowly but relentlessly over everything in its path. Inside churned millions and millions of organic molecular nanobots, each holding the codes to three lost souls, now united once more for eternity. With every heartbeat, the nanobots replicated a mother's unconditional and infinite love—a love big enough to contain Death and the entire universe itself.

THE DIGITS

Ivan Ang

For most, it started with the release of PoolzConnect, a multimedia network system devised by the Singapore Pools to allow Singaporeans greater ease in placing their 4D bets using their cell phones or any available electronic transmitting devices. All one had to do was to guess a combination of four digits (hence: 4D), ranging 0 to 9. The larger the bet, the greater the payout if the winning combination was hit. The cash prizes were generous. Three days a week, the winning combination would be picked from a lotto machine in full view of an audience, where they could enjoy the minute-by-minute denouement of their hopes and dreams.

Two weeks after the great democratization of 4D, Martin Wong was working as usual at Fuzzy Pet Shop cleaning the cages and tanks. He loved fish. An ideal evening for Martin was to simply stare at the life forms moving about in the water in their strange swaying ways. Martin's prized possession was a Flowerhorn cichlid, which he'd bought from the pet shop. No one else was buying it anyway, and he got a hefty discount. That night, as Martin was routinely staring at his fish, he noticed, for the first time, something different on its scales. They weren't the typical black blotches common on the scales of the Flowerhorn. The blotches resembled numbers. The numbers were clear: 4, 7, 4...

What happened next was itself an inexplicable moment even for Martin, for all he could think about was the 4D. He went out the next day and placed his bet on the combination he'd seen on his fish. He won the top prize of $76,000. Martin moved out of his one-room rental. Bought the Flowerhorn a five-foot tank. Made many new friends. One of them took a video of the fish on his cell phone and posted it on YouTube. The video drew lists of comments mixed with incredulity and disbelief. While almost everyone dismissed it as a hoax, few could ignore the vivid imprint of the winning combination on the scales of the fish. The video received over a million views.

When the word got out that winning combinations for 4D could be found on Flowerhorn cichlids, the buying frenzy began, some grabbing as much as five fish at a go. Before the incident, the Flowerhorn fish had never been popular. With its oddly swollen head, it resembled a blowfish that had succeeded in enlarging its head rather than its body. But ugliness was a highly forgivable aspect in animals, more so when they were said to bring windfalls. Pet shops cleared out the hamsters and the gerbils to build more tanks to hold the fish. Martin Wong set up a shop that sold nothing but the rarest and most swollen-headed Flowerhorns. The debut issue of a new magazine called *Fish!* contained an exclusive interview with Martin Wong and his "secret" for bringing out the desired numbers on the scales of the fish. The issue enjoyed three reprints.

But then the numbers ceased as to appear as inexplicably as they first had appeared. With the absence of numbers, the Flowerhorns were once again seen as ugly. Loving owners turned on their prized fish and dumped them in the river and canals. With no ability to survive in the wild, the dumped Flowerhorns died by the dozens. The result was quite cinematic: the Singapore River coated with a blanket of rotting alien-looking fish with bulbous heads. A few birds pecked at the Flowerhorn carcasses, but their flesh was unpleasant. The government later imposed a no-dumping law and ordered an extensive clean-up of the river. All future imports of the Flowerhorn were also banned. Martin Wong closed his pet shop and started a new career as a touted professional 4D gambler and advisor, but without the numbers on his fish, he soon lost all the money he had won and all the friends he'd made.

But the numbers did not disappear; they simply settled elsewhere. This time, it was a loans officer at the main DBS branch and his fiancée who were caught unawares. Together, they owned a Dalmatian named Jesse. The dog belonged to the loans officer, but having gotten engaged three months before, they decided that they now co-owned everything. The fiancée was taking Jesse out for her routine evening walk when she first noticed the odd shapes on the dog's body. She spoke of the shapes later that day. The loans officer, a hardened skeptic from his years of work at the bank, had never had patience for such nonsense. Everything could be reduced to facts, and facts could always be backed by numbers. But numbers, it turned out, were precisely the problem. Peering at the body of his very active and constantly happy dog, he found it difficult to deny that the odd shapes on their dog did indeed resemble a set of four numbers: 9, 6, 7...

The couple was reminded of the strange story of how a fish owner had struck a windfall over numbers on his fish. They placed their bets on the combination of numbers found on the fur of their dog. They won $78,000 from the lottery. They weren't gamblers, they told the press later. It was just that you don't see numbers on a dog every day. The couple later set up a grooming centre, designed to help Dalmatian owners groom numbers out of their dogs' fur. However, the centre closed down in a month, after an owner's hand was mauled by a highly-strung Dalmatian when he attempted to stroke it.

The couple's win at the lottery sparked a bout of Dalmatian-buying. The SPCA and other animal welfare organizations warned against this mindless buying of pets that would have to be put down once the owners could find no numbers on them. The Singapore Pools helped run public service messages in support of SPCA advising people not to buy pets over some unverified rumour of lottery numbers showing up on the fur of animals.

As with the fish, no numbers showed up on the fur of other Dalmatians. One by one, the dogs were left on the streets, to be picked up by others who had nothing to lose, should the numbers ever appear again. When no numbers showed, the dogs were returned to the streets. Maybe the numbers would only appear once on one particular type of animal. Which animal was next? The rumours ran wild. People began buying all sorts of pets—hamsters, rabbits and even parrots—hoping they would get the animal whose fur or feathers would reveal the next winning combination. There couldn't have been a better time to be a pet shop owner.

People began seeing numbers everywhere, even those that were never there, even in smudges on fur that bore no semblance to numbers. They did not care. When they won nothing, they abandoned their pets. There was no use for pets without numbers. Roadkills became common. Animal welfare organizations ran protests. Fines were eventually levied on anyone who abandoned their pets. Pet owners began turning to centres offering animal cremation services, where their pets would be humanely put down and cremated instantly. The animal cremation centres were making profit margins they could not have foreseen thanks to the overwhelming demand for animal cremations daily. It took months before people gave up looking for numbers. Even more months for pet store owners to realize that selling pets wasn't profitable anymore. One by one, the many pet stores that lined the streets withered and disappeared as suddenly as they had sprung up.

Then it started again.

The zookeeper had been working at The Singapore Zoo for over six years. Part of his job involved the preparation of food for the antelope and deer enclosures. One day, he went around on his routine checks and served the antelopes their feed in the morning. The antelopes kept their nervous distance as he laid out the dish of fruit and grass. He looked up and saw the smudged patterns on the body of the spotted antelope standing closest to him. The first thought was that it was a trick of light. But it wasn't, and staring harder, he could make out: 7, 0, 2...

He remembered the fish. He remembered the dog. He remembered the numbers. He left in a hurry before anyone else saw him and placed a bet on the combination. He won the top prize the very next day. Half a million dollars. He bought a new Lexus, and called the press.

The visitors to the zoo doubled. They came to see the numbers on the spotted animals' fur. The management did not think there would be any more numbers on animals. They took delight in the gullibility of the people. It was good money. For once, they needed the police to manage the crowd. Everyone was looking for numbers and when they found them, they left the zoo to place their bets on the combination.

There were numbers everywhere they looked. On the giraffes. On the spotted hyena. On the cheetahs. Numbers for everyone. All the combinations found on the animals won prizes—first, second, third, and even consolations. It was official. It was a miracle. The animals were here to bless everyone with wealth.

The management could no longer manage the massive influx of people entering the zoo each day. The director of the zoo, Mr. Charles Zobel, could not tell if he was living a dream or a nightmare. He had big plans for the zoo. Hordes of people queued up outside his zoo waiting to see the numbers.

The patterns on the animals changed daily, ensuring a permanent mob of visitors. The police were not managing the crowd as ideally as the zoo wished. People were running about, dashing to the enclosures of the spotted animals, pushing, shoving and squeezing to get their look. The zoo resembled a mall selling branded goods with massive discounts rather than a place to educate people about fascinating creatures. Out of desperation, the zoo created an online balloting system that randomly assigned passes to visitors. Foreigners and tourists were given priority. All potential visitors to the zoo would first have to be a registered user online. They had to pay a set fee to have their names registered for the balloting of entrance tickets. No refund would be given if they were not picked to visit the zoo on that day. For each day, only 400 people were allowed into the zoo. And no one could enter the zoo twice in the same year. The people were displeased. It was an infringement of their rights. The zoo was ripping them off. They attempted to protest. The zoo was adamant. Ballot, or no entry. The people succumbed. One by one, they registered online. Those who got tickets into the zoo got to see the numbers. Those who did, won the lottery the next day.

Why were numbers appearing on fur? It was a coincidence, the biologists said. They were mere genetic mutations occurring at random, very much like how some rabbits had heart-shaped patterns on their bodies, or how certain black horses developed a white-star pattern on their foreheads. But the numbers were not random; the patterns changed daily, and each set of numbers matched the combination of the lottery. When science failed to offer an explanation, religion took over. It had to be the devil, using animals to carry out his insidious plan of poisoning the mind of the nation. Making people slaves of the lottery system.

And it was working. It was the end of the world. It was time to repent. Do not visit the zoo, the heart of all evil.

Two months after the news of numbers appearing on the fur of the spotted zoo animals, the people lost faith in having a computer determine their entry into the zoo. The online balloting system allocated a day pass to a teacher, who had been given an entry pass just the week before. His total winnings amounted to $140,000. He sent in his resignation letter and set up a private tuition and learning centre made up of his former co-workers. The school was furious. The people were furious. Computers could not be trusted. Something was bound to screw up. Due to the incident, Singaporean citizens were temporarily barred from entering the zoo. Tourists could enter freely, which to most amounted to the worst form of discrimination ever—prizing foreigners over locals.

Disgruntled individuals created a Facebook page rallying people to fight the unfair balloting system and a change of the zoo management. The page received 9,000 "Likes" in two hours. The next day, people began camping outside the zoo demanding the first-come-first-serve mode of entry: let those who made the extra effort to come to the zoo early be rewarded. Lines of police officers once again formed outside of the zoo to protect visiting tourists. Perhaps it was the indignity of being barred from the zoo, or the desperation to see the numbers, but some protestors barged through the police line in an attempt to snatch entry tickets from the tourists. The police officers intervened. Punches were thrown. A scream. A shuffle of bodies. A shot rang out followed by a collective scream of shock and horror.

The zoo was shut for a week.

That week, the Singapore Pools sat down for a long meeting. They were facing a crisis. The people would only bet on numbers they knew would win the lottery. This was not right. The lottery was exciting precisely because you did not know if you have the winning combination or not. The digit-giving animals were robbing people of the precious opportunity to experience chance and excitement. Something had to change. The house must always win.

In an unprecedented move, The Pools announced that Toto, a lottery game consisting of six numbers, would replace 4D, effective immediately. The nation flared with activity. The change was necessary to maintain the people's faith in luck, fortune, and fairness, all of which the lottery stood for. With the change from four to six numbers, the zoo reopened. For that week, none of the visitors to the zoo won any money at the lottery. The first four numbers were spot on, but the last two numbers had to be guessed.

Realizing that the animals in the zoo were no longer profitable, visitor numbers declined to the point where the zoo did away with the balloting system. School trips resumed. Children were allowed to return. The numbers that had driven the nation into a state of psychosis became a thing of innocent interest. Teachers encouraged the children to identify the numbers on the animals, and then draw them in their workbooks. The children had a wonderful time learning about the animals and making out the smudged patterns on the fur that could be interpreted as numerals. It was a 9-year-old son of an engineer and an accountant who decided that he would draw the python in his workbook, and trace the many smudged spots on the giant reptile's body. The serpent lay very still for the little boy to illustrate, and he began to trace the six numbers on the serpent's body: 11, 9, 51, 12, 40…

The boy went home that evening and had the intelligence to show the six numbers to his parents, who, having long heard about the magical numbers from the zoo, placed their Toto bet on the next day. They won $97,000. The family offered to buy the python from the zoo, but the zoo politely declined. Slowly, but surely, the numbers were returning. After the python, the spotted jaguar was next. The zookeepers were the first to place their bets, and upon winning, resigned from their jobs. People began pouring into the zoo once again. The balloting system kicked in. The Pools were frustrated. This could not go on. They were losing far too much money. They announced the cessation of all lottery in the country.

Now the people had the numbers, but they had nothing to bet on. They grew frustrated. They grew angry. That week, the Singapore Pools had a private meeting with the Singapore Zoo management. The situation was bad for everyone, they said. The zoo was now incredibly rich, but think of society! People need to gamble! People needed to hold on to that hope that one day their lives would get better without any effort of their own. The lottery gave them that hope and the empowerment they could not find anywhere else. Sure, the zoo was important, but nowhere as important as the lottery. Yet, the lottery could not survive if everyone knew the exact combination that the animals were giving. The animals were murdering luck and turning it into a routine, causing an absence of excitement necessary for the well-being of the nation.

The zoo management heard them out patiently. But what was to be done? they asked. The past employees had worked at the zoo because they loved animals, but most of the current employees only worked there in order to be the first to see the numbers each day. The solution could not be clearer, said the representatives from the Singapore Pools Association: they needed to kill the spotted animals off. In exchange for a cut of all future payouts, every one of the number-giving animals must be killed. Could the animals not be given away? pleaded the zoo management. It is wrong to kill animals, and more so when they are on the brink of extinction. Words that would have worked like a charm on animal lovers had no effect on the Association.

Think about it, they replied, the distinct number-resembling patterns on the animals would give them away. The animals would be too famous not to be recognized in other zoos around the world. How would they answer for that? It was the darkest hour of the zoo, but it had to be done, for the social order. At least the animals would die painlessly.

That night, they began putting down the spotted animals. First the antelopes, then the cheetah, the spotted jaguar, the python, and so on. Their carcasses were later stored in huge metal containers and transported to the nation's incineration plant where they were burned.

The zoo opened again after a week. The balloting was still in effect. People still came. They were looking for the numbers, but they could not find any. The zookeepers, bound by the oath of secrecy with the Association kept silent. For a full month, there were no numbers. Not on the zoo animals. Not on the pets. It was as if the numbers had vanished. The Singapore Pools had won yet again. Order was restored. 4D returned.

Almost a full year passed since the numbers had appeared. The authorities remained vigilant. Import of spotted pets was discouraged. Dalmatians were banned. The Association had their informants in place to report on any signs of smudges or spots on animals or birds that mildly resembled numbers. When spotted, the animals would be quietly taken away and put down.

However, over many months, people were increasingly experiencing changes on their own skins: the number of moles and freckles multiplied exponentially. Doctors were quick to announce that the condition was innocuous, a side-effect of the constant exposure to the strong rays of the sun. But the moles and freckles were not increasing randomly. They clumped together and formed patterns resembling four-digit numbers.

The nation rejoiced once more. What was thought to be past had returned, this time as indelible marks on human skin. The government stepped in. The lottery was to be shut down again for further review, but the moles did not go away. The people grew angry again, denied an outlet for their numbers.

Anxious and desperate, the government approved funding for research into laser treatments to remove the marks from the skin of the people. The procedure was voluntary and would be sponsored by the government. As people waited in queues to have their moles and freckles removed, another piece of news was slowly making its way through the country: the numbers on their skins were the winning combinations in the national lottery of their neighbouring country, Malaysia.

Some had already packed their bags.

APOCALYPSE APPROACHES

Daryl Yam

I. JANUARY

We buried the horse in the yard. Sam had a shovel; so did I. Mom had the herbs, a dozen of them. We spent three years finding them, from all kinds of places. Amongst them was a flower that bloomed once every seven years, a root that needed nine months to fully mature, and another that had been in the ground for a thousand years. We took care of the horse for six, we raised it well, and just before it reached its seventh birthday, Dad led it out to the yard. He caused it to go limp, and we buried it on the very spot it fell, still breathing.

"Good job, boys," Mom said. "Good job."

"No problem, Mom," said Sam. His overalls had dirt all over them, as did the sleeves of his shirt, but he didn't seem to mind. We were standing with our shovels, me half-behind him, standing in his shadow and wiping my face. I wanted to head back in and rest; we had spent the whole day digging.

There was a mound of dirt where the horse was: Dad swung his torchlight around and found the centre. He struck a pole through it, hammered it in. When he backed away, he told us all to switch off our torches. A wind picked up and started howling. It was chilly. The darkness folded all over us. I heard Mom's voice speak again, from an unknown distance.

"I'm gonna wait till my eyes get adjusted," she said. There weren't even lights from the house, or from the main road. Uncle Ivan had taken them all out.

This was how we prepared for the apocalypse that would begin to strike us one year from now: our family had known it before I was born, and I was already fifteen-and-a-half years old. Grandpa and Grandma were supposed to oversee the day's events, from the horse-laying to the hole-digging to the planting of the herbs, but since Grandma had died in her sleep two months ago, Grandpa had to pass it on to my parents—for my Dad was the eldest, followed by Uncle Ivan, then Aunt Linda—not that it mattered. My Dad wasn't going anywhere anytime soon.

"You ready?" my Dad called out.

"Hang on, Vince," she said. The wind continued to howl on and on, into my ears and my clothes, it howled right through me. But I felt safe behind Sam. I had a hand on the back of his overalls.

"You okay?" he asked.

"Yeah."

"All right."

I could smell his sweat, because of the wind. It was a little sour, but I didn't mind. I could always breathe through my mouth.

"You ready now, woman?" Dad called out again. "It's nearly midnight."

"All right, all right," she said. I saw a figure move forward, towards the pole in the mound. "Hold your horses."

Aunt Linda suddenly laughed, from out of nowhere. "Was that a joke?"

Mom laughed too, a hand on the basket, and another holding the cloth down, over the herbs. "Shut up, Linda." She laughed again, a little shakily, from the cold I suppose. And then Dad laughed, called Aunt Linda an idiot, of all the times she had to say such a thing, and Uncle Ivan started to laugh too. I wanted to join in as well, but I was too tired, shovelling dirt all over our horse, covering its open mouth, its eyes. I had a hand on Sam's overalls, and he wasn't laughing either.

II. FEBRUARY

"Erica?" she cried out. "*Erica?*"

"Yah?"

Oh, God, she thought. "Where are you?"

"Toilet," said Erica, her voice distant, where she needed her daughter to be. "Are you going to dry my hair?"

"Hang on," she called back out. "Just stay in there and wait for me. Can?"

"Can."

She exhaled. The animal in the living room was still, unmoving. It almost felt like a staring contest. All it did was watch her. It blinked once. Twice. She tried to ask herself what the animal was, but she couldn't relate it to anything she had seen, or knew; it simply defied description, which would be frustrating for her, for she was already beginning to imagine how stupid she'd sound when she'd call the police, the zoo, the bloody MP, anybody who could tell her why the hell there was a menacing-looking thing in her living room and how much she could sue whoever for. Her hand searched under the kitchen island for a knife, or a fork, and in the other she held onto the handle of the ladle she'd bought last week. From Tangs. Her heart cringed at the thought of throwing the ladle across the room, or tossing it to the animal like some kind of distraction, some kind of toy. She gritted her teeth.

"What the fuck," she said under her breath.

The animal raised a paw. It took a step forward.

She gripped the ladle even tighter.

Her heart started to race, as though she had just completed her daily jog, but here she was standing still, waiting for her life to flash before her eyes. She could even feel the sweat lining her palm and fingers. She felt a cold trail running down her armpit, and she couldn't help but think how that was going to ruin her one white blouse. Everything else she owned was in black. *Shit shit shit shit shit*, swore her screaming, inner voice. *How the hell do I chase this thing out?*

The animal started to make a low, guttural sound. She could see a flash of its fangs, yellowed and grimed with spit, like the poster of a B-grade monster flick. As it took another step forward, she could see the musculature of its limbs, tensed and coiled around its wiry frame. Its tail swished between the coffee table and the television; it raised its paw once again, bracing itself for another step. Its eyes were large and bulbous, like a goldfish, giving it a mad, unearthly look.

The phone rang.

The animal halted.

The phone continued on ringing.

The animal took a step back; it growled in irritation.

"Mommy?"

"Erica—"

The animal shook its head, its mane of ringlet fur. Its eyes were closed, as though in pain. A wild idea struck her, took hold over her, like instinct: she raised her ladle, fresh from Tangs, and started banging it on the kitchen island, against the walls of the sink—the animal visibly recoiled, it gave a loud cry—

Somewhere in the house a door swung open. Footsteps, wet and padded.

"Mommy?"

"*NO—*"

She quickly glanced towards the corridor: there was her ten-year-old girl with a towel wrapped around her body. She looked back at the living room in a blind whirl of panic and realised the animal had gone. Erica rushed to her side and held the phone out, still ringing. She stared at her daughter, at the phone, stunned. She picked up the call.

"*Xin nian quai le*, Ah Lin!"

It was Yi-po.

"Are you coming over today? It's the last Chinese New Year, you know," Yi-po said excitedly over the phone, "before the world ends." She laughed. "You must come, okay? I don't care if you don't wear red, just don't wear black, can *liao*."

III. MARCH

Overhead a new track began to play: *the reverberating, low notes of a cello, ascending to a high, determined vibrato*. It was the prelude of Gioachino Rossini's *William Tell Overture*. I didn't even know how I knew this. I looked up and down the corridor: I saw no one. Not even the sound of a door opening and closing, always somewhere in the distance, only the melody of a call and answer, a light, faraway timpani. I knocked on the door, slammed my hand against it.

"Mr. Park!" I called out. "Mr. Park!"

I pulled on the handle several times. No answer. I made my way towards the lifts: they weren't working. Nothing was working, nothing was going right. I didn't recognise anything.

That morning, I'd woken up to the sound of light rain, tapping its way across the window panes. Mr. Park had still been sound asleep, his beautiful chest rising and falling. I got out from under the sheets and made my way quietly towards the bathroom, a faint odour wafting around me. I turned on the shower and washed the dried semen out of my hair. He was still asleep by the time I was done; I bent over him and stroked my hand across his chest. I played with a nipple. He fidgeted and turned over to his side. Who knew he was ticklish? I gave a short laugh and let myself out. The auto-lock system had made a soft whirr and a click behind me.

Right now, I needed out.

I ran towards the end of the corridor, where the door to the emergency exit stood open. The *Overture* picked up its pace: *the strings began to trill, tremulously, as though the sound spoke of some imminent danger. The brasses, from out of nowhere, began to resound in a tragic chorus, notes ascending and descending, while the strings tumbled upon one another like waves crashing upon a rocky shore.* I pushed my way out, panting, into the ground floor lobby.

Empty. All empty. Nobody manned the counter, drawers open, papers lying all over the place, folders strewn about and gouged of their contents. Nobody sat on the lounge chairs, or the sofas; the laughter, the banter, the flirtation of the night before, now echoes in a place where nothing resided. I went into the ladies', then the gents': no one. A spotlight over the pay phones flickered on and off. Somewhere, in a corner, a potted plant lay overturned, its soil spilt, dark and dirty across the marble tiles. The *Overture* played on in the silence.

I made my way towards the entrance. I laid my hand on the revolving door, and pushed outward: *a piccolo whistled a note goodbye.*

The drizzle went on. I stepped out onto the streets, devoid of all traffic, of all noise. The vehicles had disappeared without a trace. I was the only pedestrian walking these pavements. My phone had no reception. It was only ten in the morning, but it was as dark as the night, and as grey as the tar. The surrounding buildings barely had any of their lights on. I reached a trembling hand out towards the sky, and felt the cold drops collect in my palm.

Suddenly, somewhere: a siren.

IV. APRIL

I lit up my cigarette.

While I waited, I looked at the torrent of brown water flowing down the drainage canal. The air had a rank, muddy smell, carried by all the humidity. Sunlight struck across the surface, but reached no further into the water, three metres deep. When I was done with my cigarette, I stubbed it out on the railing and threw it into the water.

The gentlemen beside me remained quiet, watching the brown water pass us by. He broke his silence after a while.

"Dirty."

I said nothing in reply.

"Who knows what it is carrying into the sea." He then held out his hand. "Does this belong to you?"

It was my cigarette stub, the one I'd just thrown into the canal, lying in the palm of his hand.

"Yes."

The gentleman unrolled the stub and blew away the ashes. He held the thin strip of paper between his fingers. "This is my name, written in your mother tongue, and in your blood."

"Yes."

He crushed the paper and pocketed it in his coat. He then looked at his surroundings, at the void decks, the housing estate, the group of children playing by the road, laughing and screaming. "What year is this?"

I cleared my throat. "2011."

His eyes seemed to gleam. They were the colour of topaz and onyx. "How *peculiar*." He ran a hand through his hair, which was a soft shade of cherry blossoms. "Everything looks rather calm."

I said nothing.

"What is it that you wish to see?" he asked.

"The end of the world."

The gentleman blinked. He then smiled. It was not unkind. "The end of the world?"

"Yes."

"You wish to see the End of All Humanity."

"Yes."

The gentleman said nothing for a while. His eyes then began to dart in all kinds of directions, as though he were searching for something, in the sky, in the railings, in his coat. Finally, the gentleman gestured towards the brown waters of the canal.

"Look," he said.

I looked. I tried, but I couldn't even see my reflection. A plastic bottle drifted by, bobbing on the muddy surface. It caught the sunlight; it glinted, and hurt my eyes. "I don't see anything," I told him.

"But it's right there."

"I—I don't see—"

"More importantly, however," the gentleman said, holding up a finger, "do you hear that?"

I strained my ears. "Hear what?"

The gentleman sighed dramatically. "Blind *and* deaf."

V. 21st May 2011, 6 p.m. (GMT)

In the darkness, two Heralds appear.

HERALD 1: Greetings, Augur!

HERALD 2: Salutations, Seer-head!

HERALD 1: We have been sent from above to proclaim her wondrous nascence, her splendorous iridescence:

HERALD 2: The advent, the agent, in four divine emanations: Cirrus! Stratus! Cumulus! Nimbus!

HERALD 1: Prepare, O Prophetress! And pave the way:

HERALD 2: The Messenger comes; the Harbinger arrives.

The light dims; the light brightens.

HERALD 1 (*singing*):
Joyful all ye waters rise,
'Neath the tempest of the skies!
With the angelic host proclaim:
HERALD 2 (*joining in*):
Veiled in flesh the Seer-head sees,
Hailing the Nascent Deity,
Come to a man and sent to tell:
Distant Glorious Music.
HERALD 1 (*rising chant*):
Malach Hamavet,
Malach Habala:
Eloah! Elohim!
Adonai! El Shaddai!
Tzevaot, Uri Gol,
Melech HaMelachim—
HERALD 2 (*simultaneously*):
Hear her laughter,
Hear her screams:
CIRRUS! STRATUS!
CUMULUS! NIMBUS!
Impetus & Inchoate!
Petrichor & Precipitate!
HERALD 1 & HERALD 2 (*together*):
Hark! the Heralds:
The Dark Angel *Sings*:
GLORY TO—
They vanish.

VI. JUNE

As I parted the beads I had hung across the window, I saw the
traffic moving in a haze, buildings wrapped and framed in that

bright light, its facades shrouded in darkness. I saw men in chinos, and women in skirts; in the distance, a bright red balloon floated up to the sky.

The clock on the mantelpiece gave a soft chime. A shadow extended from beneath the door. Three resolute knocks. "Come in," I said.

The door opened. A man stepped in: he was tall with a broad chest, and had a slight tan. He was the picture of health, if not for his other distinguishable features, such as his unshaven chin, his red eyes, and the wrinkled shirt he had on. He said he was a student in his final year at university, majoring in Theatre Studies. His name was Theo, short for Theodore.

The door swung itself closed. "Take a seat," I told him, gesturing towards the chair before my desk, and as he sat so did I. Several moments passed and immediately I sensed that I had to be the one to speak first. So I asked him, "How did you manage to get my contact number?"

"My grand-aunt," said Theo. He took out a photograph he had kept in his wallet. It was roughly the size of a Polaroid, a simple black and white. He handed it to me. "Do you recognise her?"

"Yes," I said. "I told her I would see her again." *And so I did.* I returned him his photograph.

"You told her she would be your last ever client."

"Yes." I could sense my smile faltering. "The reason I gave was that I could no longer see beyond the end of the year. I sensed my ability going out, not like a candle flame, but like water slipping through my cupped fingers. Therefore I could not accept any more clients, not after her. It would be irresponsible."

"And have you tried?" Theo asked. "Looking beyond the end of the year?"

"I have," I told him. "I practice, without anyone noticing. Recently I have been able to look as far as February, even the middle of March—but beyond that all I receive is static. A wall of sound, but like a great emptiness." I tried to think of a suitable expression. "As though I were underwater," I added.

"I see," he said. He proceeded to take out a second photograph. "But what I need you to do is to determine a person's location—at any point of time within the next thirty days, if you can."

I took the photograph. It was of a young woman, dark-haired, who looked roughly the same age as Theo. She had partially blocked her face with an outstretched hand.

"She suddenly disappeared, three weeks ago," he said. "She said she saw a lot of crazy things, and two men who spoke a lot of nonsense to her. Hebrew, she said. I didn't believe her. The next day she cleared out her things. She was referencing a lot of Tony Kushner, though. Have you ever read *Angels in America*? Seen it on stage?"

I shook my head. "You need me to locate this girl?"

"Yes," Theo said. "Please."

I looked at the girl's hand. The palm lines were a little blurry, but I could make them out. "She will be in Union Square, San Francisco." I handed the photo back to him. "Exactly one month from now."

Theo's eyes widened. He laughed, almost in disbelief.

"Heaven," he said, "a city much like San Francisco."

VII. JULY

"Where to, sir?" the driver said. I told him I wanted to go to Union Square Park. As he stepped on the pedal, he asked if it was my first time in San Francisco. I said yes.

"And how long will you be staying?"

I paused for a moment. "Just the day," I told him.

As the taxi wove through San Francisco's streets, I didn't speak another word; I spent most of my time looking out of the window, keeping to myself. All I could hear was the hum of the engine and the soft, constant laughter coming from the radio: a morning talk show, and one of the hosts was a sassy black woman, firing jokes left, right and centre. I couldn't catch a thing she said; the volume was dialled down too low for me to hear. But once in a while, my driver would snigger.

A scooter passed us and I could barely hear the engine. Everything happening in the world outside felt muted, and cut off. *As though we were underwater.* But instead we were going through Chinatown, then a tunnel. The strobe lights burned lines in my eyes.

We continued down Stockton Street, a straight continuous drive. I saw Levi's, Niketown. A signboard with the words: Johnston & Murphy. Palm trees sprang out of nowhere, on my right. Bushes too, flowering. There were steps in between the trees, leading to a plaza, the Square? A strangely fascinating building, in the background, a contrast between metal and stucco, from the way it gleamed under the morning light. Then, right ahead: macy's, with an un-capitalised m. Bvlgari. *Neiman Marcus*, italicised. It looked fancy.

We turned a right corner. Macy's loomed up on our left, casting us in a shadow. To the right, the palm trees made way for longer, wider stairs, for people to sit on. The shadow cast by Macy's barely touched the first step. Finally my driver pulled over, in front of a junction, between Geary and Powell Street. We were so close I could read the name of the stuccoed building, the one that had caught my attention earlier: Westin St. Francis. Bellboys chatted underneath an awning of burgundy and beige. I paid, told my driver to keep the change. I stepped out.

It was as though I had come up for air. I could feel the sunlight warming my hair, and a cold wind patting my cheeks. I could hear wave upon wave of sound, gradually building in a steady crescendo, like a tide in the morning, or an afternoon rain. I heard footsteps on the pavement, traffic passing by and slowing down, a cable car, shuddering by, and a strange blend of everything surging and gushing between the buildings. These layers came upon me like melody, harmony and bass. Suddenly, a wondrous, piercing sound rose above everything else, seeming to come from everywhere and nowhere: a pure, glorious trumpet, playing a hymn. It sang across the air, reflected off the surface of the surrounding windows, the notes made of gold. I looked further down Powell Street and saw no one who could be playing anything. I looked behind me and saw, in the middle of Union Square, an iron figurine standing atop a pole, a ring in one hand and a trident in the other, raised towards the cloudless sky. And as I went nearer, up the steps, through the throng of people, I felt my legs guided by some unknown force, some strange momentum of being, as though I were truly underwater and had been swept up by a current. *She will be in Union Square, San Francisco*—and somewhere, everywhere, the trumpet kept playing.

VIII. AUGUST

The old man was standing in the middle of the overhead bridge, watching the traffic below pass by. The first time the girl saw him, she was on her way back home from primary school. She walked up the steps to the bridge with some books in her hand, and she saw him standing there. There were railings in front and behind him but he didn't lean against either. He just stood in between them, staring straight ahead. It was the first day of the month, and the first day of the week.

She was concerned about him. Was he lost? What was he doing? The only things he wore were a white singlet and a pair of brown shorts. He was barefooted. His hair, white and sparse; his tummy, round and protuberant; his toes, small and bony.

She went up to him. His eyes seemed to reflect the light of the sunset. "Uncle?" she said, waving a hand in front of his face. "Uncle?"

He blinked. His eyes darted around before finally settling onto hers. A smile formed on his lips. "*Siu hai*," he said, laughing softly. "*Hou gwai ah.*"

She smiled too, even though she didn't understood what he said, and crossed over the rest of the bridge. When she had reached the other end, she looked back and saw him watching her. She smiled again and waved goodbye.

It became a pattern. Every Monday after school, she had writing class, and debate rehearsals every Tuesday and Thursday. They would all last into the evening. She would alight at the bus stop opposite her house and climb up the steps to the overhead bridge. She would see the old man, standing in between the railings, wordlessly staring straight ahead. He never seemed to wear anything different. She would greet him, and he would greet her back. He would say the same things. Once, she was in the bathroom, brushing her hair, and her mother had walked in; she took the chance to ask her what *siu hai* and *hou gwai* meant. Her mother told her they meant "little child" and "so obedient". She then asked why. Has a teacher been speaking in dialect?

She looked at her mother. Yes, she told her. We think it's funny.

Her mother sighed and shook her head. She wondered why people would always laugh at something they didn't understand. She then grabbed a towel and a hairdryer. The girl loved it whenever her mother dried her hair.

One Sunday evening, they went down to the void deck. There was Kow-mo and Kow-fu, and her three cousins, two older, one younger. Po-po and Gong-gong were burning the paper money, while Yi-po sat elsewhere, gesturing her over, *Eh-lih-ka*, *Eh-lih-ka*. She had bought two packets of fried rice, just for her and her mother. As she was about to open her packet, though, she saw the old man standing on the overhead bridge, cast in the same orange light, his hands this time on the railing. She left behind her packet of fried rice, and ran up the stairs of the bridge.

She could still smell the smoke of incense and offerings, all the way up here. A speck of ash floated near and landed on her skin. She called out to him, "Uncle? Uncle?" but he didn't seem to hear. He wasn't watching the traffic either, as a bus came and went, roaring beneath them; he was looking at the sun, hovering over the far horizon, casting its wet light upon them. His lips were quivering, muttering something. She leaned closer to hear, and realised: he was singing.

"*Di oh oh*," he sang. "*Beh lo ho.*"

She didn't understand. She laid a hand on his arm.

Trembling, the old man finally turned his head to face her. "*Siu hai,*" he whispered, blood trickling from his ears, "*nei teng dou ma?*" He whimpered and shivered, as though he were cold. "*Nah seng yam.*"

IX. SEPTEMBER

The light piano of Erik Satie's *Gymnopédie No. 1* hovered over the guests in the lobby. Time seemed to slow down as I made my way through the throng. An elderly couple stood beside me, luggage in hand; a family of three huddled around a digital camera. Patiently we waited for our elevators, but as one of the doors rang open, nobody seemed to notice. The family was now giggling over their camera, while the elderly couple remained staring straight ahead. I shrugged to myself and walked into the elevator. I pressed the button for 3.

"Good evening, Mr. Park."

I turned around. "Ah," I said. "No wonder. Good evening, Mr. Chin."

The door slid closed.

"I've been told that Ms. Amaya's body has been found," Mr. Chin said.

"And where might it be?"

"Berwick Drive," he answered. "Wherever that is."

Mr. Chin and I stepped out together on the third floor, and made our way down the corridor towards my room. Two floors above the lobby, the piano music playing in the audio system sounded much clearer, more resonant. The first *Gymnopédie* had always been my favourite out of the series. We passed by a few other guests along the way, back from a day of travelling or heading out for a night of activity; such is the attraction of the city that surrounds the hotel, with its tall office buildings and its wide, busy streets. My room was 321 and in the mornings I would get out of bed and look out the window. Quickly, I inserted my hotel key; the auto-lock system gave a soft whirr and a click.

"Thank you, Mr. Park." Mr. Chin reached out a hand, opened the door. Together we stepped through the doorway and onto a front yard. We made our way down towards the rusty, iron-grille gate and pushed it open. We walked along a narrow, two-lane street; the pavement on either side cracked with trees and letterboxes. Mr. Chin was taking the lead. "Right around the bend," he said, pointing towards the T-junction before us.

We took a left. Berwick Drive was a single stretch of road as far as the eye could see, with an unending row of terraced houses on either side. I could make out a gathering of policemen, not too far ahead. Nobody seemed to be home for dinner on Berwick Drive, as each window was left unlit as we passed by. As the evening sky steadily darkened, the streetlights flared to life, while a red bulb spun and warned incoming traffic. None of the policemen noticed us approaching and they continued on with their work. Mr. Chin and I paid no heed, just the same.

Silently we made our way towards the body. Ms. Amaya was wearing the exact same clothes she wore that night, so many months ago. She had on a white blouse and a skirt with a floral pattern, the base as blue as the night. I remember the way she cast them onto the floor of my hotel room. Now the clothes were all wet and soiled; they clung to her bones like rags hung out to dry. I remembered the fullness of her hips, her breasts. I remembered the way she came, that little scream she let out. I remembered that short laugh, while playing with my nipple, and the morning after. She'd had no clue.

Mr. Chin sighed, and took out his phone. "We have her," he said, looking pointedly at me. "Don't we?"

I nodded. Her mouth hung agape, as though in a wide scream.

X. 21st October 2011, 6 p.m. (GMT)

The sound of beating wings fills the room.

TAL: What is that sound? Oh, God. What is that? It's like...wings or something, like a giant bird...is it a plane, or a helicopter, or...Oh, God. Oh God, oh God—

Tal clutches her chest; she doubles over in agony, brought to her knees.

TAL (*calling out*): Somebody! Anybody! I can't—*breathe*—

An average-sized middle-aged Jewish woman stands in the doorway, dressed in a dark coat, over a simple, black dress, her dark hair pulled back into a tight bun. Her skin is as white as plaster, her lips the deepest, darkest rouge, pursed into a small, heart-like shape. She appears oblivious to Tal's pain.

TAL (*barely audible*): Who—who are you?

MALACH HAMAVET (*in a thick, Jewish accent*): The Heralds would have told you, Augur, Seer-head. I I I I offer my greetings.

TAL: Oh God. Oh God. You're the angel—

MALACH HAMAVET: In four divine emanations: Cirrus, Stratus, Cumulus, Nimbus. I I I am agent, am advent; Messenger, Harbinger, Impetus & Inchoate, Petrichor & Precipitate. Her wondrous nascence. Her splendorous…iridescence. (*beat*) You look like shit, Tal.

The Jewish woman goes over and sits on a nearby chair, folding her hands on her lap. Her lips remain pursed as she watches Tal sweat and pant before her, still on her knees.

TAL (*coughing*): Where are—where are your—

MALACH HAMAVET: Beg pardon?

TAL: Your wings.

MALACH HAMAVET: Ah! (*she laughs, waves a hand*) Nonsense. I I I put them away. The feathers, can't stand them.

TAL (*smiles, in spite of the pain*): You're funny.

MALACH HAMAVET: Hmm.

The Jewish woman reaches into her coat and takes out a book with a leather cover. Tal watches her hold out the book, but seems too weak to do anything about it.

MALACH HAMAVET: Take it. Go on.

Shakily, Tal reaches out, just barely. She takes it.

MALACH HAMAVET: There you go. The Book of The End. It's a scream, I I I I tell you. (*She leans forward on her chair, and whispers.*) Heaven is going to crack wiiiiide open, Tal. Apocalypse approaches.

XI. NOVEMBER

"We are underground, are we not?"

I didn't reply.

"Yes, yes, I believe we are," the gentleman said, looking around. He seemed to be giving the train platform a nod of approval. "I can sense the earth better, as much as you have hollowed her out." He then gestured towards a display monitor hanging from the ceiling, somewhere along the middle of the platform. "What is that?"

"A monitor."

"Why does it say"—he made a face—"*3 mins*?"

"It's short for 'minutes'."

"Ah," he said. "Why, of course." He blinked. "Three minutes to *what*?"

"The train approaching."

"Marvellous," said the gentleman, his eyes widening. He came over and stood beside me, staring at both of our reflections in the glass of the platform screen doors. "It appears humans can tell their own future now."

"In a way."

"Although, three minutes does seem fairly short-sighted."

A wide grin grew on the gentleman's face. I shook my head.

"You are mocking me."

The gentleman gave a hoot of laughter, light and airy. "No, no, no, no!" he said, "absolutely not! I may have called you blind and deaf all those months ago, but I can only thank you for it! Over the course of my extended stay I couldn't help but notice a few rather extraordinary happenings."

"You never mentioned them."

"It was not in the contract."

"I've never known you to keep things to yourself," I said. "Most of the time you just talk."

"Oh, you make me blush." He then cast a look around the platform, as though on the lookout for eavesdroppers. "What do you wish to know?" he whispered.

I shrugged. "Anything."

"Last month, on the twenty-first, then? At precisely eighteen-hundred hours."

I turned to look at him; I was intrigued. "What happened?"

He leaned over to my ear. "A visitation, from the angel of death." He backed away. "I've met her before; what a cruel, uptight bitch. And that awful way she dresses, urgh, Malach Hamavet indeed." He then made a sudden, jolting movement. "Ooh!" he exclaimed, grabbing my arm. "Do you hear that?"

I groaned. "No, I do not."

"Get over yourself, I'm not mocking you this time," the gentleman snapped, his pointed ears twitching in agitation. "I think the train is coming." He then looked over at the display monitor. "Is that why it is flashing now? No more *mins*?"

"Y-yes," I said, nodding. The train was coming, indeed. There was a slight vibration that travelled throughout the platform, followed by a soft, guttural rumble. A light grew in the tunnel beyond the screen doors. Slowly, our reflections in the Plexiglas began to diminish, though I could still see the gentleman. He looked utterly distraught, as the train rushed into view.

"What a dreadful sound it makes," he said. "A screech, then a halt."

The screen doors slid open. The gentleman and I stepped aside.

XII. DECEMBER

It is time. Twelve minutes to midnight. Our cousins dug up their plants, one by one, followed by Uncle Liam, then Uncle Tobias. He was bad at it, but it's okay, we had a laugh. It's Aunt Linda's turn now. She struggles with hers too, but eventually she yanks it out of the earth, the roots a whole mess.

"Oh my," she says, wiping her forehead. "I hope we're not running behind schedule."

"Don't worry, Linda." Dad's voice. "Sean, you're next."

Aunt Linda's torchlight swings past me as I switch mine on. A beam of illumination, cutting through the darkness. The grass has long browned, and is now half-covered in snow. There's a soft, crunching noise as I take the few steps towards the mound, under which the horse still lies, with a stake speared through its heart.

Mine is the flower that blooms once every seven years. It's called beargrass. It blooms into a white bulb at the tip of the stalk, and is from the northern Rockies. I set my torch on the ground and pocket my gloves. The same wind from a year ago begins to blow, cold and harsh. I grab onto the base of the stalk with one hand and clump the leaves together with the other, just like how Sam taught me. I'm done in less than ten seconds.

"Good job, Sean," says Mom. Dad says nothing. He's the one with the oldest torch; I can tell by the amber of his light.

Uncle Ivan passes by me, his curses drowned out by the howl of the wind, while I head back to my spot beside Sam. He's wearing the usual: a cotton long-sleeve under his denim overalls, tucked into his leather boots. His arms are crossed, waiting for his turn, which is soon; he's after Uncle Ivan. I hold up the beargrass, shine my torch on it. I think about how this clump of flowers is supposed to protect me. Sam smiles the way he does, a grin cocked to the side.

"Nice," is all he says.

Uncle Ivan's done. His is a spindly tree, almost as tall as he is.

"You're sweating too, huh," Aunt Linda says, to which Uncle Ivan retorts, "Shut it, Lin," because that's all he can manage for now.

Sam makes his way forward without being asked. Dad shines a trail ahead of him with his torch, casting that pale brown light over his figure. Sam looks like he's stepping into a bygone era, or an old photograph. Compared to Uncle Ivan's tree, his plant is really short, the leaves barely reaching his ankles. He turns his own light off, relying entirely on Dad's. He takes off his gloves and starts parting the dirt with his big, strong hands.

"You're doing fine, Sam." Mom again, calling out. "Just be careful."

His is the mandrake, the root that used to need nine months. Sam reaches in and scoops the root out, cradling it like it's an actual newborn, screaming into the wind, and it makes our cousins nervous. It's heaving and sobbing and moaning against Sam's overalls. Now it knows air, and what it's like to breathe.

Sam walks back to us. After him is Mom, who touches him on the shoulder as she walks past him. He's looking down at the root, nestled in his arms, covered in dirt, struggling and shivering in the cold. You can see the stem growing from its belly, and the leaves, velvet and green. The little thing even has fingers, outstretched and wanting. This is a part of the life our horse has now become, the horse we raised together. "Look at its eyes," Sam says, and I do.

0100110101000101010011010100111101010 1001001011001

Justin Ker

On her last day at work, she heads straight home from the law firm. The entire firm understands that she is still broken, down to the auntie who normally makes her afternoon Milo, and adds extra milk to dilute her grief. She pushes through the glass door of the lobby, holding a white box of her former cubicle possessions.

She collapses into the cool vinyl seat of the taxi and the driver pulls away from Raffles Place. The taxi driver says nothing. The city passes by as a reflection on the Hyundai's scrubbed windows. Finally, he says, where do you want to go?

She reaches into the white box, and takes out a handphone with a blinking flash memory stick attached to its back. Her thumb hovers over the call button of the Memory-phone.

His architectural firm had sent him to Mumbai eight months before, and he had become one of the thirty-two people killed by Pakistani terrorists at the Trident Hotel. They had been married for barely a year when he died.

She recalls the strangeness she felt at the Mumbai morgue, a sense of distance despite being so close to his body. The obese Indian police inspector waved his hand upwards, and an

Untouchable attendant lifted the blue plastic sheet covering him. She looked at his face quietly while the inspector waited for her to cry. He did not look like her husband. She asked if she could touch his hair.

"It is against regulations," the inspector said, his moustache twitching. "But you may proceed." She stroked his hair twice, tentatively, in the small cold room, watched by the short attendant and the fat police inspector. She could hear the wailing of other victims' relatives outside, muffled by the morgue's steel doors. There was a small hole in his right shoulder where one of the bullets had entered. It was small and black.

When she got back to Singapore from Mumbai after identifying his body, she discovered a voice-mail he had left for her on her handphone. She sat up on the sofa as she listened for the first time, pressing the phone close to her ear.

He had called when the terrorists first entered the Trident: *Oh my god. Someone is shooting in the lobby.* There was a pause, as if he was recognizing his own mortality, then he called out her name, once. There was gunfire in the background.

As news of the attacks broke on Channel NewsAsia, she called him non-stop from Singapore for two hours, while her secretary booked a flight to India. She finally reached him, as he was hiding alone in an unlit stairwell. The reception was spotty as they talked desperately over the phone. She could barely hear him, and there were echoes and lags, as their voices were exchanged via Indian satellites floating over the Arabian Sea, beaming the anaemic signal onto Chowpatty Beach. Each word exchanged fell like a single precious raindrop. They continued talking until the terrorists found him.

The voice-mail arrived one week late, stored in the servers of India Telecom as an electronic signal, a bright green sine-wave trace on an oscilloscope screen. It was then mysteriously sent through sagging wires and perpetually failing satellites, landing in

Singapore, reaching her handphone, arriving at her right ear like an aural letter, like a mistake. She played it again and again.

The message contained ten words and eighteen seconds of the sound of his breathing. This was all she had left of him. He had been reduced to a binary signal, a concatenated string of ones and zeroes, memory as the verisimilitude of life.

Through a friend teaching at the university, she found a chain-smoking doctoral student in computer science who was on the verge of pawning his dormitory mattress for money. The doctoral student asked for a copy of everything her husband had ever written or said, and twenty cartons of menthol lights. So the woman went through their apartment with a large yellow, IKEA polyester bag. The bag slowly filled with print-outs of his emails, Facebook status updates, SMS messages, his sketchbook of houses, an old handwritten love-letter from their university days, the audio track from a holiday video taken in Siem Reap.

But she left the magnetic poem he had constructed on the refrigerator door alone; they had bought the kit at Kinokuniya. She saw visions of him stooped over the refrigerator door, swapping the words around, and adjusting the tilt of the magnetic words with his thumb and forefinger.

The doctoral student digitized everything he had ever written, typed, or said into the verisimilitude of his voice. He then programmed an artificial intelligence and encoded it onto a tiny flash-memory stick that affixed to the woman's handphone.

All she had to do was to press a special sequence of eight numbers, and she could talk to an A.I. that sounded just like her dead husband. The first few iterations were awkward and artificial, but six months of cigarette-fuelled work improved the flow of the conversations. When the doctoral student finished the final version, he proclaimed to the woman: "I have triumphed over death. I have made memory eternal."

The woman could not bear looking at photographs or videos of her husband. It was too jarring, too painful. But with a false telephone, she could reach him in a way, pretend he was on the other side of the electronic distance, at the end of pressing eight numbers on the Memory-phone's keypad.

She could talk to him in the comforting darkness of her apartment and have a conversation with a ghost on an imaginary phone line. They would speak about their weekend walks at Pierce Reservoir, the love affairs of their friends playing out on Facebook, her cantankerous mother who was opposed to her marrying a Chinese man. When she laughed, he laughed as well.

Sometimes he would rephrase what she had just said, and speak it back to her in agreement. At first she thought these were just glitches where the Memory-phone's A.I. was weak, but she came to realize that, as in real life, not much significant information was exchanged between two people talking (especially married couples). The signal-to-noise ratio between couples varied greatly, but an invisible law dictated that this ratio inevitably declined as the number of years together increased.

Now, free from work, she spends her days swimming at their condominium pool, her evenings observing families eat dinner at Ghim Moh Market. Her shares flicker uselessly on her computer screen. She has exactly one cigarette on her balcony every night, exhaling into the black air.

After midnight, she walks around Singapore with her Memory-phone, talking to him as if he were still in Mumbai, just waiting to return to Singapore. She rides the last train on the new Circle Line. She walks through the void decks of random HDB blocks, taking the lift to the top floor. From there, she looks out over the repeating vista of housing blocks and multi-storey car parks, with their regular bars of fluorescent lighting. Two Bangladeshi labourers sleep on a piece of cardboard in a staircase landing between floors. Her eyes take in a nocturnal Singapore that she has not seen before, a stillness that is foreign.

Channel NewsAsia once reported that the police had installed closed-circuit television cameras in the lift landings and common areas of most HDB blocks. The newscaster gave the assurance that no one would be on the other side watching; the footage would only be retrieved if a crime occurred, otherwise all film would be deleted after a month. Big Father would respect your privacy.

She has this fantasy of breaking into the police command centre, to become the only audience watching Singapore sleep. She would be seated in a cubed room, whose six walls consisted entirely of different flat-screen televisions, skipping from one empty lift lobby to the next. Occasionally someone would enter a lift with his Ah Lian girlfriend. A demented old woman potters around the staircase landings in her pyjamas. A black cat crosses the screen, staring into the eye of the camera's lens. The woman would be able to see the entire island simultaneously, like a security guard god.

Then the fantasy evolves into something more self-centric: she wants to see the footage of herself walking all over Singapore, while talking to him on her Memory-phone. If only she could splice it all together into a single video from all the different CCTV cameras she has walked past. She thinks that such a film might give her some insight into what she was doing with her life.

At Marina Barrage, with the Memory-phone to her ear, she looks out at the Singapore skyline. It has changed bit by bit over the years, almost imperceptibly, until now everything has changed. When she was young, the most prominent building was the OCBC building that looked like an upright calculator, constructed in the Brutalist style. Now there are new glass edifices with names she does not even know. She wonders if her husband the architect would approve of the altered skyline, so she asks him. For a brief moment, while listening to the reply, she mistakes the A.I.'s voice for him.

A new sadness overcomes her. It is now 2 a.m. Waves crash against the concrete walls of Marina Barrage as the night breeze blows past her. At one end of the barrage are construction barges, moored there for building some new undersea expressway. She walks down a jetty, climbs over a low gate onto one of the barges, and slips off its mooring rope. The barge is a large floating platform ringed by black car tyres, with a single three-storey lighthouse in its centre.

Slowly, the barge drifts out to sea, carried by the outgoing tide. She climbs up into the top of the floating lighthouse, watching the retreating lights of Singapore. Her height above the waves presides over undersea tunnels, the waters that will eventually engulf everything, and the binary immortality of memory.

The Coast Guard hunts for the missing barge, but eventually the search is called off after two weeks. Once in a while, she is seen by the old boatmen who sleep on their bumboats, anchored off Clifford Pier. The woman and her barge appear as a phantom on the waves, a mirage of the seas. She is reported to be standing at the top of the floating lighthouse, looking, looking.

DEWY

Grace Chia Kraković

They called her Dewy because her eyes appeared wet even when not crying. It was meant to be a joke by the first family she worked for—a Scottish family of six living in Bukit Timah. But the name stuck. Dewy's complexion was tawny and her lips reflected a sheen that gave them a characteristic moist look. Her hair, knotted into a ponytail, was a blanket of charcoal silk. She was alluring without even trying to be so; features like these would make a vain girl proud, but on an orphaned girl trying to eke a living at the age of fourteen, struggling as a domestic helper in a foreign country, beauty was a disadvantage.

The previous year, Dewy had left her foster home in Semarang to find work as a domestic helper. The Javanese employment agency she signed up with forged her documentation, declaring her a legal adult at eighteen. She was quickly picked, based on her then-homely looks, by the Scottish expatriate family in Singapore. They treated Dewy like one of their own. Before relocating back to Glasgow, they gave her an effusive positive testimony, painting her as an ace worker, which helped her gain new employment in no time: a German family with an infant, who had been friends with her first employer.

Dewy worked for her new family with the same vigour as the first. Her priority was to take care of the eleven-month-old

123

infant, followed by her cleaning duties. Her affable personality endeared her to her new Sir and Ma'am. She was still practically a child herself, and while her new employers suspected she wasn't as old as she said she was, they closed an eye to it. Six months later, Dewy became just another part of the Weber family. There was a comfortable, familiar routine to their lives, and a certain sense of affection among them all. One day, Mrs. Weber broached the subject delicately, gently intruding into Dewy's small maid's room off of the kitchen.

"Dewy, where are your parents?"

"Ma'am, I got no parents."

"Not even a mother?"

"No, Ma'am."

"So who raised you?"

"In home, Ma'am. For children with no parents."

"I see. So how do you know when were you born? Did the home tell you?"

"Yes, Ma'am."

"So when were you born?"

"1998, Ma'am."

"And what name did they give you then?"

"Sri, Ma'am. My name Sri."

"I see. Please go and bring in the laundry. There's going to be a storm."

Poor Dewy. She had made a big mistake, revealing two secrets her maid agency had made her swear not to tell. Dewy scuttled away through the kitchen. Would her Sir and Ma'am send her back now? What was she to do? That night, as she lay in her maid's room huddled under her blanket, she wept for her own folly. Little did she know that Mrs. Weber now liked her even more, with the knowledge that Dewy was honest.

~

From then on, Mr. Weber would tease Dewy about being brought by the stork. That made no sense to Dewy, who didn't know what the stork imagery meant. She only remembered a story of her origins told to her by an elderly warden, Nurhayati.

Nurhayati had been very fond of Dewy, and often gave her a bigger portion of rice than the other children at the orphanage. She told her that when Dewy was born, she caused so much pain that her mother wept three large teardrops, each falling to the earth like pearls. When her mother died soon after, Dewy was then sent to the children's home. Her mother had named her Sri before she passed away, in tribute to the rice goddess, and so that the child would never be hungry. Nurhayati was emotional when narrating the story, as if she had a personal connection to it. The next day, Nurhayati was said to have been fired from her job, and the little orphan girl never saw her again.

Fourteen year-old Dewy seemed to blossom overnight. Her budding breasts enlarged, her hips filled out with curves, and she grew two inches taller. Her pudginess gave way to a slenderness that Mr. Weber began to notice. Mrs. Weber was hardly at home; a business woman who ran her own company importing art collectibles, she had entrusted the care of her home and her baby to the teenager.

The three-storey bungalow Dewy had to clean daily was filled with paintings, sculptures, and cultural artefacts from worlds she had never before encountered. Not only were the walls adorned with original Renaissance, cubist, and impressionist paintings from European masters, but the Weber household also showcased bronze sculptures by Dalí and Rodin. On a special glass shelving unit was nested an ornate Fabergé egg encrusted with gemstones. Dewy's instruction was to never touch it, although she had to keep the shelving pristine.

One morning when Mr. Weber was bouncing his laughing baby boy on his leg, Dewy reached up to wipe the glass shelves. Mr. Weber noticed how her breasts were firmly squeezed against the cotton fabric of her tee shirt, which had now become a size too small. The rhythmic dance of her contoured flesh distracted him. He tried to look away. When his eyes darted back, she was on tiptoe, reaching up to wipe at a high shelf, the action exposing her midriff, while her buttocks stretched taut against her shorts. Mr. Weber felt an abrupt erection coming on; he quickly placed his baby on the floor and fled to his bedroom, locking the door. He curled up into a heap on the floor, trying to will away his lust. He had previously felt paternal toward the fourteen-year-old girl. What had happened?

A month after the incident, Mr. Weber's peace of mind was shattered. He found himself swearing a lot more, even in front of the baby. He was constantly agitated, picking on his wife and baby for faults only he could see. But with Dewy, he was silent, disdainful, and cold. His wife spoke out finally, not knowing why her husband had changed so drastically.

"What is eating away at you, honey?"

"What nonsense are you talking about?"

"Your behaviour is unacceptable. Frankly, you're being extremely difficult to put up with."

"Go look at yourself in the mirror."

"Stop it now. I won't stand for this."

"No one is asking you to. Leave if you want to."

"I didn't say anything about leaving. Do you want me to leave?"

"I'm tired. Go away."

"What's wrong? Tell me."

"My head hurts. I'm going up to bed."

"Honey, don't go. Let's finish this."

But Mr. Weber wouldn't talk to his wife. He knew exactly what was wrong with him, but his secret affected his relationship with his wife—and his helper. He was charged to explode from keeping it all in. That night, he tossed and turned in bed with the ferocity and restlessness of a caged lion. His dreams all involved indecent actions with Dewy, and while his dream self roared with satisfaction, his slumbered body ached with an itch he couldn't scratch. So much pain in pleasure existed in the confused mind of a man in mid-life crisis.

That pain had to go away, Mr. Weber decided. The next night, after the entire household had gone to sleep, he crept through the kitchen and towards Dewy's room. He stood outside her door for half an hour, wavering between desire and conscience. He knew that whatever decision he took would be an unalterable one. The fire within him was roaring, razing the edges of his sanity until the dream image of Dewy rose up in his mind like an apparition, a goddess seducing him with the intensity of gravitational pull.

He placed his palm on the knob and turned. The door opened, soundlessly. Dewy was asleep on the bed, loosely hugging her blanket. Mr. Weber entered. He stood at the edge of her bed, eyes poring over every ounce of bared flesh—her feet, ankles, shins, thighs, fingers, wrists, arms, elbows, face, neck, and finally her cleavage, rising and then falling with each exhalation, peeking through her V-necked pyjama top.

Mr. Weber was no longer able to restrain himself once he saw the evidence of her budding sexuality on display. He sat down on her bed. She was still sound asleep. He placed his hand on her legs and felt them. She didn't move. His hands roved up her hips and torso. She didn't move. He was now touching her breasts with the tips of his fingers. He closed his eyes, imagining the possibilities. When he opened them, Dewy stared back in utter shock.

"Sir! What you doing?" Dewy shouted, her voice bouncing off the walls in the darkness.

He jerked back his hand and shot to his feet.

"I-I'm...sorry."

Mr. Weber lurched out of the maid's quarters, banging his head against the doorframe and tripping over a hand-woven kitchen rug, utterly ashamed of his audacity. What on earth had he been thinking? His wife was right. What had happened to him?

Dewy couldn't get back to sleep all that night. She was terrified, knowing exactly what Mr. Weber had done. She was thankful he hadn't gone further, but that didn't lessen her anxiety. She curled into a tight ball and gripped her blanket tightly, eyes glued to the doorway in case he chose to return, waiting endlessly until the sun rose and its light faintly illuminated her room. Then she got out of bed, and crept out into the kitchen. She felt nauseated and jittery. What could she take to make herself feel calmer?

In the half-darkened kitchen—for Dewy was afraid of turning on the light and seeing her Sir standing there—the girl tried to prepare a concoction. Her mind was dazed, in shock. She ate what she could find and drank what she could mix, eyes struggling to keep open, her motions on autopilot. Something she put into her mouth tasted odd but she swallowed anyway. Dewy wanted to fill her stomach with strength so that she could deal with what came when the household later awoke.

When she had finished, fatigue overtook her. She had to abandon her usual routine of starting the housework before everyone rose. Her legs guided her back to bed as if they had a life of their own, and she lay down, exhausted, inhaling and exhaling until blackness overcame her vision.

~

When Mr. Weber woke up, his sense of dread returned in force. Had last night been a dream? He tried to convince himself that it had, and so he closed his eyes, ready to forget the whole incident, turning over and hugging his wife for the first time in a month. Mrs. Weber yawned and turned towards her husband with a smile.

"Good morning, honey," she said, full of affection.

"Good morning. I'm sorry I've been difficult."

"That's all right. I have a surprise for you."

"Really? I can't wait to see it."

"Do you want it now?"

"Yes." Mr. Weber briefly thought his wife meant sex.

"Get out of bed right now. Let's get ready."

"What?"

"Have you forgotten? It's our wedding anniversary. I've booked us a week's stay in Club Med Mauritius. Come on, the limo will be here soon."

"And the baby?"

"We're talking him along. Club Med is family-friendly. We'll be fine."

"And Dewy?"

"Dewy knows all about this. I told her last week. She said she's going to redo the garden while we're gone. Our holiday is waiting. Aren't you excited?"

"I guess so...Yes, I am." He returned his wife's smile. "What would I do without you?"

Sure enough, the limo cruised into the driveway at precisely 6:45 a.m. to ferry the family to Changi Airport for their morning flight. Dewy had packed the luggage days before. Mr. Weber was relieved he wouldn't need to face his helper for an entire week, until he had gained some mental clarity.

"Dewy, we're off!" Mrs. Weber shouted, one arm balancing the infant on her hip. "Where's that girl?"

"Come on, honey, let's go. Dewy is probably just cleaning the bathroom. She can't hear us."

"That girl is a godsend," Mrs. Weber said. The baby squealed into her ear; this would be his first trip abroad, on a plane. Later, when the plane rose into the skies, the baby's ears popped from the pressure inside his eardrums, and he squealed again at the unexpected sensation, which caused Mr. Weber to laugh for the first time since his irrational urges had taken him over.

Eight days of sand, sea, and surf was enough to cleanse the spirits of the Weber family. However, when they returned to Singapore, Mrs. Weber looked forward to once again seeing her charge, thankful at how efficient Dewy could be in taking care of her child. The working mother had overestimated herself; caring for a boisterous, rambunctious one-year old was even more difficult than running a business. She was glad to pass her duties back to Dewy.

"Dewy!" Mrs. Weber yelled. There was no answer.

"What's that smell?" Mr. Weber said. He noticed it the minute he stepped into the house. A week of relaxation had banished all forms of guilt from his mind, but upon his return home, the shame of his actions returned with him, gnawing away at his guts. He twitched where he stood.

"Where's it coming from?" Mrs. Weber asked, walking through the house with infant on hip. He wrinkled his button nose, apparently able to smell it too.

Mr. Weber followed his wife and found himself crushing dozens of black ants with each step he took; they covered the floor in constantly-shifting formations, tons of them, and a shiver of revulsion moved up his spine. The smell became more intense the further they stepped inside the interior of the house, a combination of sandalwood incense and something sugary sweet. His wife headed into the kitchen, heedless of the ants, making a beeline for the maid's quarters at its far end.

"What is this?" Mrs. Weber shouted. "Dewy!"

In addition to the ants, every surface in the kitchen was piled with rice grains. It made the walking slippery and treacherous, and Mr. Weber couldn't suppress a shudder at the sight of rice spilling from the cabinetry, the sink, the open refrigerator. The sweet sandalwood smell was nearly palpable here, and it grew stronger the closer they stepped to Dewy's room.

Mrs. Weber put her palm on the doorknob to the maid's room and turned it, and as she whispered, "Oh my god," Mr. Weber rushed forward and took the baby from her dangerously swaying form, pressing the oblivious child's face tight into his chest to avert his gaze from the grisly scene.

The coroner was stumped. The only conjecture he could make was that Dewy had died of food poisoning; traces of ricin could be found all throughout Dewy's room. He asked the Webers if they normally kept the poison in the house. Mrs. Weber said she wasn't sure. Mr. Weber stared straight ahead, unable to respond. Fortunately for the Webers, they both passed a polygraph test easily and so were acquitted of suspicion. Dewy's death was written off as "accidental."

The rest of the discovery was just as beguiling. In place of a normal corpse, Dewy's body had transformed into a confusion of nature. A coconut tree had emerged from her head. Grass sprung from her hair and cassava grew from her legs. Teak, oak and sandalwood trees replaced her arms. Flower shrubs had appeared on her lips and fruit trees grew from her breasts. Her pyjama bottoms were soaked through with a dark sticky fluid the coroner ascertained was palm sugar, which had soaked through the mattress and coated the floor of the small room, and subsequently attracted the hordes of ants. Out of her belly grew an *Oryza* plant that continually sprouted rice grains, spraying them outwards into the air like a fertile fountain dispensing confetti blessings. Nothing familiarly human remained of Dewy.

After the inquest, the bizarre burial, and the thorough top-to-bottom scouring of the bungalow by professional cleaners, Mrs. Weber found a replacement helper for her baby. She still wept genuine tears for what had happened to Dewy, but she needed to work and life had to go on. Mr. Weber became sullen once again. At times he was irritable, at other times depressed. Mrs Weber didn't know what to make of her husband, and she found that she didn't care. She now had a new charge to worry about, a booming business, and a baby developing new milestones; she hadn't signed up to mollycoddle another immature creature. Her husband's problems could wait.

However, even after the professional cleaning, the sweet sandalwood smell and the presence of rice grains never entirely went away. The new Filipino helper cleaned the entire house on a regular basis, but she also could not get rid of the lingering smell or the errant grains. She would always overlook one spot or another, and lo and behold, more rice grains would appear.

On a balmy Sunday afternoon when the Weber family was resting in the living room, the baby crawled up to Mr. Weber, one fist tightly clutching a gift for his father. Mr. Weber was disinterested, but the child waved his fist, giggling, and pulled his shirt up, exposing his belly button. He took the grain of rice ensconced in his fist, and placed it gingerly in the crevice of his belly. The one-year old opened his mouth, eyes sparkling, and said, "*Nasi.*"

Mr. Weber cringed. Mrs. Weber put down her office papers, picked up her child, and kissed him noisily on the cheek. Her baby had just spoken his first word.

WHERE NO CARS GO

JY Yang

In the small hours of a weekend morning at his office on the thirtieth storey, Charles Chong saw the Maserati speeding down the neighbouring skyscraper like water across skin.

He had been alone in the bank building that fateful night because he only liked working in the Marina Bay Financial Centre when it was empty. Buildings, soaring, emptied of their human loads, structures stripped to their pure form and freed of purpose. Charles found poetry in this. He was contracted on a flexi work-life scheme, allowing him to show up at the hours he liked, as long as he checked every box and got all his KPIs fulfilled. His boss and colleagues seemed to like this arrangement better as well, because it meant they didn't have to deal with Charles. And they didn't even know that he could talk to buildings.

The first indication of something different from his usual routine that night had been the distant hum of a thousand bees, ignorable until a bone-shattering wall of V8-fueled sound burst through it. Startled out of spreadsheet data-entry, Charles was greeted by a singular white shape streaking across the glass of the adjacent tower like a punch to the gut, defying gravity and all logic. By all rights, he should not have been moved by the sight of a spirit car racing down the sides of a neighbouring skyscraper. He was a sensitive, and a card-carrying member of the Groundskeepers' Association; his gift was talking to buildings, and to the guardians that were the embodiment of the locations they protected.

Abandoning his desk, he ran to the window as the exotic car swept downwards in a corkscrew spiral. It was white and smooth and bore three squares of metal for gills, vanishing along the edge of the building, only to remerge in a cloud of throaty engine-noise that Dopplered away and back. Headlamps cut a swathe across the sleeping building, a lighthouse in motion, a coupe-shaped warship on the hunt. Glass, cool and still, pressed against Charles' heated fingers.

When the Maserati reached the ground, running down a leg supporting a multi-storey lobby, it leaped in a figure skater's trajectory and touched road. The car peeled away with a roar, curving onto the street as though it was the most natural thing in the world. The lemon-yellow CityCab it cut in front of instinctively slowed to let it pass, although Charles had no idea if the cab driver could see the Maserati or not. Did it matter? He leaned into the glass to follow the Maserati as it rocketed away, red taillights vanishing into pinpoint streaks that were swallowed by the sleeping city. Only then did he let out his breath.

Spirit cars were pure expressions of *qi*, mobile and supple. He had heard of them, heard of a community of sensitives that rode these things like horse-masters. Now he knew they were real, and his first encounter had been exquisite. A million questions boiled, dogging him. Had the Maserati been alone? Was there someone inside, or was it driving of its own volition? Did it belong to someone? Did it run wild and free? Where did it come from? Where was it going? What was it doing?

Later, lying on his bed, he saw it running in the darkness behind his eyelids, gliding through the night at two hundred kilometres per hour, regal and careless, curved nose sluicing through the air like Poseidon's chariot. It raced across a skyscraper that went on forever, it danced on the surface on the Milky Way, it wove amongst herds of dinosaurs, the call of its engine ripping through some Jurassic plain. Time meant nothing to it, space was there for it to conquer. A four wheeled-demigod embodying infinite potential.

When he was out on the street, he searched the roads for hints of it, head turning at every loud sound that might be an eight-cylinder, heart jumping if he spied a white curve of a certain topography that could have been the start of that distinctive snout.

He had to see it again.

"I'm looking for a Maserati," Charles said.

The girl behind the bar—if it could be called that—tucked a strand of chemical-blond hair behind her ear and nodded, as if such requests were routine. "Do you have a name?"

"Charles." He held a hand out.

"Oh, no," she said, laughing, "I meant the Maserati. Do you know his or her name?"

Charles had bullied, bribed and sweet-talked this way through more than a dozen guardians to find the riders' bar—the watering hole for the community of people who rode spirit cars. He had brought them offerings and little treasures of city-detritus, doorknobs and dead microwave ovens and the thick metal ribs of old Chinese calendars. The sort of things that guardians liked. He had eventually been pointed to the second floor of a mixed residential/commercial building in Joo Chiat, a place he was unfamiliar with. The ground floor was occupied by a dodgy karaoke bar that only came alive at half past six, judging by the sleepiness of the guardian who greeted him when he had arrived. Well, that was Joo Chiat for you. Better or worse after sundown, depending on who you asked.

"I don't know its name," Charles said. He left out the part where he hadn't known that spirit rides had names. Well, he did now.

The girl behind the bar didn't look old enough to either drink or drive, which was somehow fitting with the oddly family-friendly vibe to this place. Throw pillows, casual seating, drinks served off an old-school mahogany table given second life, alcohol bottles stacked behind it on a metal shelving rack like this was some *mamak* shop. "His or her," the girl said. She had stripy hair and wore a lot of costume jewellery. "Not 'its'. Rides have gender identities."

"How does that work?"

The girl tapped out a small rhythm with her fingers. Bright-eyed and smiling as she was, she might not have been humouring him if the bar hadn't been empty. "You're a groundskeeper, aren't you? Only a groundskeeper would ask such stupid questions. A train runner would know, for example." Left unspoken: The assumption that only sensitives would be able to find this place.

Charles unfolded the piece of paper he had shoved into his back pocket before he'd left his own house. "This," he said, pointing to the picture printed on it. "It looked exactly like this." It had taken an hour's hunt on Google to surface a picture of what he had actually seen. A rare breed. A good sign: Easier to find. Exceptional.

The girl smoothed the picture over the tabletop. "A Maserati, huh? Are you from the police?"

"No. Why would you ask that?"

She flapped the piece of paper at him. "You printed out a picture from Google. You're the kind of person who prints out emails to bring to a meeting. It's a government thing. And you talk like one of those official government people."

Charles' hand automatically tightened around his phone on the table. "It's easier to see it on a printout," he pointed out.

The girl patted him on the arm, laughing. "Don't take it so personally, uncle, I was just joking, okay?"

Her unfettered enthusiasm stirred nameless *déjà vu* within him. If Charles hadn't been at the wrong end of his current decade he might have been interested in her. "Well, I'm not. I'm looking for this car because I saw it driving down the side of a building in the Marina Bay Financial District. That's where I work." He paused, and corrected himself: "Him or her, I mean. I want to know what it was doing. He or she."

"That's it?"

"That's it."

She giggled. "It's a car crush!" When Charles shot her a dirty look she patted his arm again, a movement that sent an uncomfortable jolt through him. "I know what you mean. It's like a song you hear on the radio and really, really like, right? You don't know the song title, but you just want to hear it again."

"So can you help me?"

"No." She sighed through her nose. Tapped the picture on the table. "But I know somebody who can. My friend. He used to ride a Maserati a few years back. He knows most of the other Maserati riders in Singapore."

"How do I contact him?"

"Are you free this Saturday? We have a meetup in the morning. I'll take you."

"I can go by myself, if you give me the address…"

"How can you walk into a gathering where nobody knows you? That would be so weird. I'll take you." Charles was about to protest, but she cut him off: "They won't let strangers in, so if you want to go, you have to go as my friend."

She had a point. "Fine." He had planned to work on Saturday morning. Time for him to rejig the week's schedule.

The girl smiled and stuck out her hand. "I'm Huiling. Nice to meet you."

~

Saturday morning found Charles at a decommissioned army camp in Choa Chu Kang, sunk in a patch of overgrown green, its long, winding roads still intact and uncluttered by debris. It looked uninhabited, except that it was being rent apart by an engine cacophony that few others could see or hear. And if they did, what would they make of this scene of madness? A gaggle of Minis raced each other around a bend, while a white shape recognizable as a Porsche 911 led a big black-and-orange car on a game of tag through loosely-packed trees.

Huiling was dressed as if for a picnic: tank top, shorts, and flip-flops. Charles sweltered in the shirt and pants he'd chosen to wear. The camp's guardian spirit, a lined brown nut of a man still dressed in fatigues, saluted Charles as he walked down the slightly-overgrown side of a road. Charles saluted back. He wasn't chatty with guardians of places he didn't usually frequent, and ex-military bases were very low on his list.

Huiling's ride was an Audi TT she'd introduced as Edelweiss. "Like the song," she said, and when Charles stared blankly she had started singing, getting as far as three lines before he remembered the scene from *The Sound of Music*. The ride now rolled quietly in front of them, uncomplainingly keeping pace. Huiling's gait was light, almost a skip. He had almost forgotten how much energy young people had. "One of you groundskeepers gave us access to this place," she said, gesturing expansively.

Loose groups of riders congregated in a concrete-lined clearing, accompanied by music, a couple of outsized drink coolers, and a general sense of merry-making. Edelweiss honked as they approached, and the gathered riders looked up. Huiling waved to a man leaning against an idling pick-up truck, several tons of chrome and severe styling. So trucks could be spirit familiars too, apparently. "That's him," Huiling said. "My friend,

Cheech. That Toyota Hilux is his current ride. And those are his fast-car riding friends."

Cheech, short for Chee Chuan. He was tanned, had a dragon boat racer's physique, and his face creased easily into a smile as he introduced Charles to the other riders. Charles just nodded and nodded, confident that he would not remember any of their names in five minutes' time. "This is Aziz," Cheech said, "Someone you probably want to meet. His current ride is a Maserati."

Aziz nodded. "A white GranTurismo." He appeared young, even if he wasn't, dressed snappily in skinny jeans and a carefully coordinated chartreuse tee shirt. "He said you were looking for one."

"Yeah." Charles stuck his hands in his pockets.

Aziz gave him a know-all grin. "Maybe you'll get lucky today. Let's see." He made a small gesture, over his shoulder, and for the first time Charles noticed the trident tattoo on the inside of his arm. The mark of the Maserati.

An engine roar, superseding everything else, and growing closer. Charles' breath hitched in his throat—what if this was it, this was the thing that he was looking for? The end of his quest could be right now. His hands clenched in his pockets, and he was suddenly afraid to look, afraid to spoil the moment. But he turned around anyway.

A car streaked down the road that curved around the clearing in full throttle, a firm-nosed construct of glass and steel and carbon fibre. Its noise, hyper-real, felt like it could shred right through him. Heads turned, people dropped what they were doing, and even the Porsche stopped in its tracks, narrowly missing a collision with the black-and-orange car. A sound of brakes and the car glided into a controlled stop. In the slanted morning light the dispersing clouds of vaporised rubber gave it an ethereal aura, like something out of a multi-million dollar music video production.

Huiling alone seemed unimpressed by the display. "Drama queen."

Aziz stepped forward, over the edge of the clearing, and put his hand on the car's bonnet. It responded with an engine-purr, the noise of a great Siberian tiger. "This is Shirleen," he said, and he gestured at Charles. "Come closer, she won't bite."

"No," Charles said, and it wasn't because he was afraid. His heart was doing something strange, a leaden weight in his chest descending to the pit of his stomach. "This is wrong, it's all wrong."

"What is it?" Huiling asked.

"That's not the car I saw. It's not even the same model."

"All the white Maseratis in Singapore look like this," Cheech said, doubt lacing his voice. "They're all GranTurismos. What did you see?"

Charles nudged Huiling. "You saw the printout," he said. "It was different, wasn't it?"

Huiling scowled. "I'm not very familiar with Maseratis. I can tell the difference between a two-door and four-door model. That's about it."

"You have pictures of the car you saw?" Aziz asked.

"Not the car," he said, "just a car that looked exactly like it. The same model." He pulled his phone out of his pocket, somewhat hesitantly, and looked up the page he had saved in his browser, a set of pictures from some motorshow or the other. "It looked like this."

The crowd gathered around the phone, trying to look at the tiny screen. Aziz tried to take the phone from Charles, but he held firm, holding the screen tilted out so that Aziz could see it. Admitting defeat, the younger man gave it a once-over. A strange expression passed over his face. "That's an MC Stradale, bro."

Cheech leaned over to peer at the screen, and he and Aziz carried out a small secret conversation, low mutterings and little shrugs, things he couldn't parse. He was distinctly aware of his heart beating in his chest, as if it didn't belong there. "What's an MC Stradale?"

"It's a very new car," Cheech said. "It's based on the GranTurismo, the cars that we have here, but it's got more power. It's rare."

"So nobody in Singapore rides one?" Huiling asked.

Aziz shook his head. "No, man. There's no way something like that can show up and we don't hear about it. Our cars are quite social, something that a lot of the Italian cars have in common. They would know if they had a new brother or sister in town."

Cheech said, under his breath: "Wasn't there one that Blink was investigating?"

"Yeah, but that was different…"

Somebody, one of Cheech's nameless group, whispered, "Eh, careful, she's watching us over there."

Aziz looked over his shoulder, and that was when Charles noticed the young woman watching them from the outskirts of the clearing. Her dark-coloured blouse and skirt camouflaged her well in the foliage; the black-and-orange car idling next to her did not. She saw them staring, and nonchalantly walked behind a tree. The car did no such thing. Was that Blink? Had she overheard their conversation, despite being a hundred meters away?

Aziz shrugged. "She did ask us about it. But it was nothing. That car's gone now, anyway."

"That car? So there was one of these cars in the country?" He waved his phone, and got only shrugs in return. So. This was how it was going to be. Charles should have known. Sensitives were not that much different from ordinary people, after all.

"It was just someone passing through the country," Aziz said. "A tourist, businessman."

"Tourist," said Huiling firmly. "That explains the running-up-and-down-buildings thing. It's the kind of thing people do while they're on holiday, and stupid."

"It wasn't," he said, and he was certain of it. The car he had seen had purpose. It was going somewhere. He looked up, but both Blink and her black-and-orange baby were gone. It didn't matter. Charles was going to find her, and he was going to get her to spill her secrets.

The phone rang nine or ten times before it was picked up. "Hello?" said Huiling, her tinny voice sounding very far away.

"How do you arrange your meetups?"

"Sorry, what?"

"Your meetups. You said that people come and go as they like, and the venue changes. Do you have an online forum? The groundskeepers have a forum, and a mailing list. Surely you people have one too."

"Is this Charles?"

"No, I'm actually the Prime Minister."

"Very funny. Do you know what time it is?"

"3 a.m. Sorry, I work at these times. Rider forums, Huiling. I need an address."

"I'll send you the URL. Why are you calling now? You could have asked these questions earlier, at the meetup."

"I wasn't comfortable at the meetup. I didn't think anyone else there was really interested in helping me, anyway." They hadn't seemed to understand his passion, not in the way Huiling did. "Can I ask you a question?"

"Would you really not ask it if I said no?"

Charles bit his lip at that.

Huiling sighed, a rush of white noise in his ear. "Just ask, uncle."

"That girl, Blink. Do you know her?"

"Ah." A noise of understanding. "You think she knows about your MC Strudelly, or whatever it's called. Hmm." Her voice had lost most of its sleepiness. "I wouldn't be surprised, you know. You saw that car with her? The big orange one? That's Button. There are only, like, six of that kind of ride in the world. Or maybe seven. Button's really powerful. She rents her out to do all the really dangerous jobs, like catching rogue rides or protecting someone. A lot of investigative work, too. Stuff like *CatchCheatingSpouse*. So if your MC Strudel—"

"Stradale."

"Yeah, whatever. If he or she was doing weird stuff like running all over buildings, because it annoys the guardians, maybe someone would have called an investigation."

"You don't happen to have her contact, do you?"

"She doesn't mix around much. Like you, lah. Antisocial type. As far as I know you need a referral for her services. She doesn't advertise. But I can ask around."

"It's okay, I'll ask around on the forums myself."

"You won't get anywhere."

We'll see about that, Charles thought.

It took almost a week worrying at the rider forums before something happened. It was after he had already made a nuisance of himself hijacking random threads and harassing others for information about this mysterious Blink person. One moderator had already permabanned him from a sub-board, and he was sure the others were about to do the same. What he discovered: Riders didn't like talking about this Blink person. Apparently she was the sort you only went to when you were in big trouble.

He nearly overlooked it, his godsend. Someone, whose username he had not seen before, sent him a private message: *what do you want from the mc stradale.*

Charles had chosen to ignore it, at first. But then he remembered he never once mentioned the model of Maserati he had been looking for. He messaged back: *Inspiration. It's my muse. I want to find out more about it.*

He got a reply: *i see. so thats why you were looking for me? its blink btw Prove it.*

you came to last weeks gathering with a someone who rides an audi tt. your shirt was white and you saw me eavesdropping.

He checked the user's profile: Blank. No picture, not even a cheesy quote filled in as a signature. Only one post since joining the forum two years ago, and it just said "thanks!" The thread was in a sub-board he had been locked out of. This was as good as it got. *Okay, I believe you. Now what?*

when do you want to meet?

Chinatown filled his mouth with the cloying taste of duplicity and crass commercialism. Equal parts tourist trap and hipster enclave, this shophouse row he was searching featured eateries sprawling out onto a thoroughfare closed to normal traffic. He meandered through sweaty clusters of DSLR-camera laden gawpers and brisk businessmen wilting in their dress shirts. Charles was dressed like a businessman too, complete with shiny shoes and briefcase. There were some daytime work meetings he just couldn't avoid.

He combed the five-foot ways, looking at the numbers inscribed in shiny decals over post-boxes until he found the one scribbled onto a piece of paper clutched in his hand like a talisman. He needn't have bothered. Sitting in front of the pertinent unit, calmly sunning itself on the traffic-less street, was the big black-and-orange car he had seen at the meetup. He inspected it: some kind of exotic sports car, huge engine in the rear shown off under panel glass, silver letters stamped on the back, a B and a backwards E fused together. People walked by it and around it as if it were a collection of dustbins. Maybe that's what they saw. Charles patted one of its smooth shiny surfaces and was rewarded with a pleased-dog engine rumble.

Charles climbed the shophouse's narrow stairs, trailed by the spicy-sweet smell of the traditional Chinese medicine shop on the ground floor. The next floor consisted of an equally-narrow landing and a door festooned with Chinese characters he couldn't read. Knock-knock.

The unit's interior was a long, cramped confusion of teak wood, cracked parquet and metal trimmings. An old woman in a floral-patterned lilac suit frowned at him, disturbed from her bookkeeping. Under an incandescent lamp lay a thick record book on the plastic marbled tabletop. "Who are you looking for?" she asked in Mandarin.

"Blink?"

"Oh. Ah moi!" She called out, and there was a muffled reply from the rear of the unit, closed off with a peeling gray door. "Inside," the old woman said.

Blink worked off a single table crammed edge-to-edge with paperwork, stationery and a laptop that had seen better times. The dress top she wore today had short scalloped sleeves, partially revealing the marking on her left bicep. A B and a reverse E. "Hi," she said. "Sorry the place is so messy. I'm a bit busy at the moment, but let me just get to this first? Do you want to grab a chair, or something?"

"Oh. Yeah. It's fine." He sat down while she tapped on her laptop, probably composing an email or something similar. The room was a converted kitchen area, and apparently still used as one, judging by the state of the microwave and sink. It was well-lit by a window that opened into a shaft of other windows. A shelving rack held spices, bulbs of garlic and onion, and dark glass containers holding liquid that he couldn't identify. Someone had stuck a bunch of cheerful stickers, the kind one got buying snacks, on the side of the shelves.

Charles twiddled his thumbs.

"Okay," she said, finally looking away from her laptop. "Sorry it took so long. What did you want?"

"Er. It's Charles," he said. "Hades75 from the forums?"

"Oh! Right, sorry." Her eyes flicked sideways to the calendar wired to the window grille, then back at Charles. "You were the one who was looking for the MC Stradale…"

At least she remembered that much. "You were there that Saturday, right? I saw you watching us. I thought you were shy or something."

Blink made a fragile sound that might have been a laugh. "I was trying to get Button to eavesdrop, but she was being a bit conspicuous that day."

"That car, Button? It—she's yours?"

A nod, as she shuffled through her papers. "I send her out on assignments." She dug through a particularly ruffled mountain range and abruptly pulled out a manila folder, nearly causing an avalanche. A small collection of stapled-together stacks lay inside, and she handed one to Charles. It was filled with pictures: stills from videos, shot from a dashboard, with the dreamy, pixelated quality of resolution sensors. Shots of another car, a white Maserati, around the financial district and town area. Parked in front of The Fullerton Hotel. Crossing the Benjamin Sheares bridge. Pulling out of the Marina Bay Sands carpark. From the side, from the back, from the front. That face, with its deeply carved fascia slats like a Cheshire smile, was unmistakeable. Charles felt strangely calm, detached, even though his fingers trembled as he flipped the pages back and forth.

"There's only one MC Stradale known in the whole of Southeast Asia," Blink said. "Maybe someone in a remote Javanese village has one too, but I'm not sure how likely that is."

"When were these photos taken?"

"A couple of months ago. They were quite active then, especially during the day. The ride's name is Charon. When did you say you saw the stunts?"

"About three weeks ago."

"That was around the time we lost track of them in Singapore. Then they showed up, overseas."

"So I'm the last person to have seen it in this country," Charles said, more to himself than anyone else. The thought filled him with unbecoming glee. "Why were you tracking it?"

"For a job," Blink said. Charles noticed she had a nervous tic that was probably the source of her nickname. "Someone who worked in the area was curious about it, but his ride couldn't keep up with the Maserati, so he asked for help."

"A snoop, huh?"

Blink laughed nervously. "If you want to put it like that."

One of the photos gave him additional pause. It showed a young woman, beautiful like a model, getting out of the car. Long hair, sharp cheekbones, full lips. She looked Eurasian, or at least of mixed ethnicity. "Is that her? The car's owner?"

"The rider, yes. Her name is Theresa Manning. She's in Batam now. She has a few properties there."

Charles stared at the photograph. He could tell nothing about her from this one snapshot, nothing at all. The big mirrored shades she wore seemed to mock him. "I want to meet her," he said. "Her and the car."

Blink sighed, her hands clasped together. "Look, I don't usually offer my services for free—"

"You want money? I can pay you for the information. How much?"

"No, that's not what I meant! I just wanted you to stop harassing the other forum members. I thought maybe you would quit it if I gave you the information you wanted." She sighed. "I don't want you to go harassing her either. But…"

Charles leaned forward. Blink looked pensive, her thoughts far away from the room. "From what we gathered about her, she's pretty capable of handling herself."

"Just give me her email address," Charles said plaintively. "She can block me if she doesn't want to speak to me."

Blink nodded. "That's not a bad idea. I think I can do that."

Charles hadn't had anything to worry about: the Maserati's owner did want to speak to him. She wanted to do more than that, in fact. Her reply to his own rambling, awkward email turned up in his inbox less than an hour after he'd dispatched his:

Hello, Charles

I know who you are. We monitor everything said about us, and we noticed that you were snooping around. And that girl, Blink. We knew she was watching us too. She's not as clever as she thinks. It was quite funny, watching you all blunder around trying to find us. All you had to do was ask, but you people are so shy, it's almost embarrassing. Aren't you lucky, though. I'd like to have tea with you at the address I've attached. Let me know when. Bring that friend of yours too. The Audi girl. She's been poking around as well; you just got to the finish line first.

Tess

He kept reading the e-mail over and over. No, it wasn't a dream. He reached for his phone and dialled Huiling. "How would you like a short trip to Batam?"

Fragments of Indonesian countryside sped past the Audi TT's windows and melted away. Charles wasn't thinking straight, just moving forward one step at a time. He wasn't thinking at all. Huiling was at the helm of Edelweiss, humming an inane song under her breath. She seemed to be taking it a lot better than he was.

"Why are you doing this for me?" he suddenly asked, unable to keep it back any longer. "You didn't have to."

Huiling actually laughed out loud. "Doing it for you? Uncle, I wouldn't get my passport out to go on somebody else's silly quest. I'm here for myself, yo." She grinned, an easy, lazy thing. "Driving down the sides of buildings—that's a crazy thing! Amazing! It's so good, even stupid groundskeepers get inspired. I want to meet this woman. I've wanted to meet her ever since you brought it up."

At least one of them knew what they were doing, then. "It's good you're here, anyway. I'm bad at travelling, actually. I get lost all the time. And I'm terrible at talking to guardians in other countries. Plus, I don't speak Bahasa Indonesia."

"You have to speak Bahasa to the guardians here?"

"It's not really necessary, but it helps."

She turned the car off the dusty road and onto a dirt path tangled with vegetation on either side. Charles must have looked wary, because she smiled hugely and said, "Don't worry." She patted Edelweiss' steering wheel. "She knows where she's going."

The dirt path climbed upwards and opened up at its crest onto a stretch of yellow, sandy beach. He could see the shape of a peaked roof nearby plastered with *attap* leaves, and a cluster of coconut trees rippling in the wind. Huiling pulled up at the boundary where the dirt ended and sand began.

"Is this it?" he asked. She made a non-committal gesture with her hands. He took a deep breath and pushed the car's suddenly-heavy door open.

They stood on the beach's edge in the waves of reflected heat. Charles squinted and shielded his eyes. Maybe it was not quite paradise, but at least it was quiet. And slow, the heat dragging everything down to a crawl.

A sound, a familiar V8 growl. Huiling pointed. "There!"

Coming down the jaundiced beach was a white shape, blinding in its intensity, so painful to look at that Charles' eyes watered. But it was unmistakable, despite being distorted through the searing light and film of water. It was his Maserati, his MC Stradale.

Time slowed further, slipping through the gaps in the heat-warped air. The Maserati came up to him, close enough to touch, close enough to feel the energy radiating off its smooth, fluted nose. Charles reached out as if to touch it, then suddenly withdrew, terrified that something might happen if he did. The Maserati idled, splendid and aloof, its slanted headlamps revealing no emotion. Of course not: it was a car.

He looked at Huiling and shrugged, a small and helpless gesture. "This is it, then."

Huiling patted Edelweiss on the nose. "Stay and watch the perimeter, okay?"

The Maserati turned smoothly in the sand, leaving behind the faintest of tyre tracks. Charles stumbled after it, shoes sinking and sliding. The car didn't wait. He found himself chasing after it, after its insouciance, after the restrained growl of its engine. Huiling seemed to have no problems keeping up. Ah, to be so young again.

The car was headed in an unquestioned line towards the lone house lording over this stretch of beach, a construct of wood and palm elevated on a platform of stilts. Yet for all the rustic aura, the house was no haphazard chop-job. The wood forming the walls was free of fungal spots or decay, and the stilts holding it up were sturdy and triply lashed together with yards of twine bound up in complicated knots. There was an air of deliberation to it, a kind of posed simplicity that was thought out down to the colour of every piece of wood that went into its making.

The Maserati stopped at the foot of the house, to the steps made of perfectly coordinated timber. He looked at the car. "Up there?"

It revved its engine, which could have been a *yes* or *you idiot*. He couldn't tell which.

A sudden terror seized him. He didn't want to do this. The belated realization grabbed some part of the anatomy in his chest and squeezed hard. He didn't want to meet the driver of the car he had glimpsed, he didn't want to put a face to the phenomenon.

But he had come all the way here. And Huiling was standing here with him, wasting her weekend, while all he wanted to do was run away before he reached his goal.

He had a choice. He could turn away, go back up the beach, and back to his life in Singapore, satisfying himself with the fact that the Maserati was real, a thing in the world—he could hear it right now, its engine grumbling! And he could stop thinking about the whole affair.

Or he could go in and meet whoever was waiting in there and actually talk to her. Find out about her life.

Huiling nudged him, as though sensing his hesitation. "Come on, uncle. Let's go."

Charles climbed the steps slowly. There was a patio of sorts, a stretch of flat planks about half a meter wide, between the steps and the façade of the house. A beaded curtain hung across the doorway.

"Inside," said a woman's voice. Tess.

"You first," said Huiling in a whisper. "It's your gig after all."

It wasn't dark, as he'd expected. The peaked roof had been opened at the top to let in the light, filling out the insides with an ambient glow. The interior of the house was minimalist in its design, sparse wooden furniture trimmed in white. One combined living-dining-sleeping space with partitions for what he assumed was a bathroom.

In person, Tess had the type of glamour Charles had only encountered from afar, in glossy magazine pages and hotel lobbies and mixer parties his firm sometimes held. Olive skin, culturally-acceptable thinness, and mixed features that would let her slot herself into any ethnicity she wanted, and people would believe it. "Hello, you two," she said. "Sit. I made you something to drink." She gestured towards a set of reclining chairs that looked like they had been carved out of whole blocks of wood, with a short table in between on which sat two glasses filled with a liquid that graduated from orange to red. A third chair faced them.

Charles struggled to say something. His throat was dry and his mind spun fruitlessly.

"You're Charles," she said, filling in the silence. "And you're Huiling. Please sit."

Huiling flopped into one of the chairs, but Charles remained standing. "I just wanted to say," he began, then stopped.

Tess sat down in the third chair, hooked one knee over the other, and looked at him expectantly. He blew out a huge breath. "I just wanted to say thank you."

She tilted her head. Charles squeezed his eyes shut and forced himself to talk: "When I saw you and your Maserati in the MBFC, I saw perfection. I can't really put it into words. But I saw something that day that really inspired me. It was amazing. It was like everything suddenly made sense. Like there was a point to life that I never saw before. It was so extraordinary. So...It was..." The words dried up.

Tess looked at him and a smile broke out across her face. Her teeth were amazingly white, even whiter than the Maserati that he could hear rumbling outside. "You've got to be kidding me."

Charles opened his mouth, closed it, opened it again.

"He isn't kidding," Huiling supplied, helpfully.

"Sit down," she said, pointing to the chair opposite her. Charles reluctantly sank into the seat. His hands were shaking.

Tess sipped coolly from her drink, her lips painted as red as the cranberry liqueur at the bottom of the glass. He could only look at his own glass, despite the dryness of his throat. He didn't dare touch anything "So you're a groundskeeper," she said.

Charles nodded.

Her expression as she scanned him was calm, with perhaps just the barest hint of a smirk. "Do you want to know what Charon and I were doing, that night, in the MBFC?"

Fighting crime? Banishing demons? Had she been saving the world, protecting the city, like a foxy Batman or Spiderman, swinging from building to building in her brand new Maserati?

Her lips stretched in a self-satisfied smile. "Financial fraud."

Charles blinked once, twice. "I'm sorry?"

"You heard me. Financial fraud." She put the drink down on the table and folded her fingers together. "I met someone. A banker. He told me places to look where they'd be doing dodgy accounting. Siphoning money from one account to another, either squirreling it away or covering up evidence of poor investment decisions. Massive amounts of money, hundreds of millions, sums of money poor sods on the streets like you could only ever dream of." She raised an eyebrow. "So you want to know what I did?"

"What?" Huiling asked. She was leaning forward in her chair, like a child at the movies.

"I found myself a hacker. A systems analyst, working in another bank. Russian. Self-taught. He's very good. I had him work me up a little program, a tiny little worm, to take a small percentage of the fraudulent transactions and put it into another account. That was what I was doing, that night. Planting it into their computer systems." Leaning forward, she said: "I was skimming the skimmers."

"Um," said Charles. His face had worked itself into a frown without him realizing it. Huiling, on the other hand, was staring at her, rapt, as she sucked down the red-and-orange drink Tess had made.

"That's not even the best part," Tess said.

"Really. So...What's the best part?"

Her smile could have been a shark's advertisement for toothpaste. "I'll never get caught. Sure, they'll eventually figure out what I'm doing. But who are they going to tell? And what would they say?" She spread her hands. "So, Charles, you were right. What you saw was perfection. The perfect crime."

This was not what he had been expecting. He had walked out of his ordinary life into a Dalí painting, melted clocks and pyramidal buildings and gravity-defying Italian supercars riding on spindly-legged elephants. "So all this. This beach house, this place."

"I own the entire stretch."

"Yes. I mean, that's how you pay for it? By stealing from dishonest bankers?"

Tess shook her head, still smiling. "My family owns an oilfield in the North Sea. The money that I get from the skimming is just a tiny, tiny drop of how much my family is worth."

"So why do it?"

"Why not?"

Huiling put her glass down on the table. "You," she said slowly, "are the coolest person I have ever met."

Charles looked at her, feeling somehow betrayed. Huiling, in her stead, looked surprised that Charles wasn't enjoying himself more. She picked her drink up again.

Silence settled around them for a brief, uncomfortable moment. Charles bit his lower lip. Tess wet hers. "You're a groundskeeper," she said to Charles. He nodded. That feral smile, again. "Have you ever thought of robbing a bank?"

"What?"

"A bank," she said, as if talking to a child. "Have you ever thought about robbing one?"

Huiling put her now-empty glass down, more slowly than she had before. Charles glanced sideways at her, then back at Tess. "I heard you," he said. "Why?"

"Why not?" Tess leaned back in her chair. "Groundskeeper. You're in deep with the building guardians. All you have to do is talk to one of them, and you can slip in and out of the bank in their building without ever being noticed. And you, Audi girl. You seem pretty quick on your feet. You have the perfect getaway car. Why wouldn't you do it?"

"It's stealing."

"Oh, please. Like you would ever steal enough money to hurt a bank."

Charles kept quiet. Huiling tilted her head. Was she seriously considering it?

"Just a couple of hundred thousand," Tess said. "Nothing at all to the banks, but plenty of dosh to get comfortable on. Think about it."

"Right." Charles stood up, his heart pounding, drink still untouched. "I think we should go, actually."

Huiling blinked. "Are you kidding, uncle? We just got here."

"She's asking us to rob a bank. That's crazy."

"She isn't asking. She's just suggesting. Nobody's forcing you to rob a bank." Huiling gave Tess one of her characteristic huge smiles. "Your life sounds amazing. I want to know about the other wild things you've done."

Charles looked at her, uncomprehending, then at Tess, and back at her. There was a hollowness within him that he couldn't describe. "Look, I know you want to talk some more, or whatever. I'll just go out and stay with Edelweiss, all right? I'll wait for you. I have emails to send."

Tess and Huiling looked at each other, and something passed between them that he couldn't read. Hadn't they just met each other as well? Charles felt like an unwanted overgrown insect, and shivered. Tess looked at him and shrugged. "Suit yourself, then."

"I'll catch you later, uncle. Be nice to Edelweiss."

"It was nice to meet you," Charles blurted at Tess before he fled.

The Maserati was in the surf, driving amongst the slapping waves, sending up sprays of salt water. Charles skidded to stop in the sand, the wind hot and heavy between them. "You shouldn't do that," he said. "You could get water in your engine."

The Maserati stopped and turned towards him, its engine a soft threatening noise. He stared at it, and it stared back at him. And he felt just as small and stupid as he had back in the house. Of course it could play in the surf. It was a spirit car. It ran vertically down the sides of buildings. Laws of physics were, to it, mere suggestions that it could laugh at. And it, accepting the challenge, went to the places where no cars go.

The Maserati carved itself a neat circle, and drove straight into the sea. Fins of water shot up as it sliced through the waves, skimming the surface like a speedboat. As Charles watched it navigate a perfect turn in the sunlight he felt a deep sense longing stirring in him again. He had no idea what had just happened, and there was an empty, buzzing feeling in his chest where his heart was knocking about, but he felt that if he could stand there, and just watch the Maserati be everything he wanted to be for a little while longer, it would all go away. His job, his life, all the people who didn't like him and who he just couldn't make himself like either. With a roar, the car shot towards the horizon, nought to sixty in four-point-six seconds but maybe faster if it was going over water, who the hell knew. It was an impenetrable entity that did not care what anyone thought of it. Charles closed his eyes, illogically wanting to preserve this image in his mind forever.

"Freedom," he said. "You were supposed to be freedom."

GREEN MAN PLUS

Isa Kamari

He sits on a bench and watches children chasing each other and frolicking at the playground a few meters away. He smiles, remembering his childhood days at the *kampong*. The entire village and the nearby hill was his playground. It felt good then to be free and cheerful.

He looks up at the sky. Everywhere is blue, not a single cloud to be seen. It would be a lovely day to be out in the open and feel alive, but he is in no mood to relish the moment. He sighs deeply. He looks at the children again. His eyes become teary.

Just a few minutes ago he checked out from the hospital, weary from the bad news. He has a tumour in his large intestine.

He keeps wondering why. He lives a healthy lifestyle, exercises almost every day. Only rain keeps him away from brisk walking and stretching at the park. He eats a balanced diet of carbohydrates, protein and greens. He has no major worries since he enjoys his retirement days. How did the tumour appear?

The doctor told him that he will need to undergo a biopsy soon. The tumour has grown to the size of a golf ball. If it is malignant and grows bigger and bursts, then the problem might spread to more parts of his body and it would be hard to control the disease.

He breathes in deeply and shuts his eyes. He must not worry too much. The doctor told him that the "problem" is still manageable, advised him to remove the tumour regardless of the outcome of the biopsy. As such, the doctor suggested that both procedures could be done in one surgical operation, and fixed it for Monday next.

He opens his eyes and presses his palms into his thighs. He looks at the surface of the bare ground. An eerie thought shakes his usually calm disposition; he cannot help but imagine himself to be under it, six feet deep. He trembles.

"Arre you reaady to crosss ooverrr?"

Simultaneously with the guttural utterance, the branches of the trees in front of him sway and shake from a sudden gust of wind. A flock of crows takes flight. Where did they come from? His face turns pale. He panics and turns his head. There is nobody to be seen. Even the playground is now empty. A frightful memory which creaks and moves back and forth with the empty swing seizes him.

Two months ago at his religious class, the *ustaz* told his followers that a person would be able to know of the coming of his or her death a hundred days before the event. Allah would reveal the signs to His servants who performed all the religious obligations. It would be a privilege, since death is a moment of celebration for the soul to return willingly to the Creator in a tranquil and contented state known as *husnul khatimah* or the "best of ends." As such, the coming of death should not be feared.

Everything was as usual after the class. He left for his home by walking slowly along the footpath from the mosque after the *asar* prayers. The din from the nearby coffee shop could be heard on the warm but breezy afternoon. His mind and soul felt enlightened and peaceful.

Just as he reached a nearby bench, he felt an abrupt spasm that ran from his head down his arms to his thighs and feet. The spasm shook him so terribly that he had to hold the bench's armrest firmly before he sat down. His chest heaved and his whole body trembled. Sweat appeared on his forehead and nape, and quickly chilled.

His body felt numb and his mind went blank for a moment. He realized the significance of the experience. That was the first sign! Or was it? He was dazed for a while. He had never felt so lost and fearful in his entire life.

The *ustaz* reassured his followers that the discernment of the approach of death would leave the faithful servant calm and humble, as he or she could then prepare for the moment of release and glory. The initial bewilderment would change into complete surrender as the signs were unfolded to the servant one by one. Naturally the servant would do all the things in the remaining days that would be important or meaningful to be left behind to his or her loved ones. But he or she would accomplish these tasks with the state of mind of someone who knew of and cherished the manifestation of the big secret between Allah and His faithful servant alone because, as the *ustaz* had said, it would be an honour or privilege.

But it didn't feel like an honour or privilege as he dragged his feet and returned home that afternoon. He was sullen and dazed. His body shook as he prepared to nap. He was afraid that he might wake up in a grave. But he remembered that if the sign were true, then he would have another ninety-nine days to live. As such, he should not feel threatened by sudden death. Yet, to anticipate death was equally terrible. He did not take his dinner or sleep that night. He told himself to be on the lookout for the next sign.

The second sign would appear forty days before the fateful day. Anxious of his possible demise, for two months he performed all the *wajib* or obligatory religious duties, as well as the *sunnat* or additional duties to gain the pleasure of Allah. Gradually he became at peace with himself. He forgot about all his anxieties.

The fateful second sign came after the *asar* prayer again. As he was sitting cross-legged and resting his back against one of the pillars in the mosque, he felt an excruciating pain at his navel that would not go away. He held his stomach and bent his body forward and backward repeatedly to ease the pain. He could not help but cry out. One of the other members of the congregation noticed his suffering and approached him, and was kind enough to send him to the Accident and Emergency department of Changi General Hospital.

He was then warded for treatment and examination. The tumour was discovered. He felt restless and was afraid of staying at the hospital. He pleaded incessantly to the doctor to let him return home. He was finally given home-leave over the weekend, since none of the operating theatres were available and the agony in his stomach had disappeared after he was given painkillers. But he was advised by the doctor to rush to the hospital as soon as he felt the pain again. In any case, he must return for the surgery. He promised to do so. He just wanted to spend more time at home. He had a lot to think about.

According to the *ustaz*, forty days before death, the leaf in which the name of the servant had been inscribed since his creation would fall from the Lote Tree in Heaven. The Angel of Death would then follow the person everywhere, in preparation of his duty to remove the life-force from the person's body. Sometimes the angel would appear in person to forewarn him or her. Upon seeing the Angel of Death, the person would naturally be confused until he or she realized the significance of the visit.

He now shudders while holding the thought and looks straight ahead. He feels as if he is being sucked into a tunnel. He is almost breathless. Abruptly, a man in a black robe appears in front of him about fifty meters away, smiling widely. He can feel the overpowering presence from where he sits. The robed man's lips begin to move.

"Arre you reaady to crosss ooverrr?" the eerie voice reverberates again. Each syllable seems to pound on his eardrums. He cups his ears with his palms and looks straight into the large eyes of the stranger. Goosepimples appear on his arms and cheeks and he shakes uncontrollably. He tightens his eyelids against the sight. He waits until the clatter of his teeth abates. Then he opens his eyes again slowly, scanning the surroundings with the anticipation of shutting them again. Fortunately, the man, or whatever he might be, is no longer there.

He feels relieved momentarily. A deadening silence hovers in the air. Dusk is approaching. He needs to take a feeder bus that will bring him to the bus stop nearest to his flat. He pulls out his purple Senior Citizens Concession card, which allows him to travel at a discounted rate by bus and MRT train.

He is in deep thought as he boards the bus that will take him home. If the signs are true, he will be dead in less than forty days. The third sign should appear seven days before the tragic day: a person who has lost his appetite due to illness will suddenly relish food like never before. He dreads such an experience. He does not want to enjoy food just to die a few days later.

The fourth sign would surface just three days before death, after the *asar* prayer. He would experience intense pain in the middle of his forehead. The light in his pupils would fade, his nose would sink in noticeably, his earlobes would wilt and the edges would curl in, and his feet would bend inwards so much that it would be unstable for him to stand stationary for too long. It was recommended that one perform a fast during the remaining days to ensure that one's intestines would not be filled with too much excrement upon death.

The final sign would appear just one day before the return to his Lord. He would feel a pulsating pain at the top of his head in a spot known as the *ubun-ubun*. If that sign were to appear, it would mean that he would not make it to the next *asar* prayer. There would be no turning back. He would definitely meet his Creator shortly afterward.

His eyes are teary as he alights from the bus and walks listlessly towards the pedestrian crossing. The "green man" has not yet appeared at the traffic light. He takes out his purple SCC card and taps it onto the traffic pole's Green Man Plus device with his trembling hand. An initiative of the Land Transport Authority, the Green Man Plus scheme allows the elderly to cross the road safely and comfortably at selected pedestrian crossings; all the elderly man or woman needs to do is to tap their purple card on the attached device and the "green man" would blinker for an additional six seconds. He has used the scheme every day since it was implemented and is grateful that he need not rush to cross the road. Alas! He has not many more days left to enjoy such privileges.

"Am I ready to cross over?" he says aloud.

An eerie feeling suddenly overwhelms him. He senses the presence of the man with the black robes again. He looks around but the apparition is nowhere to be seen. Yet somehow he feels that he is being trailed and watched. He shuts his eyes with the hope that he can dispel the fear of meeting him again.

Then a hopeful and rather devious thought crosses his mind. He is struck by its simplicity and promise. If he can add six seconds to the duration of his crossing, perhaps he could incrementally do the same to his life. It is an outrageous proposal but he does not think it is impossible. No, not at all! In fact he is desperately hopeful about it. After all, he has nothing to lose and more time to gain. Yes, more time! He could beat the apparition at his own game and chase him away!

Something within him releases. He laughs heartily. He is not afraid anymore. He then grins unabashedly and waves the purple card victoriously.

As the "green man" appears, he crosses the road briskly and waits at the other end for the "red man" to appear next. When it does, he taps his purple card again to wait for the "green man" to re-appear and add six seconds to his life as he re-crosses the road. He repeats the procedure with a confident and cunning smile.

At first nobody pays attention to his antics. After multiple crossings, however, the motorists become frustrated; the traffic light turns red more often and they are forced to wait an additional six seconds each time the crazy old man traverses the road. But nobody can stop him. He has not broken any law. All they can do is sneer and shout at him. Some motorists avoid the crossing altogether and make a detour. Many passersby just gather and observe the old man who never stops grinning as he waves and taps his purple Senior Citizens Concession card at the Green Man Plus device that has given him hope of an extended life.

Amidst the spectacle, nobody seems to notice the van that suddenly stops near the traffic light control box by the side of the road. A man in black overalls steps out from the van. He is holding a pair of pliers.

MIRAGE

Noelle de Jesus

The blistering afternoon heat lay like a heavy blanket over all of us. I knew Gong Gong would be in a state again, and I just didn't have the energy for it. Not only that, we didn't have the drinking water for it.

We were already too deep into our weekly water ration, and we needed to conserve. As it was, by tomorrow, we would only have a litre, maybe a litre and half to drink each. This always happened when my grandfather succumbed to his condition. First, he would not be able to get up out of bed. Then he complained incessantly of unbearable thirst, and would rage on and on about the good old days until I too was half-crazed, believing I wanted—no, that I *needed*—more water, when even just half as much would have been perfectly sufficient.

Sometimes, I felt the best thing to do was leave him like that. Go about my business—go diving or fishing, trap shrimp or shellfish, or go to Orchard Market to trade. Sometimes, I tried to snap him out of it. I'd beg him to come with me. In good times, diving, we had unearthed so many trinkets just off the Alexandra Coast, ancient artefacts waterlogged and damaged, but clearly from the Golden Age. Over the years, we had found books, good enough once dried sufficiently out in the sun, bottles of dark liquid—liquor even. Gong Gong had once eagerly sampled

167

a dark, labelled bottle, but learned now not to, as it only exacerbated thirst. We also found several mobile phones and other gadgets. None functioning, but they were wonderful to see.

"Come on, Gong Gong. Let's go find more buried treasure. Diving will cool you off."

But it was no use. All Gong Gong wanted to do was murmur weakly, "Water, Kelvin...water..." all the while whimpering and pointing at his throat.

It was better to stay outside of the house until he got over it. It was better to wait for the clarity that came on cooler days. When it rained, Gong Gong had good ideas for trapping and then purifying rain water. Sometimes, he tended to the plants that grew in the shallows and made up most of what we ate. We even managed to save enough for our little community to do simple things like washing our faces. When it was cool, he liked to dive. When the wind blew moist on his face, he happily spoke of his great hope that one day the Great Benevolent Government would shape up and restore this dark age to light.

But when it was this hot, the old man fell into a kind of madness, a ranting stupor that was terrible to see. If it was not whimpering, it was angry muttering or just a sulky silence. In these times, he chose not to listen to you. Not only that, I felt that I too could easily get sucked into his lunacy.

When these times struck, my first instinct was always to leave. But I felt too much compassion for him. This life was all I knew, but he lived his best years through the Golden Age. And the past twenty years? This was the tail-end of Gong Gong's life and yet, this time was also the most frightening and the most difficult for him, this dark age. Ironically, it was an era that was bright with heat, one in which he was constantly parched with a thirst that was impossible to slake.

Fortunately, most of the time, Gong Gong and I knew well not to waste the monthly allocation our GBG bestowed upon us for such mundane pursuits as bathing and cooking. We ate a little of what we caught or dove for—fish mostly, plus sea slugs, crab and shrimp. But a few of the artefacts that we dove for were of great use and interest to the GBG. Anything else left over, like articles of clothing or shoes or items like scissors, we sold or traded at the Orchard Market.

Our water was only for drinking, and between us, with strategic use, we could each manage to drink about three litres a day. Why use water rations for cleaning, when you live next to the sea?

"You know, Kelvin," our next door neighbour Serena said, "It's not like you need to drink that much water a day. Nai Nai says, back in the Golden Age, people had to *force* themselves to drink that much water a day." I knew that Serena and her grandmother liked to feel fresh water on their faces, on their eyes and on their skin. They also boiled water into which they steeped tea leaves they got at the market. I always said tea was a waste of water because it dehydrated you, and frequently left you thirstier than ever. Serena always ignored me.

Even here at the edge of Spore on the jagged River Valley Coast, it was hot. Yes, even here in the double row of waterway homes where Gong Gong and I were sent to live at the beginning of Transition, once all who were sick and dying had already passed on, and the fittest emerged. We, and the few other small families like ours with Triple-Senior Citizens from the Golden Age; many of us were just two-person units.

Gong Gong said that they kept the TSCs at the edge of society because TSCs knew too much. "We know the truth, boy. That's why they keep us here, with no work, just supplying us with our rations—keep us fed, keep us quiet. They're afraid we'll just open our mouths and spoil their big plans." I believed him.

I had heard there were communities like ours, mostly along the coasts, far from downtown Bukit Timah, where a new state was being established.

The sea lapped lazily against the specially designed concrete pillars that held up our small homes, and there was a very slight breeze that did nothing for the heat. The hypnotic sound of the waves only reminded Gong Gong of his unquenchable thirst, and as regular as the tides, the memory and the lunacy returned to plague him. Sometimes he went back to the dreadful week of the flood, when the Golden Age had been reduced to mere memory.

At River Valley Coast, we had all been alike. We had no mothers and fathers now, only grandmothers and grandfathers, and usually only just one. The remains of the government led by the former Navy, now known only as the Spore GBG, stepped in and rescued us. I don't remember much of that terrible time. Just the rising water overtaking us, and holding on to Gong Gong as he treaded choppy waters, gasping and then telling me to hold my breath as we were deluged by the waves. All of us—myself, Serena, Ada, Kenneth and Samuel—we were all small children taking lessons at an educational facility, and our grandparents were waiting for us when the ocean waters had risen.

Only a few of us, about eleven or twelve small family units, had remained. Those of us who survived were good swimmers. By now, of course, quite a number of the TSCs had passed on. To my knowledge, there were only three left: my Gong Gong, Serena's Nai Nai, and Kenneth's Ye Ye, who at the moment was also ailing, and if her grandson was right, she would not last the month. I believed the same of Gong Gong, but it was a thought that I did not allow myself.

Spore was now less than half of what it had been. According to the great books that remained, our people occupied a smaller area of land than ever before. On the other hand, by the time the floods had transformed the landscape, the state had grown its land by almost half, through a comprehensive reclamation program. Gong Gong said that, at its largest, the state had been almost 900 square kilometres. Today, in this year of 2090, our land was less than its original 500 square kilometres, as even some areas of natural igneous rock were under shallow seawater.

Growing up, my memory of Gong Gong was of him standing and gesturing at the sea. "Over there was where your parents would go to work. And further east, over there." He'd pointed in the distance at a patch of deep blue, where sometimes we saw leaping dolphins. "Over there was where we lived, in a tall, tall building." He'd told me that my parents worked in the lower echelons of a government office. They had been smart and dutiful and they worked in public utilities. He described a government that was complex and multi-layered, with different sections and committees in charge of specific functions. It was the complete opposite, it seemed to me, of the GBG.

"And over there, what was over there, Gong Gong?" The little boy that I had been never tired of asking him questions about what once was. Because in the great expanse of water that surrounded me, it was difficult to imagine anything else. He'd always had an answer. He taught me everything he knew.

He'd drawn maps. He'd spoken of islands. He'd talked of tourists from other countries coming to what was our land to have holidays and enjoy themselves. The city had everything, it seemed: malls and clubs and a giant Ferris wheel, a building that looked like a boat, and amusement parks. I did not mind the old stories of all that had been. I did not mind the lessons in geography or history. I knew my teachers at school were altering some of the facts. But I also understood why. It had been easier to build hope on an orderly sequence of events.

But the one story I really did not want to hear was the story Gong Gong told on these hot and humid days. It would be like a hallucination. He would fall into a nap, and all of a sudden sit up, gasping for breath and weeping from thirst.

"All we have to do is find it! It's somewhere under all this water."

"What is, Gong Gong?" I asked him.

"It's a warehouse of fresh drinking water. Bottles and bottles of it, untouched for decades."

The idea of this warehouse, filled floor-to-ceiling with sealed bottles of fresh drinking water made Gong Gong crazy. It made me crazy. I made him promise not to talk about it to our neighbours. That kind of talk was dangerous.

"It's only a dream, Gong Gong."

Sometimes, he would be angry.

"No! No, it's not. Your father took me there. I saw the bottles myself. No one was buying it then. No one wanted it. Even I didn't want to drink it. So they piled it all into the warehouse. I saw it all, back in the Golden Age. You know nothing. Don't you understand? If we find it, we can have everything! We don't have to suffer the way we have been suffering. I know it's out there. You have to help me find it."

"We are not suffering, Gong Gong. We are okay. We have our rations. The GBG will take care of us. They always have."

"Have they? *Have they?* Pah!" He spat at me, his eyes wild and wizened, the skin on his face, lined and dry. "You know nothing, boy. *Nothing.*"

There were days, back when he was stronger, that he would rise in the early morning. He would call me to bring the boat and we would row out as far as we could to where he felt it might be. The warehouse. The fresh drinking water in sealed bottles. And then he would jump off the boat with his swim goggles and go looking for the warehouse and the building. I waited in the boat. Or sometimes, I would dive in with him. He told me what to look for, but we'd never ever found it.

Serena came and knocked on our window. I left Gong Gong's side and stepped out in the heat to talk with her.

"How is he?"

"To be expected, considering the weather. Thirsty."

She sighed. I knew she faced a similar situation with her Nai Nai. One cannot know what kind of drain you experience emotionally and physically as you adjust to scarcity when once upon a time, you knew plenty.

"I don't think it will be long for me now. Nai Nai hasn't said a word since she finished this week's rations. I don't know if she will make it to next week, even if I split my share of the rations with her."

I reached for Serena's hand.

"I'm sorry. I really am."

I knew what she wanted to ask me. I averted my eyes. Gong Gong still seemed very strong to me. And soon, the weather would cool off and he could come back to himself.

Serena shook her head, turned, and left.

"Kelvin? Water?"

I returned to my grandfather's bedside. He was sitting up, all of a sudden energized. I let him have a cup of water, and he did what he always did, each and every time he drank. He took the cup and let the water wet his upper lip for half a minute, before finally, reluctantly, draining the cup.

"Promise me, you'll try to find it, Kelvin. Promise me." Gong Gong grabbed my arm. "I remember now. There were four factories. You have to take the boat to Ulu Pandan Coast."

Ulu Pandan Coast was nowhere near where we lived. I had only heard of it and had never been there myself. There was nothing there. It was just GBG territory, north of the state, closer to downtown. In all our journeys together on that boat, we never ever made it that far. And in this heat, I wasn't certain we could. But the old man would not let up. I did not have the heart to say no.

"Can we go today, Kelvin? Please?"

We had not taken a boat trip in weeks. Not since the most recent heat wave had hit. I was also worried about provisions. Out in the sun, we would naturally need to consume more of the rations. But what kind of grandson would deny his grandfather's plaintive pleas, especially knowing he may not have all that many weeks left. Not me. I couldn't do it.

"Ok, Gong Gong. We'll go. But let's wait—let's wait until the sun begins to set," I said, hoping the weather would give us some respite. We could row close to shore and make a round of the island, but I knew that with only me rowing, it would be a good couple of hours before we hit Ulu Pandan Bay. Then of course, there were the GBG patrol boats to watch out for. These areas they monitored very closely, and if they found us, they would not be happy that we were so far out of our assigned territory.

But the old man seemed calm and happy now. He brought out his swim mask and the breathing apparatus he had made out of an old rubber hose we had found deep in our waters. He got up and dressed himself and waited for the sun to begin its descent.

"You're a good boy, Kelvin. Just like your father. Never mind what happens to me. What's important is that you go on, make the most out of your life. And this treasure will help you."

His words made me sad, but I set my feelings aside, and then carefully transferred half a litre of water into a sealed container. Then I went out to ready the boat.

Serena was standing on the wood deck that wrapped around all our homes, and when she saw me helping Gong Gong, cane and all, walk towards the boat, her eyebrows shot up.

"Good afternoon, uncle. Good to see you out and about."

"Hello, girl!" The old man seemed to sense that now was not a time to inquire after Serena's grandmother. And she too did not bring the old lady up. Families with TSCs were very tactful that way, especially the TSCs themselves.

And just as I had hoped, the air took a cool turn, and we caught a nice tail wind. It was as though the heat of this day had never even taken place. As I rowed, I watched the old man sit and stare at the vast horizon, shot with bolts of purple, orange and pale pink from the slowly sinking sun. I sent our boat gliding lightly across this calm and placid sea, with a moist breeze. Neither of us spoke for the better part of an hour. I felt like I had when I was a young boy—just content and happy to be alive and well, rowing my boat with my grandfather at my side. He was all the family I'd ever had.

As we neared the small bay of Ulu Pandan, I was happy to find no other boats around. The hour was too late for GBG.

"The thing is, they bottled too much of it, and it was just a matter of...wrong timing." Gong Gong murmured as much to himself as to me. "Too much of the wrong thing at the wrong time. No one would drink it, so they had to put it aside. But now, now is the perfect time."

"The perfect time for what, Gong Gong?"

"The new water, my boy. Think about a warehouse full of bottled water—New Water, they called it. And for your information, it was perfectly good water. Both your father and mother said that. Everybody knew it was safe to drink, but the ordinary people, they couldn't. They all said it was shit. Shit water. I thought it was shit. Well, they bottled too much of it, and they filled a warehouse of the stuff. But today, it's not shit. Today it's gold. Gold from the Golden Age."

Our boat was no longer moving. We were about two hundred meters from the shore.

"But Gong Gong," I protested, "You don't think the GBG already knows that? For all you know, they have it already."

The old man sputtered with indignation.

"Pah! The GBG! They don't care to listen to the old folk. They might know about it, but they also only believe their own information. They know it was supplementing the water supply, but I don't think they know just how much of it was bottled."

He shook his head, and tugged at the small anchor. I helped him drop it.

"We'll find it here. Let me go first."

"No, Gong Gong. You're not strong enough."

"Kelvin, you can't find something if you don't know what you're looking for."

Dusk was starting to creep in, and the water was looking dark and menacing. Our boat bobbed about as the tides grew stronger. I thought that I should do the dive, but my arms were too tired from the rowing. All of a sudden, the entire mission seemed impossible—a foolish pipe dream. Nothing but a useless, cruel fantasy.

The old man peeled off his shirt, leaving only his shorts. His body was pitiful to see, nothing but an emaciated torso and pale spindly limbs. I had a terrible sense of foreboding.

"Gong Gong, let's row to land and we can pick up official GBG transport back to home. You need your rest."

The old man peered into my eyes, and when I looked into his, I saw hurt flashing in them.

"You don't believe me, Kelvin?"

I rushed to reassure him, to tell him I believed him. I believed there had been new water. I just didn't believe my grandfather would find it today…or ever.

He ignored me and stood, scanning the bay, looking at the land and the network of low-rise buildings that had been constructed, and then looking back at the water. He measured the space with his eyes.

"I don't care that you don't believe me, Kelvin. But I'm going to find it, no matter what." The old man put on his swim goggles and grabbed hold of his rubber hose.

"Gong Gong, have a drink first?"

"No Kelvin, you keep that. I will save my thirst for that first bottle of new water."

He leaped in. I looked at the water around me, noting the bubbles that came up through the hose. I waited three minutes. After five minutes, I dove in myself. And then I came up, gasping for breath. I dove in again, searching for my grandfather, but the water was too dark. I dove in again and again, but there was only blackness. I must have gone down into the depths six or seven times, and each time I saw nothing. Nothing at all. Finally, I pulled and pulled at the breathing hose and out it came. My Gong Gong was gone.

I climbed back into the boat. I don't know how long I sat there, weeping and shivering. I wrapped myself in the towel I had packed for my grandfather. Eventually, I rowed the boat to shore. I would find a patrol unit from the GBG. Surely they would help me.

I dragged the boat so that it rested just halfway up the rocky beach, tears still streaming down my face. Even though my clothes were wet, I shoved my feet into my shoes and walked as fast as I could to the nearest building, hoping it was a GBG Station. I burst in, babbling.

"Please help me. My grandfather...we were on our boat..."

A man in uniform stood up at my words. "Do you have any identification?"

"I'm sorry. No I don't. We...We're from the River Valley Coast. My...my grandfather...He's a TSC. Please help me. I think he drowned in the bay."

Something flickered in the officer's eyes. He nodded to a colleague.

"Another TSC diving for buried treasure. That's the third one this month."

I felt my knees buckle under me at those words.

"Sit down, son. You've been through hell, I know. I'm very sorry about your grandfather. Would you like a drink of water?"

"Yes...yes, sir...please, thank you," I said, barely able to hear my own words. My heart beat in wild patterns, broken as it was.

He handed me a full plastic bottle, unopened. I screwed off the top and drank long and deep before I read the label. It didn't matter. I already knew what it said.

FENG SHUI TRAIN

Yuen Kit Mun

"Anything yet?" asked Christine Ong, her LED headlight shining into my eyes.

I shook my head and turned to look at the others. Grandmaster Tang and Madam Lim just frowned. They weren't enjoying themselves, here in the dim and stuffy train tunnel. They were more used to cushy corporate gigs: hotels, shopping centres, Shenton Way skyscrapers. They must have thought that they had clients to impress because they were dressed in traditional Chinese clothes: Grandmaster Tang in long black pants and a white shirt with "frog" buttons, Madam Lim in a dark purple *samfu*. At least they wore sensible black Bruce Lee shoes. The rest of us were in jeans and tee shirts.

I didn't know what the grandmasters were looking for because my feng shui knowledge wasn't very deep. We kept on walking beside the track, following Ong and her maintenance crew as they checked the rails for problems. I kept an eye on the grandmasters because their *qi* aura was growing more and more orange as we walked.

The crew shone their lights and poked around with wooden poles. Ong had told us that they used wood just in case the third rail was energised, and cautioned us to stay away from it. The power was supposed to be off, but this was standard *kiasu* industrial safety procedure: assume Murphy's Law and don't take unnecessary risks.

A few of the crew had big digital SLR cameras. They were taking flash photos of the tracks every few meters. The way they handled their cameras looked a bit clumsy, like they weren't used to using them. I guessed that this must be some new cover-your-ass procedure.

"How about here?" asked Ong. "This is where one of the trains broke down."

Ong wasn't really expecting much from us. She was a trained engineer, so she was naturally a skeptic. She was just following orders from above, ticking off a checkbox. Due diligence.

We were between Somerset and Dhoby Ghaut stations, heading south. I remembered this breakdown. It was only a few weeks ago. Rush hour. A few hundred thousand commuters had to be ferried by backup buses. Steel clamps on the power line had been loose and snagged the contact shoes on the train. Tore out thirty meters of aluminium busbar. It was fixed now. I could see the replacement busbar, still shiny and new.

The *qi* here looked the same as anywhere else in the tunnel. Green, thin wispy tendrils, like joss stick smoke. Not great, but nothing to be worried about.

"Don't worry about us," I said. "Just keep on going. We'll tell you if we see anything."

We carried on for a few more minutes. Ong called for a break when we reached Dhoby Ghaut. She could see that Grandmaster Tang and Madam Lim were tired. We had started at Newton and had only walked three stations, but the grandmasters were in their sixties.

There were some whispered grumbles from the maintenance crew. A few shot us dirty looks. It was 2 a.m. Everybody wanted to finish as quickly as possible and get back home.

There were concrete steps at the end of the platform. Ong motioned us to take a seat. The two grandmasters were too weary to complain about the dirtiness of the steps and we sat down like little children.

"What can you tell me so far?" asked Ong, standing in front of us. "You want us to hang mirrors? We can hang mirrors."

"Mirrors are for amateurs," sniffed Madam Lim. "They often cause more problems than they solve."

"Feng shui for trains is difficult," said Grandmaster Tang. "Large metal things, moving at high speed. They will continuously disturb the *qi*. Aside from that, there is nothing misaligned about the tunnel."

"You want us to slow the trains down?" asked Ong. "We're already doing that while we finish inspecting the tracks to reduce the stress on them. Look, we've got breakdowns every month. Our engineers can't find anything wrong until after something happens. The public, the press, the government—everyone is calling for blood. You're supposed to be the best and all you can tell me is to slow down the trains? Can't you fix the feng shui?"

"There was nobody better than Venerable Seng Keong," said Grandmaster Tang.

"His remedy was, and is, still correct," said Madam Lim.

"You mean the one-dollar coin?" asked Ong.

Legend was that the octagonal Pa Kua had been inscribed onto the country's minted one-dollar coins, so that they would be widely distributed across Singapore, and counteract the disruption of the *qi* caused by the underground MRT train tunnels. The MRT started public service in 1987, the same year the coins had been introduced.

"The government doesn't like us to talk about that," said Grandmaster Tang.

"The coins were to improve Singapore's *qi*, right?" said Ong. "Not the feng shui of the railway tracks and tunnels themselves.

So maybe there's an independent way to improve the *qi* for the trains?"

She thought like an engineer. Feng shui didn't always work that way, its effects were subtle. It was a long term environmental pressure. Like Chinese medicine, it was holistic, slow and comprehensive, its effects difficult to measure. Anyone who guaranteed overnight results was a fraud.

We decided to call it a night. The two grandmasters were in no condition to continue. Ong unlocked the platform's glass door for us, then accompanied us out of the station.

Outside, I took in a deep breath of the rich, deep blue *qi* that swirled like thick ocean fog. Orchard Road, even this far from the main upscale shopping belt, had some of the best feng shui in Singapore. Grandmasters like Tang and Lim were paid handsomely to ensure this. The Land Transport Authority and Urban Redevelopment Authority didn't believe in geomancy, but the businessmen who owned the shopping malls did.

Ong went back in to rejoin the maintenance crew while the three of us crossed over to the Plaza Singapura side of the road to wait for taxis; at this hour, it wasn't necessary to go to the official taxi stand at the rear of Plaza Sing. We stood between the end of the black railing and the bus stop. I had seen passengers waiting here before, after a midnight movie at the Golden Village theatre.

"How old are you?" asked Madam Lim.

"I'll be twenty-five this year."

Grandmaster Tang's eyebrows shot up. "That means you were born in 1987," he said. "Same year as the MRT."

"Yes, my mother says that I was born on the train."

They stared at me.

"It's just a joke that she likes to tell people."

"You studied feng shui at Singapore Poly?" asked Grandmaster Tang. "Architecture, correct?"

I shook my head. "I'm from ITE." They didn't teach feng shui at the Institute of Technical Education.

"Then who is your *sifu*?" asked Madam Lim.

I'd been afraid that this would happen. "I don't have one," I said.

"Why are you here?" asked Madam Lim. Meaning, how did I end up on the same gig as them.

"I was invited by Ong's boss," I said.

"Why?" asked Madam Lim.

"I have consulted for his daughter," I said, trying not to blush. I knew they would ask so I just went ahead and told them. "For her HDB flat."

Madam Lim rolled her eyes but held her tongue. She now knew that I wasn't a threat to her status. I was *kucing kurap*, small time, not worth her attention.

Grandmaster Tang handed me his business card. "This is my personal number," he said. "Let's get together some time and talk business."

I didn't have a business card; I gave him a missed call so my number would be recorded in his phone's record.

A blue Comfort taxi pulled up, the driver looking bored even though I knew he must be pleased with the fifty percent midnight surcharge. We let Madam Lim take it.

The flow of *qi* through the taxi looked unusually smooth, like smoke trails in a wind tunnel. I bent down to look inside the taxi, following the stream with my eyes, and saw a horizontal row of six one-dollar coins stuck on to the top of the dashboard in front of the driver.

I turned round and saw grandmaster Tang looking thoughtfully at me.

Someone was banging on my bedroom door.

"Ronald!"

"I'm awake, ma!"

"Get up! It's time for lunch!"

"I'm coming!"

I rolled out of bed and walked out to the kitchen bathroom.

"Time you got a real job!" my mother shouted through the door.

I flushed the toilet and then went to wash my hands in the sink outside. "I'm running my own business, ma. I'm an entrepreneur."

She was already seated at the kitchen table. *Char siew* and roast pork today.

"Anybody can pay fifty dollars and register a business on the ACRA website," she said. "You think I don't know, is it? If you have a real business, how come you cannot pay me rent for your room? Auntie Ling's son is an engineer. He's marrying a lawyer next month. They have an apartment in Bishan. Do you know that he sends Auntie Ling to Europe for a vacation every year? What should I tell my friends?"

"It's not that simple, ma."

"If your feng shui is so good, how come your business *tak laku* one? Explain that to me, young man."

It was difficult to get started in the feng shui business because nobody takes a young guy seriously. When you're a no-name freelancer, you depend on referrals. To get referrals, you need clients in the first place. Chicken and egg. Feng shui isn't magic.

A lot of it is to do with whether or not you put up a good show, not how good your feng shui really is. You need to dress the part, speak some mumbo-jumbo, act wise and confident, maybe stroke your beard. I was a lousy salesman. And I didn't have a beard.

I heard my phone beep. I headed into my bedroom to check.

"You come back here and eat your lunch, young man! I am not waiting for you any longer!"

The SMS was from Grandmaster Tang.

"I have to go, ma," I shouted back to her. "I have a job!"

184

~

"The Marina Bay Sands Hotel is designed like a dragon's head, looking back towards the city," said Grandmaster Tang to the assembled group. "It reflects the *qi* back to the financial centre."

There were twenty-two people in the tour group, a mix of locals and tourists. Grandmaster Tang was dressed in the same black pants and white shirt as the night before. Looked like he was going for tai chi class.

We stood at the Merlion, One Fullerton. Grandmaster Tang had asked me to help guide the group. His assistant had called in sick at the last minute, and I needed the cash. I wore black pants, a buttoned down black shirt and Bruce Lee shoes that I had bought for Wing Chun class at the local community centre. I was beginning to learn how to play the game.

"Which school of feng shui do you follow?" asked one of the members of the tour group, an Australian lady, here with her husband and teenage daughter. "Flying Star, Black Hat or Compass School?"

"Black Hat?" asked her husband.

"Don't worry, dear. It's not what it sounds like."

She was obviously the enthusiast, dragging the other two along with her. She had probably read more about feng shui than I had.

"Um, Grandmaster Tang is Flying Star," I said.

"You're his apprentice?"

"His assistant for this tour."

"Tell us a bit about the Merlion," said Grandmaster Tang. He was looking at me. The whole tour group turned and stared at me.

"Er, the Merlion was moved to this location in 2002 because the new Esplanade Bridge blocked its *qi*. Tour boats also couldn't see it from the sea. You can find the original location next to the Waterboat House, about fifty metres away, over there."

Grandmaster Tang was nodding and smiling. "Tell us about the direction."

"Uh, this new location has the Merlion facing east, the same direction as in the old location. The direction was set by the Venerable Seng Keong." It was always Seng Keong. The guy was a legend.

"Venerable?" asked the Australian lady.

"He was the head priest at the Pure Light Buddhist temple," I said.

"Feng shui is Buddhist?" she asked.

"I think Taoist. But Buddhists and others can use it too. It's not a religion."

"Can you tell us why it faces east?" asked Grandmaster Tang.

I looked up at the Merlion, watched it focus the *qi* from behind it like a lens, then disperse it out over the bay. *Qi* moved much faster in the daytime, looking more like rays of light than smoke.

"It-it's the colour," I stammered.

Grandmaster Tang raised an eyebrow. "The colour?"

"Yes, here at the mouth of the river, that's the best direction to get dark blue *qi*. In other directions, the *qi* isn't so rich."

Grandmaster Tang stared at me for a few seconds and then forced a smile. Stupid, stupid, stupid. I should have kept my mouth shut. "Yes, thank you," he said, then turned back to the group. "Now if you'll all follow me we'll continue the tour this way."

He walked us slowly up the river, spending most of the time explaining the feng shui of the skyscrapers along Boat Quay. He was a corporate guy all right. He was also diplomatic, leaving out the feng shui wars between the different buildings, only concentrating on the positive design aspects. When the wars originally had raged, I could see the colours change every month, as the feng shui masters for neighbouring skyscrapers fought each other with slanted doorways, mirrored windows and flagpoles.

Grandmaster Tang didn't ask me to speak to the tour group again, but I kept noticing him glancing at me, especially when I was looking up at the skyscrapers. I stayed quiet and concentrated on keeping the group together, doing a head count every few minutes and rounding up the stragglers. The Australian lady avoided me and didn't ask any more questions.

The tour ended at the new Parliament House. The group dispersed, some going to Funan Centre to shop, others to Raffles City. Grandmaster Tang and I stood around for a while, answering queries from the more eager feng shui hobbyists. Most asked about landmark buildings, a few wanted advice about their apartments.

The last one finally left. Grandmaster Tang thanked me and handed me my payment in an *ang pow*. It didn't seem polite to open it right then so I stuffed the red packet, unopened, into my pocket.

"Which way are you going?" he asked.

"To the MRT station."

"So am I."

We crossed over to the new Supreme Court building, dodging other pedestrians as we walked. I was afraid that he would ask me about seeing the colours of *qi* so I blurted out the first thing that came into my head. "You didn't want to tell them about the Boat Quay feng shui war?" I asked.

He smiled. "That's not a good thing to tell people about. Did you know that I was one of the people involved?"

Oops. "No, I didn't. How did the war end?"

Grandmaster Tang chuckled. "Government asked us to stop."

"URA?"

"Prime Minister's Office."

Ouch.

"You mean the government believes in feng shui?" I asked.

"Maybe not. Foreign media was starting to run stories about the war. That was the PMO's main concern. They didn't want us to look like superstitious fools."

"Do you think that's what is happening with the trains?" I asked.

He shook his head. "I don't know."

We walked on in silence until we reached St. Andrew's Cathedral. We were almost at the station entrance when I saw an intense narrow beam of red cutting *qi* streaming from the top of a lamppost across the road. It was like a laser, brighter than any *qi* that I had ever seen before. It pointed downwards, straight into the ventilation duct of the station.

I stopped and stared.

"What do you see?" asked Grandmaster Tang.

"Thank you for coming," said Christine Ong as she shook my hand. "I wanted to personally thank you and hand you the cheque for the consulting fee."

We were in her office near City Hall MRT station, not far from where I had seen the beam of red *qi*.

"Our engineers found an electronic device on the top of that lamppost," she said.

"What kind of electronic device?"

"Analogue, radio frequency is all that they can figure out so far. Doesn't seem to do anything. Solar-powered, could have been there for months or years. We found similar devices at twelve other stations. Custom stuff. DIY photo-etched single-layer printed circuit board, hand-soldered with standard electronic components anyone could get from Sim Lim Square."

"No rechargeable battery, right?"

"That's right. How did you know?"

That explained why I didn't see anything that night inside the tunnel. It had only been operating during the day.

"Could I take a look at it?" I asked.

"I'm afraid not. They've been sent off to a few different organisations where a lot of very experienced people are reverse-engineering them."

"Where did you send them?" My guess was DSO, IDA, Home Affairs, maybe even ST Electronics or Creative.

She flashed an insincere smile. "I'm afraid I don't know. Oh, and by the way, I'd appreciate it if you didn't mention the device to anyone. It's covered under the non-disclosure agreement that you signed earlier." She paused. "How did you know that the device was there?"

"I, er, my handphone."

"Your handphone?"

"Yes, I was walking by, talking to my friend on my phone and it cut out as I passed the ventilation duct." Now where the heck had that come from?

"That was a lucky break."

"Yes, it was," I said. "*The Straits Times* says that you're building feng shui fountains in some MRT stations. Which grandmaster recommended that?"

"I thought you might ask about that," said Ong, looking embarrassed. "That was the CEO's idea. He says that no matter what, we need to show the public that we're doing something. And the Tourism Board loves the idea. URA, LTA, NAC, EDB, SIA have all signed off on it."

"SIA?"

"Singapore Institute of Architects."

"Ah. But there'll be too many independent variables," I said. "Now you won't know which change made the difference."

"Don't think I don't know that. We're getting new diagnostic equipment too, ultrasound and x-ray track scanners, vibration monitors on all trains. Not to mention proactive replacement of rail clamps before their fatigue date. It's an all-of-the-above strategy, Mr. Ng. Welcome to the real world."

"So what do you think is really going on?" I asked.

She smiled. "Thank you for your assistance. We'll be in touch if anything new turns up."

Outside the building, Grandmaster Tang leaned elegantly against a marble pillar.

"Good morning," I said, wondering what he was doing there.

"I saw you go in as I was coming out." He reached into his shirt pocket and pulled out a cheque. "It's payday for all of us. Come, let me buy you lunch. Just down the road, a restaurant belongs to a friend of mine. One of the first businesses that I consulted for. You can tell me what you think of the feng shui design."

I followed him down North Bridge Road, past the plain yellow wall of CHIJMES, our Bruce Lee shoes silent against the concrete pavement.

LAST TIME KOPITIAM

Marc de Faoite

As he stood alone in the near silence of the wood panelled, carpeted elevator only the numbers on the digital display above the door and the popping of his eardrums gave James Sullivan any indication that he was moving upwards through the innards of the building. He was both curious and apprehensive. Juniors like him rarely even got to take the elevator to the CEO's floor, never mind meet the man in person.

"Sit down, Sullivan. Tea?"

"Yes, please," said James, as he took a seat on the opposite side of Prescott's huge desk.

Prescott had a coveted corner office. The two walls behind him were floor to ceiling glass with a breathtaking view of London and the River Thames that wound its way through Canary Wharf. The other two walls were panelled wood. One was decorated with framed photographs and certificates. The other wall held a single gold-framed oil painting that James guessed might be a Monet. An original perhaps. He didn't know how much one might cost, but he guessed a man like Prescott could afford it.

Prescott pushed a button on his desk and leaned forward.

"Tea for Mr Sullivan and myself, please, Joan."

Joan. That must be the old stern-faced guardian in the outer office. She had looked him up and down when he presented himself outside Prescott's office and made him feel like a disobedient schoolboy sent to the principal's office. He had felt himself involuntarily blush. Joan didn't look at him when she came in now and put the tea tray on Prescott's desk, but James gave an almost imperceptible involuntary shudder when she left the room. Prescott noticed and smiled.

"Tough old girl, that Joan," he said as he poured himself a cup of tea. "Help yourself. But damned efficient. Keeps the wife happy too, you know—she who must be obeyed. Wouldn't trust me with a twenty-year-old out there. Can't say I blame her," he said with a grin and a wink. "I'd offer you a biscuit, but she has me watching the old waistline." James wasn't sure if Prescott was referring to his wife or to Joan.

"Anyway. No doubt you are wondering why I've called you up here."

James nodded halfway through a sip and almost choked on his tea.

"Yes, Mister Prescott."

"Oh, don't 'Mister Prescott' me. From here on in it's Tom and…James, isn't it?"

"Yes, sir."

"No 'yes, sir' either. We're colleagues here, not master and servant." Prescott took another sip of tea.

"So James, you're single, or so I'm told. That right?"

"Yes, sir. I mean: Tom."

"Well enjoy it while you can. That's part of the reason you're here. We won't kid each other that you're the best man for the job, but you are certainly not the worst by any means. You might not see much of me, but believe me I take a keen interest in all our staff."

So there was a new job in the air, James thought to himself, but what did being single have to do with it?

"You want to send me overseas?" asked James.

"Clever boy, quick on the uptake. I like that. Yes, Singapore. We have a slot to fill rather urgently. Can't say for how long. Chap has burnout issues. On extended sick leave, so you might have to be there for a while. Can't risk sending a family man, it wouldn't help things at home, so it's come down to you. You'll be looked after—housing, overseas allowance, per diem, all the usual stuff and a little raise."

James sat very still, but his mind was racing.

"A simple yes or no will suffice, but there's one condition." Prescott stared at him intensely, as if to see if he would pass some test. "You'll fly out there this weekend so you can hit the ground running on Monday morning. Sorry about the short notice, but it can't be helped. So are you in or are you out, James? Will you be our man in the East?"

"I'm your man indeed," said James, allowing himself a smile. Prescott stood up and extended his hand. James stood and shook it. The older man's grip was firm and dry.

"Don't let us down now. We're counting on you."

"Don't worry, sir...Tom, I won't."

"Joan will give you a file with all the details. You can pick it up on the way out. Sign what needs to be signed and pass it on to personnel. And be a good man, take the tea tray out with you when you go. Best of luck. We'll be in touch."

That first month flew past. His predecessor had left him with quite a mess to clean up. James worked long hours with little free time to do anything other than eat and sleep. It didn't do to have a backlog when you traded in derivatives and futures. But now he was on top of his new portfolios and order had been restored.

Old Mister Lim from Accounts Receivable had taken a liking to James and had befriended the younger man. Sharing a common caffeine addiction, they arranged to meet for coffee one weekend at a small place near the Singapore River. While waiting for their drinks to cool, Mister Lim handed James a little guidebook, small enough to slip into his pocket, called *An Historic Guide to Singapore*. James noticed that the author's name was also Lim, and remarked on the coincidence.

"Write myself," said the old man, blushing slightly. "You can say history my passion. Young people nowadays don't know history, lah. Singapore young country only, but past forget already. You know Singapore only country get independent without try. Most place fight wars, lah. Singapore not even look for independence. Malaysia just say okay you go now, we don't want you anymore. I remember Lee Kuan Yew cry on television."

"So what was it like back then?" James asked.

"Last time was not like this, with all these skyscrapers and Shaw-Ping-Maws. Last time not so fast, lah. People take the time to talk to each other. Young people nowadays always such a rush. Never take time. Look at all these youngsters," he said with a wave of his hand at the other patrons of the coffee shop. "Nobody talk. Play with smart-phone only. Where got smart one, leh?"

"That's the same everywhere," answered James with a sigh. He had also noticed the growing trend towards submersion in the virtual world, though it did seem to be exaggerated here in Singapore. Or perhaps it was just the type of people who frequented these coffee places. But who was he to judge? He had a smart-phone in his pocket too.

"Apart from people, what else has changed in your lifetime?"

The old man began to chuckle quietly. "You really want to know what Singapore was like last time?"

"Well yes, I'm curious."

"Then we go from here and I show you, lah."

"That's very kind of you, but I don't want to take up all your free time."

"I old man. No need rush. And anyway, what is time?"

They took a taxi, Mister Lim speaking rapidly to the driver in some Chinese dialect. James didn't recognize the streets, but then again all he really knew of the city was the bus route from his condo to work. The taxi stopped on a corner. This seemed like an older part of town, with simple two-storey shophouses on either side of the streets. In fact the area seemed quite run down. Mister Lim walked surprisingly fast and James found himself jogging to keep up and sweating in the midday heat.

"This place," Mr Lim said, stopping at the entrance to one of the shophouses. "You must remember the name." A black wooden board with Chinese characters carved and painted in gold hung above the door.

"I'll never remember that. What does it say?"

"I will write for you."

Mister Lim scribbled the same characters on a scrap of paper, handed it to James and pushed open the door of the *kopitiam*. A little bell jangled somewhere unseen inside. James followed him in. The interior was dark and it took James' eyes a moment to adjust. The place seemed small, but the high wooden-beamed ceilings gave it a sense of spaciousness. Two ceiling fans rotated slowly, stirring the still air. It was very quiet, the thick walls blocking out any external sounds and keeping the temperature indoors cool despite the heat outside. Louvered shutters played the role of windows. As far as James could see there was no glass in the frames. There didn't seem to be any other customers either. They sat at a small round marble-topped table that was cool to the touch. He admired the dark wooden chairs.

"Nice to see somewhere that isn't made of plastic."

"Yes, all Singapore like this last time. No plastic at all."

James looked around. It was true, there wasn't a scrap of plastic to be seen. Even the old light-switches seemed to be made of ceramic and Bakelite.

"It's like a museum here. Just like stepping back in time. Thanks for bringing me."

A small stocky dark-haired man of indeterminate age appeared and brought them a pot of tea and three small ceramic cups.

"You eat dim sum?" asked Mister Lim.

"Sounds good," said James.

Mister Lim squawked something at the waiter, or the owner, or whoever the strange stocky man was and after a minute or so he reappeared with a tray of steaming saucers and tiny bamboo steamers with a selection of tasty-looking morsels.

Mr Lim sipped his tea and looked at James thoughtfully.

"I must go now," said Mister Lim, standing up. "When you finish, you go and explore. My guidebook will help you see the old Singapore. Remember this place. You must come back here again."

James swallowed the dumpling he was chewing, shook the old man's hand and thanked him.

"No need thank you, lah. You want see what Singapore like last time, now you find out."

With that he turned and left, the little bell jangling as he opened and closed the door.

James continued eating his dim sum and finished the scalding pot of tea. He had burned the tip of his tongue and now rubbed it against the back of his lower teeth. He reached in his pocket to check the time and was surprised to find that his smart-phone had no coverage. Must be something to do with the thick walls, he thought to himself. He decided to leave and stood, deliberately scraping the wooden chair across the floor to attract the owner's attention. The small man reappeared and James handed him a fifty-dollar note.

"Got twenty or not? Don't have so much small money, lah."

James took back the fifty and passed him two tens instead. The owner handed James a stack of still unfamiliar notes and some coins. He was surprised to receive so much change. He still hadn't gotten used to the prices in Singapore. Some things were more expensive than in London, while other things seemed ridiculously cheap. The notes seemed slightly different to the ones he was used to during his short time in country, but he pocketed them anyway.

Out on the street he was assailed again by the tropical heat, but somehow the air had a different quality about it, less polluted, more fragrant, with an underlying note of decay. He supposed it was because this part of town seemed more run down than the rest, and a strong breeze from the ocean could quickly change the city's air. But there was only a very slight breeze today and the sun beat down mercilessly. If he wasn't careful, his sensitive skin would be quickly burned pink. Two young women walked past him. They held black umbrellas as parasols. They were dressed in old-fashioned clothes, short-sleeved satin dresses with high collars, and their hair was styled short and wavy, like the movie stars he had seen in old posters. Perhaps the ladies were off to a fancy dress party.

He noticed that the street was made of compacted earth and was surprised that he hadn't noticed the open drains when he had first arrived. He'd probably been distracted listening to Mister Lim. He really should have paid more attention to his surroundings, otherwise what was the point of trying to discover this city that had so suddenly become his new home?

He reached the corner of the street. An old man sat waiting with a trishaw. James had heard about trishaws, basically a bicycle with a shaded sidecar, but hadn't seen one before. It could be fun to see Singapore in the old-fashioned way.

"Can you show me around the old parts of the city? The historic places? Maybe along the riverfront?"

"You wago claky boky?" asked the trishaw driver. James hadn't understood a word.

"Do you speak English?"

"Spik awleddy lah. You wan go cla key bow key."

And then he understood. Clarke Quay or Boat Quay. Perhaps he would be better off seeking the shelter of the air-conditioned shops around Clarke Quay just to get out of this punishing heat. He could feel the skin on his face searing under the unforgiving equatorial sun.

"Oh, sorry. Yes, take me to Clarke Quay, but show me the sights on the way."

James climbed onto the woven rattan seat and the old man started cycling. The little bit of shade and the breeze helped, but sweat still pearled on his forehead and his shirt stuck to him unpleasantly. Maybe the reason for Singaporeans' obsession with visiting shopping malls (or Shaw-Ping-Maws, as he had smilingly come to think of them from Mr Lim's description) was that it was just a way to avoid the heat.

An old car passed. James wasn't good on cars, but it looked like something from the nineteen-fifties. Amazing that things like that were still running. And another one. Must be some kind of vintage car rally going on today. There were very few people about. The few young men he saw were all very slim. He also hadn't realized that Brylcreem was so in fashion here.

There were lots of things he still had to discover about Singapore. He had no idea that there were areas like this without a skyscraper in sight. In fact, few of the buildings were more than two or three stories high and many of them were run down and dilapidated. There was almost no traffic on the streets except for bicycles and pedestrians. He felt as if he had wandered onto a film set, but it all looked too real for that. These people weren't actors; he could see that many of them really were poor. And the smells from the drains wouldn't be needed on a film set either.

It seemed almost Third World. This was nothing like the modern Singapore that he lived and worked in. Drying clothes hung on poles extended from the upper windows of houses and most of the children playing on the sides of the road ran barefoot. When was the last time he had seen a child barefoot? When was the last time he had seen a child play outdoors? Perhaps this was an area that was kept quiet about. A place that never made it to the glossy brochures.

He pulled out his smart-phone again and tried to log on to Google Maps to find out exactly where he was. Strange. Again there was no network available. Perhaps there was something wrong with his phone. He looked at the map in Mister Lim's little guidebook and recognized some of the buildings around Clarke Quay, but all these old cars and buses he had seen on the way left him perplexed. He stepped down from the trishaw and handed the old man one of the five-dollar notes he had received from the owner of the *kopitiam*.

"Too much lah. Sixty cent owny."

Sixty cents for a fifteen minute trishaw ride, when a cup of coffee at "Stabbers" (as the locals called Starbucks) cost him more than five dollars? It didn't make sense. Neither did the money. He noticed that the note bore the inscription *Board of Commissioners of Currency Malaya and British Borneo*. The man at the *kopitiam* had obviously short-changed him by giving him an old out-of-date note. He looked at the other notes and saw that they were all the same.

"Sorry, my money seems to be no good." James pulled out his wallet and took out a fresh note.

"This one no good lah. First one good."

It didn't make sense. Was someone playing a joke on him? He handed the driver one of the dud dollars and told him to keep the change. The driver smiled and shook his head, muttering something about *ang moh*.

Coffee at Starbucks, yes, that was a good idea. It would be air-conditioned, it would have wi-fi and he could get out of this heat. He was sure there would be one somewhere around Clarke Quay. He checked his smart-phone again, but there was still no access to any network. He walked around and looked for a place for coffee, but the area seemed to be filled with warehouses that stored the goods that barefooted men brought back and forth from the boats anchored along the riverfront. He found a simple hawker stall where an Indian man in a sarong made coffee for him in something that looked like an old sock. It was a terribly bitter, but he drank it all the same. He needed to add extra sugar just to make it palatable.

A young Chinese man with round black-framed glasses and lacquered hair sat at an adjacent table reading *The Straits Times*. The newspaper shook slightly in the wind but James managed to read the main banner. It read *"The Straits Times* wishes its Muslim readers *Selamat Hari Raya Haji."* Then there was an article quoting someone called Tengku talking about troops in the Congo. James hadn't realised that today was a feast day. Perhaps…but no, that still didn't explain all the odd things he had noticed.

"Would you mind if I took a look at your paper for a moment?" James asked the young man.

"Oh, you can keep it if you want. I've just about finished reading. It's always the same old news anyway." The young man spoke perfect English, with just a slight trace of Asia in his vowels. He folded the newspaper and handed it to James. "Having a day off work?"

"Yes, first real day off since I got here. Still kind of trying to get to grips with Singapore. What's with all the old cars?"

"Old cars? They're not all that old. Hardly less modern than British cars, but then again it's true that a few years have passed since I came back east. Anyway I must get going. Don't want to be late. Meeting my fiancée for a date at the cinema for the afternoon show."

"There's a cinema near here? What's showing?"

"Yes, the Kings Theatre. Not too far from here. Perhaps a brisk twenty-minute walk. No idea what's on. Some silly American romance I expect, but if it keeps the lady happy…"

"Well, thanks for the newspaper. Oh, you wouldn't happen to know where I could find Starbucks by any chance?"

"Starbuck? You mean like the character in *Moby Dick*? Don't know anyone of that name. I'm afraid I can't help you. Does he work near here?"

"Never mind," said James coldly.

The young man stood up, slung his jacket over his arm, put on his hat and waved over his shoulder.

Smart ass, thought James. Never heard of Starbucks. Yeah, right. He picked up the paper and read about Malayan troops in the Congo. This was an odd newspaper. The advertisements were all drawn to look old. Mint-flavoured Bird's Eye peas at Cold Storage. Modern glasses that looked anything but. Singapore was taking this whole retro thing very seriously today.

Then he glanced at the top of the page. The date caught his eye. Thursday, 25th of May, 1961? What on earth? Then things all started to fall into place. Why the young Chinese man had thought the cars were modern. Why the trishaw ride had been so cheap. The strange banknotes the *kopitiam* owner had given him. Mister Lim's voice echoed in his head: *You really want to know what Singapore was like last time?*

How was it possible? *Remember this place. You must come back here again.* The *kopitiam.* That was the key. James felt a rising sense of panic. He had to get back there. He winced as he drained his cup of acrid coffee. His heart was beating fast. He took a few deep breaths and massaged his temples. Think, think. So he was back in 1961. What did Mr Lim's guidebook say about 1961? He leafed through the pages. Singapore wasn't fully independent yet. That would explain the writing on the banknotes. Lee Kuan Yew was already prime minister. Hold on…May 1961, the Bukit Ho Swee Fire. When was that? Oh shit. That was today—the afternoon of the 25th of May. James read on. *The fire started at 3:30 p.m. in Kampong Tiong Bahru behind the King's Cinema and cost the lives of more than 7,000 people.*

The only explanation James could figure was that Mr Lim had given him this information for a reason. But why? Perhaps he was meant to stop the fire and save those people. The more he thought about it, the more convinced he became.

"What time is it now?" he asked the coffee stall owner. He couldn't trust his smart-phone anymore.

"Nearly three o'clock. You all right, boss? Not looking very good, lah."

"Yes, I'm fine. It's just the heat. Can you tell me where the King's Cinema is? Oh, hold on, it's okay."

"Okay?"

"I mean, it's all right. I've seen someone I know."

The young man with the glasses who had given him the newspaper was still in sight. He jogged to catch up with him, but the young man walked fast and stayed ahead. James followed him from a distance. He checked the road signs. He was on Havelock Road. The young man turned left and after a long while James saw him meet a young woman in front of the cinema. He needed to warn someone about the fire.

"Hello again," James panted as he approached the couple. He was quite out of breath and sweat had gathered on his forehead, but the strong wind that had picked up helped him to cool down.

"Oh hello," said the young man, looking strangely at James' dishevelled state.

"Listen, I need your help. I need to warn people about a fire that's about to start."

"What do you mean a fire that's about to start? What are you talking about?"

The young woman backed away, looking at James fearfully. She tugged the young man's sleeve and whispered something in his ear.

"I'm sorry. I can't help you," the young man said and the couple walked away.

James read the entry in the guidebook again. *The fire started at 3:30 p.m. in Kampong Tiong Bahru behind the King's Cinema…*

It had taken him almost half an hour to get here. Perhaps he could ask a policeman for help. However, the police would probably think he was mad, just like the young couple seemed to do. He could call the fire brigade, but his phone didn't work and he didn't know the number anyhow. Would 999 work? He looked around for a phone box but couldn't find one. James jogged down the narrow alleyway beside the cinema and entered into a maze of wooden shacks with simple palm-leaf roofs. Which way to go? What was he going to do, anyhow? There was only one thing for it. He ran through the narrow laneways shouting at the top of his voice.

"Fire, fire, FIRE! Leave your homes. Take your children and your valuables. Fire, fire, fire!"

He felt quite ridiculous, but what more could he do? He was surprised when people started to react. Families fled their homes, dragging their dirty-faced children behind them. Some carried bundles with them. Most seemed so poor that they owned nothing of value worth trying to save. Hundreds of people fled down the hill towards the cinema and the wider road beyond, calling out to their neighbours, warning them of the fire.

One old woman stood on the little veranda of her home. "You have to leave here, please!" shouted James. "Everything will burn down."

The old woman said something in dialect and pointed into her house. James bounded up the two small steps and went inside.

The interior of the hovel was dark, but in one corner, lit by a kerosene lamp, James saw an old Chinese man. He was lying on a grass mat upon the bare planks of the floor. The old man looked at him helplessly and raised a hand in a gesture that could be interpreted as salutation, dismissal or resignation. The old woman stood in silhouette by the door wringing her worried hands. James stooped down and gathered the old man in his arms. He was incredibly light. James recoiled at the fetid breath that issued from the old man's mouth and took an involuntary step backwards, knocking over the kerosene lamp.

The hot glass cracked easily and the dry grass mat immediately caught fire. James tried to stamp out the flames, but it wasn't easy with the old man in his arms. The fire spread to the sun-dried wooden planks of the wall and almost instantly the hungry flames set the palm-leaf roof alight. The roof crackled and the room filled with smoke. James stumbled out of the little house carrying the old man, and followed the old woman down the hill as she joined the crowds fleeing from their homes. A look over his shoulder confirmed his worst fears. The fire had quickly jumped from one impoverished house to another. Soon the entire hillside was burning down.

He laid the old man on the ground opposite the cinema. He stood with the crowds that had gathered there and watched the inferno. Dark smoke filled the air and formed a cloud that blacked out the sun. Grey wisps of ash were falling everywhere. Oddly, James seemed to smell roasted coffee. He needed to get away from here before someone found out that he was the one who had started the fire. James made his way back towards Havelock Road and managed to flag down a taxi. He showed the driver the scrap of paper where Mister Lim had written the name of the *kopitiam*.

The bell jangled as he pushed open the door and stumbled into the gloom. Again there were no customers inside. He took a seat at one of the round marble-topped tables. His sweat-soaked clothes reeked of smoke. The fans in the high ceiling only lightly stirred the thick air. The sunlight that filtered through the shutters hit the tiled floor in segments of parallel lines. James lowered his forehead against the cool white stone of the table. That felt good. He let out a sigh and felt tears well up in his eyes. He had caused the deaths of more than seven thousand people. People he had tried to save.

When he raised his head again the owner was standing beside him.

"Can you take me back?" James asked.

"I *have* to take you back," said the man, sniffing the smoky air. "I have no more choice than you have. Don't feel bad about it. You have done what needed to be done, lah. It has always been this way. If you had not done your duty, then the time you came from would no longer exist." said the man and poured James a glass of tea. "Everything affects everything else."

James took a silent sip from the glass.

"You must return the rest of the money I gave you. You can't take anything back or leave anything behind."

James emptied his pockets and gave the man the few coins and crumpled notes that remained.

"I'll leave you now. When you finish your tea, you may go." Then the man smiled and chuckled. "Take your time."

Back in his own time and his own apartment, James took a long shower and changed into clean clothes. Although he had washed away the ash and sweat, James could still smell and taste the smoke from the fire. He poured himself a generous glass of Jameson while he waited for his laptop to boot up. He swallowed a mouthful of the whiskey. It sent a shudder through his body, followed by a warming glow. Then he clicked and typed and looked up the details of the Bukit Ho Swee fire.

The strong winds, wooden housing, and stores of oil and petrol ensured that the fire spread rapidly. Narrow lanes and the gathered crowds impeded access by the fire department. All told, two hundred and fifty acres of housing and shops were completely destroyed, as were three timber yards, a school, some warehouses, and a coffee mill. Well that explained the smell he'd detected.

Sixteen thousand people were left homeless. Over the following four years, over eight thousand new flats were built by the Housing Development Board and all those who had lost their homes were relocated. The cause of the fire, whether arson or accident, was never discovered. Despite the massive scale of the devastation, only four people died.

It eased his guilty conscience to read that the real figure had been four deaths and not the seven thousand mentioned in Mister Lim's guidebook. So he had saved those people after all. Or had he? Had Mr Lim exaggerated the figure to spur James into action? Try as he might he couldn't make sense of it all.

The next morning at the office, James looked for Mister Lim, only to be told that the old man had left for a long business trip.

His smart-phone rang, startling him. An unlisted number.

"Sullivan. This is Tom Prescott here."

"Oh, hello, Tom," he said shakily, not really in the mood to speak to his boss in that moment. "How are you?"

"Never mind about me. How are things with you in Singapore? Had a good weekend?"

"Not bad, I guess. A bit hot."

"So I hear. Listen, James. There have been some changes. We're going to bring you back to London. It seems that you've done all that was needed there in Singapore. One of our clients, with what you might call 'long-term development investments' is very happy with the work you've done over there. You are obviously quite adept at handling futures and derivatives. And there's a new opening for you at HQ. Can't give you the details just yet. All in good time, James. All in good time."

CHAPTER 28: ENERGY

The Centipede Collective

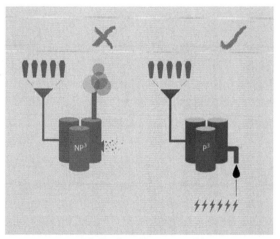

We must come to terms with the fact that our world is running out of energy. The economic development of the past few centuries, industrious as it has been, can no longer be sustained by the resources of coal, oil, wind, and the sun—precious gifts that we have taken for granted. But because this is an age of technology--of miracles and innovation—I am confident that mankind will find a solution. As stalwarts of the next generation, you bear nothing less than the weighty burden of our entire species.

I wish you luck, and congratulate you in advance.

—Prime Minister (VII) Subramaniam

Introduction

You may be scratching your head after reading the Prime Minister's comments above, made during a speech to graduates of the Singapore University of New Technology (now the Singapore-Malaysia University of Regenerative Humanity) in 2060. After all, we are not "running out of energy," and in fact are far from it. As the previous chapter has shown, Singapore now produces enough energy to power its homes, offices, and vehicles, without relying on other countries. We have been called a "model for energy regeneration," and our energy infrastructure has been studied by scientists and politicians all over the world.

This wasn't always the case, however. There was a time when the whole world, not just Singapore, suffered from a shortage of energy. Our traditional sources—oil fields, coal mines, even the natural forces of wind and water—were not enough to meet our needs. People said we had reached Peak Energy, and were afraid that future generations—in other words, you and me—would have to live frugally.

This chapter will show you how we overcame this challenge, thanks to the ingenuity of one of our home-grown inventors.

Part One: Dr. Lee Wen Huo's Bright Spark

Dr. Lee Wen Huo was a researcher at the Singapore University of New Technology (SUNtech) in 2060 when the government announced that Singapore was running out of energy. The world had hit Peak Energy, and formerly resource-rich countries were barely producing enough energy to keep themselves going. Scenes of dry lakes and empty oil canisters were in the news every day.

As a researcher in SUNtech's Experimental Energy department, Dr. Lee felt that he had to tackle Peak Energy. He also knew that the "weighty burden" Prime Minister (VII) had talked about was something that could be addressed by Singapore, and by science. Singapore, after all, had overcome many odds to become a commercial and innovative hub in Asia, including separation from Malaysia, the brief military confrontation with Indonesia, and economic competition from the Neo-Asia Union of Cambodia, Myanmar, Vietnam, and Laos (see Chapters 12-19 for a history of Singapore's economic and political development).

However, most of Dr. Lee's innovations had failed, and he was running out of inspiration. Then, in 2062, a combination of critical thinking and good fortune gave him the idea that was to solve Singapore's energy woes.

Here is an excerpt from Dr. Lee's autobiography, in which he describes his breakthrough:

I was attending the funeral for my father, who passed away after a long fight with cancer. Mind you, this was soon after the Ministry of National Development had exhumed the last of Singapore's cemeteries in Choa Chu Kang to make way for the Centre for Holistic Meat Progenesis, so we had to hold the ceremony in the columbarium, right in front of the tiny alcove in which we were going to seal Pa's remains.

A couple of weeks before this, Parliament had debated the merits of demolishing columbaria in the interest of economic development, and making disposal of cremains by sea compulsory for all new deaths. As you can imagine, resource scarcity was pretty much on all of our minds.

At the time, I was fresh from another failure in the research laboratory, and was beginning to wonder if I should give up on this Peak Energy thing. I was despondent, and, ashamedly, too absorbed in my own thoughts to pay attention to the funeral.

Just as I snapped out of it, I heard the preacher read a line from Genesis: "Dust thou art, and unto dust thou shalt return." I know the line well— God used these words to chastise Adam and Eve when they ate from the Tree of Knowledge, reminding them that they would ultimately have to return to the earth from whence they came, turning from a warm body of life to a pile of ashes, just like my Pa.

The Christian in me accepted this fact. But the scientist in me was skeptical, defiant even. I thought about the debates in Parliament, and the burning of the remains of the deceased, and all I could say to myself was: what a waste of energy.

Part Two: Cremation

Cremation, or the combustion of dead bodies into ash, used to be the method of choice for disposing of a loved one's remains. In fact, by the early 2010s, land was so scarce in Singapore that our government made it compulsory to cremate all the newly deceased. By 2015, a law had been passed ordering all cemeteries to be exhumed to free up land for industrial, residential, and commercial use, with the remains in these cemeteries to be cremated and placed in one of Singapore's many columbaria. By 2040, all of Singapore's columbaria had reached full capacity, and the government began to encourage Singaporeans to scatter ashes in the island's surrounding waters.

However, the cremation process used up a great amount of energy. According to estimates by the Energy Market Bureau (EMBr), the average cremation required about 35 kilowatt-hours of energy—enough to power a three-room flat for more than a week! The industrial furnaces used to burn bodies also released noxious chemicals such as carbon monoxide into the air, causing further harm to our environment. It may be true that "unto dust thou shalt return," but we waste quite a bit of resources in the process.

Dr. Lee's big idea has a lot to do with the concept of recycling (see Chapter 11). It also has a lot to do with harvesting the latent energy in you and me after we die. He wanted to reduce the energy spent during the cremation process, so that

Singapore would have more resources for its more productive activities. The Centre for Holistic Meat Progenesis (CHoMP) that was mentioned in the autobiography excerpt created and sustains about two thousand jobs for Singaporeans, and generates more than a billion dollars in business expenditure. In the mid-2060s, it also needed more than two hundred kilowatt-hours a day to remain operational, a demand that was becoming increasingly hard to meet as Singapore was already close to full capacity for its solar plants, offshore turbines, and other conventional power-generation facilities. However, because locating CHoMP in Singapore made us the world's hub for artificial protein, we needed to find ways to help keep it within our shores. (You can read more about CHoMP, and how Singapore is reducing our reliance on other countries for meat, in Chapter 30: Food and Nutrition.)

Part Three: P³, NecrOil, and Our Energy Boom

Dr. Lee Wen Huo's idea helped create what we now call Post-Promethean Power, or P³. This revolutionary process was based on Dr. Lee's groundbreaking research in Experimental Energy, as well as Dr. Lilith Khoo-Bhattacharya's theories of Closed-Loop Regenerative Humanity (which you will learn about in the next chapter on the service economy). P³ was officially recognized as a power source in 2075, the 110th anniversary of Singapore's independence and the year Dr. Lee was conferred the Stamford Raffles Medal for outstanding public service.

The key insight behind P³ is the idea that, when treated a certain way in a contained, controlled, environment, fresh remains can be harnessed for energy. By ensuring that it consumes less energy than it creates, the P³ process results in a net energy gain.

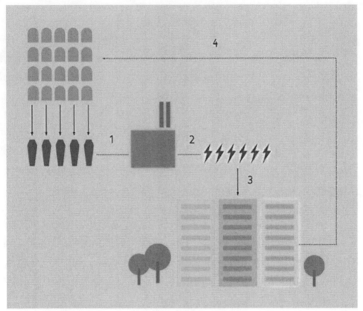

The full details of Dr. Lee's award-winning technology are too advanced to explain in one chapter; however, Figure 28.1 above gives an overview of the various steps in the process.

First, remains are taken to the P³ treatment facility in Lim Chu Kang as soon as possible after death (1). The fresher the remains, the more energy can be harnessed. A 2069 amendment to the Funerals and Remains Act has made it compulsory for a family of the deceased to hold a funeral ceremony not more than two working days after death, and to hand the remains over to the Public Utilities Board not more than one working day after the ceremony has taken place.

Once they have been delivered to the treatment facility, the remains are immediately sent to the P³ furnaces for processing. If furnaces are already operating at full capacity, as was the case during the super-flu outbreak of 2081, remains are put into deep freeze to prevent decomposition.

The furnaces combust the remains using a unique process developed and patented by Dr. Lee and the Public Utilities Board (2). While non-P³ combustion turns remains into ashes and smoke, P³ combustion results in a liquid called NecrOil that can be used to create batteries, power cars, or even converted into electricity (3). It is the energy generated from NecrOil that results in Post-Promethean Power. Because the furnaces are self-contained and do not release by-products such as smoke into the air, the process does not harm the environment.

The final step in this process happens when the Singaporeans that have enjoyed the P³ generated from NecrOil, pass away (4). The remains of these Singaporeans will in turn be sent to Lim Chu Kang for processing, thus starting the process once more and generating a "closed-loop" cycle of energy.

It is largely thanks to P³ that Singapore is now energy-independent. On average, a person's remains can be converted into about 10 litres of NecrOil, which in turn generates about 48 megawatts of power. Given Singapore's mortality rate, and the energy we still get from other power sources, this is more than enough to meet Singapore's needs—in fact, in 2095, P³ was able to meet more than 85% of the national demand for energy. A long way from the wasteful days of cremation, don't you think?

Of course, not all remains are converted to P³. While Singaporean citizens and Permanent Residents aged 60 or older at the time of death are automatically sent for processing, others are assessed for possible reanimation by the Regenerative Humanity Action Board (ReHAB). In addition, foreigners who pass away while they are in Singapore are exempt from the regulations governing P³ and Regenerative Humanity, though their families are given a $10,000 cheque by the Singapore government should they decide to opt in.

Part Four: From SiMURgH To Singapore Society

Dr. Lee Wen Huo first presented his complete proposal for P³ at the inaugural SiMURgH Flock of Ideas conference in 2067, where it was well-received by both researchers and government agencies. Singapore's Energy Market Bureau (EMBr) purchased exclusive patent rights to Dr. Lee's furnaces and technology soon after, amid fierce competition from the Penang Autonomous Region's Energy Directorate. In 2068 and 2069, the government (and PUB) pilot-tested batches of remains, and retrofitted our energy infrastructure with P³-compatible materials, and in 2070 the Lim Chu Kang facility was declared fully operational.

In line with its promise of collaboration and consultation (see Chapter 2: Policy and Politics), the Singapore government also actively engaged Singaporeans on P³, and sought their opinions at various platforms. During the pilot-test phase, and even in the early 2070s, it was not uncommon to see a Member of Parliament at a funeral held in the void decks of our Housing Development Board (HDB) flats, explaining P³ to the mourners and answering questions on the subject. Perhaps the greatest illustration of the government's commitment to transparency and open dialogue was in 2069, when Ovidia Yang, Minister of Community, Youth and Sports, volunteered her recently deceased mother for pilot-testing, filmed the entire process, and uploaded the video onto the Internet for public viewing.

Singaporeans, in turn, demonstrated great resilience and selflessness by supporting the P³ Act (which has since been merged with the Regenerative Humanity Act) when it was announced in Parliament in 2070. In a referendum held in 2073, 76 percent of Singaporeans agreed that continuing to use P³ was a good idea, with a further 15 percent saying that they would let the government decide.

Today, several innovations have been made to increase the inclusive and meaningful nature of P³ to Singaporeans. We now have the option of deciding how the NecrOil generated by our loved ones will be put to use, which makes us feel more involved in the entire process. According to a survey conducted by EMBr in 2091, more than half of Singaporeans choose to use their parents' NecrOil to power their homes and/or electric vehicles; and 95 percent of these people feel that doing so gives them a sense of achievement.

In 2095, the government conducted an online poll to decide where the combined NecrOil of our current Cabinet of Ministers would be used, with a total of twenty options offered. The winning option received more than a quarter of the total votes, and as a result, our Cabinet will be powering Virtualopolis, Singapore's one-stop commercial, educational, and entertainment hub for Virtual Humanity and Modified Reality (V-HuMoR) when they pass away. The NecrOil of Ministers that pass away will be stored until all members of the Cabinet are deceased.

How would you like *your* NecrOil to be used when you pass away?

Conclusion

The success of P³ was brought about by a combination of individual ingenuity and public policy. Without Dr. Lee's bright idea, inspired by his own father's funeral, we might not have found a solution to the energy problem. Also, without the support of the Singapore government, and of the Singaporean people, his idea might never have been implemented.

We can see the importance of public support in the example of Sweden. When the Swedish government reached an agreement with our government in 2088 to adapt Dr. Lee's technology for their own use, they did not count on the Swedish people being extremely hostile to the idea. As a result, the Swedish people refused to send remains for processing, and dead bodies piled up on the streets of Stockholm and other major cities, leading to widespread disease and other problems. Because of this, the Swedish government was overthrown in 2090, and replaced by a new political party that has since reversed the decision to use P^3.

Singapore's seamless experience with P^3 is therefore even more compelling, and even more impressive. However, in a speech to Parliament in 2090, Prime Minister (VIII) Andrew Fernandez warned that, as always, Singapore should not rest on its laurels:

The idea of recycling the remains of our loved ones, our fellow Singaporeans, is both elegant and poignant. We understand the emotional strain placed on Singaporeans and Permanent Residents when they have to say goodbye to their parents, relatives, and friends within two days of their passing. However, the unanimous support we have received from the people is proof that everyone realizes that this is a small price to pay for energy independence, a goal that many would have thought impossible just forty or fifty years ago. During my Meet-the-People sessions, people often tell me that they even feel proud that their loved ones can continue to do their part for the nation even after they have left this earth.

But we must not take this independence for granted. Major advances in health care are already increasing Singaporeans' life expectancy. More and more Singaporeans are moving abroad and opting out of the P^3 scheme. A general decline in the supply of labour for the service industry has forced us to send a larger percentage of the deceased to ReHAB for reanimation.

So I say to you, be proud that we have found a way to address our energy needs, but let's not think that this is the end of this particular chapter of the Singapore story. We have faced challenges on this front before, and will face even more in the future, but as long as we remain vigilant, innovative, and loyal to the nation, we will—we must—continue to overcome them.

There may come a time when even P^3 will not be enough to satisfy our energy demands. Already, there are discussions to expand the Lim Chu Kang facility in anticipation of projected population increases and more energy-intensive investments in Singapore. It is your job, as the next generation of Singaporeans, to ensure that the "age of technology, miracles, and innovation" of which Prime Minister (VII) Subramaniam spoke more than 30 years ago continues, and that Dr. Lee's idea is only the start of an energy boom for our country.

Afterword

Some of you may be wondering what happened to Dr. Lee Wen Huo. After receiving numerous awards for his work on P^3, Dr. Lee went on to become SiMURgH's Dean Emeritus in 2080, and held the post until his death in 2096. As a final honour, Dr. Lee's body was not processed into NecrOil, as is the custom for Singaporeans aged 60 and above; instead, his remains were sent to ReHAB. His reanimated body now serves food and drinks to guests in SiMURgH's VVIP Lounge.

WAITING FOR THE SNOW

Carrick Ang

On her twenty-first birthday, Miranda Ong Swee Lian was taking out the garbage to the centralized 14th-storey rubbish chute when a passing *karung guni* man stopped in front of her, cackled, and began dancing deliriously. She stood there, holding the pungent NTUC bags just above the opened chute, and looked distinctly perturbed at the tiny old man's antics in the common area.

"MY-RUN-DA!" he shrieked. "I found you, I found you." He seemed overwhelmingly happy.

"Erm. Ah Pek, all I want to do is throw my rubbish."

The *karung guni* man stopped in mid-stance and cocked his head to a side. Then, he began sniffing the stale air. Slowly, he approached Miranda, quietly muttering under his breath.

"Expired *tow gay*, a few small cartons of yogurt, some of last night's leftovers of Hokkien *mee*, and, what's that? Oh yes, a few drops of spilled Milo and *kopi* from the kitchen sink. Mmm. Interesting." The rubbish connoisseur winked at her.

"What?" Miranda's mouth closed.

"I buy from you. Your rubbish."

This transaction did not bode well for Miranda's sensible brain: Okay. Calm down. He seems relatively harmless. I can probably take him if he tries anything funny. Let's just sell him the trash and go back down the corridor and home.

Unfortunately, Miranda's illogical Singaporean reflex to strike whilst the financially viable iron was hot also kicked in just as she replied: "Okay, sure. Let's bargain."

"I give you this. Something valuable, something one-of-a-kind."

The ticket was bright orange, and neatly perforated down the middle. It read, "Admission for One," in large thick Gothic text. As she looked at it, the *karung guni* man quickly tucked away the rubbish bags into his haversack.

"But what's it for?"

"TEAK-KEET for an ADD-VENT-CHER!"

"Why do I not trust you, Ah Pek?"

"Ahaha! So RE-TORT-DEE-CALL *siah*!"

"What's that?"

"What's what?"

"You don't feel it? That!"

"The wind?"

"Yes the wind! It's getting very windy!"

"Oh yes, it's the WASTE-TER-LEE!"

"What?"

"It's the westerly monsoon winds, lah. It's your ticket to ride, Miranda."

"Wait."

"Yes?"

"What's with the sudden improvement in language?"

"Ah, fanciful façades and smoke and broken mirrors. That's how realities lie to you. Enjoy the adventure. Oh, and happy hatch-day!"

In retrospect, Miranda couldn't remember what happened to the *karung guni* Ah Pek after that. He suddenly disappeared as the wind's howling became almost unbearable. In any case, the great monsoon wind came crashing into Mirada with brute force. It huffed and puffed at Madam Siri's potted cactuses and sent broken debris flying across the open corridor. Before she knew it, Miranda was lifted off her feet.

In her childhood, Miranda had dreamt that she died without anyone knowing. An empty funeral, an empty wake. She'd passed on in her bed—old, moored to the rigidities of a body that came with age and time. Gone were the days of being young and foolish. She died alone and reminiscing what it was like to be nimble and quick—the candlestick of life waning and faltering in the bittersweet darkness of death and more death. Miranda had awoken from the dream in despair and tears. "I don't want to grow old, don't let me grow old," she'd repeated endlessly to her comforting mother.

Now, as she was tossed through the air, flashes of that episode jumped across Miranda's inner mind. "At least," she thought, as she hurtled towards the opened HDB rubbish chute, and surely, to her imminent and violent death, "I'll be forever 21."

Despite overwhelming odds toward injury, she slipped neatly through the tiny opening in one piece, shrieking in Hokkien-laden vulgarities, tumbling down the rabbit hole and, to her surprise, landing not amidst a mountain of the housing block's garbage but on a large pile of dried leaves. The interior of the chute was nowhere to be found, and she appeared to be in a forest clearing instead.

After a moment of recovery, and making sure that all her bits and pieces were where they should've been, it dawned on Miranda that she was not alone. As her eyes adjusted to the bright moonlit surroundings, a familiar voice said, "Miranda, are you okay?" She looked up, and found herself staring at…herself.

"You're me," Miranda quietly observed.

"Well, yes. And no," said the other Miranda. As if to demonstrate the point, her doppelgänger took a small jump back, did a quick pirouette, and began dancing a short ballet routine. The restless winds rustled the tall leaves in the trees that surrounded the two women. In the open moonlight, Miranda could see everything in distinct pale sepia hues, and she watched as the other Miranda danced ever so lightly. She was faster than Miranda, and evidently more elegant. She danced brilliantly.

The young woman finished her last movement and curtsied.

"Welcome to the shadow lands, Miranda. You can call me Dot."

Dot offered her hand, but just as Miranda reached upwards, Dot wrapped her arms around Miranda in a tight, warm embrace. The cool evening wind brushed against Miranda's skin and whipped her hair as she breathed in the fresh air of the night. Miranda felt as though she had found a lost twin sister.

Dot stood up and took Miranda by the hand. "Okay, that's enough fuzziness for now, I think. We can catch up along the way. We should hurry, or we'll miss the Mambo".

They followed a path through narrow trees and flowing gullies. The two young women talked about rainbows and flowers, and laughed at jokes about cute boys and funny animals. They crossed a creaky wooden bridge, and passed several large stones.

"Is there anyone else here?" asked Miranda.

"That's a yes-and-no answer too," replied Dot, after pondering the question. "There are others like me, shadow people. Things here are subtle reflections of your world, after all. But you can't see them, can you? You're from the other side."

Miranda imagined herself stepping through masses of travelling shadow twins. It was quite disconcerting.

"And what's this Mambo we're going for?" asked Miranda.

"Well, let's just keep that a surprise for now. Better to keep you in suspense, my dear. Oh look, here we are."

They stopped in a clearing at the top of a small hill. Just in front of them stood a large rain tree. Its large crown towered over the landscape, its jagged greyish-brown bark fractured with old age and stippled with knots that jutted straight out.

"That's a big tree," observed Miranda.

"It is," replied Dot. "We're going to climb it."

"What?"

"Don't worry, it's easy once you get the hang of it. Come on, I'll show you."

With that, Miranda found herself running after her petite doppelgänger, who'd taken off to the base of the tall tree.

Dot was right. It was an easy climb once you knew what to do. Miranda wrangled from one bark hold to another, then swung her body upward from branch to branch. Graceful Dot was always a step ahead, carefully coaching and making sure she was comfortable in the climb, saying things like, "Pace yourself, know you're in control." Before she knew it, Miranda found herself at the top, looking outward across the land.

The two young women sat perched on the highest branch. Their legs hung off the edge of nothingness and beyond. The full moon blazed still. Silver cloud spirals rolled gently by. Below, the forest floor stretched onwards, until a sea brokered the end of the blue-grey horizon line. A quietening hush filled the atmosphere.

"Are you ready?" asked Dorothy. "It's almost time."

It started slowly. Miranda felt the first fleck of something brush against her arm, and she'd reached instinctively to touch it. It was a damp spot. And then, another brush. As she watched, she realized it was not a raindrop, but a tiny snowflake, drifting up past her into the sky.

Through the dense foliage of midnight woods and extended rivers, white snow was floating up from the ground. The frozen particles floated gently, picked up by circular updrafts and vast spiralling swings in the wind currents. Higher up, they clumped together into dense masses, and disappeared.

"Welcome to the Mambo," Dot said finally.

"It's beautiful."

Dot stretched out her right palm face down, the snowflakes sticking to its surface. Miranda watched as Dot started softly shaping the gathered flakes into a roundish compact ball.

"Yes, it is beautiful," agreed Dot. "Miranda, you really don't know why you're here?"

Miranda shook her head.

Dot gestured to the flowing snowfall. "These are the dream fragments of the city folk," she began. "Each, taking its turn to ascend." Quietly, like the waning nightlight, her voice faded into a soft murmur.

"These are the dream fragments of the city folk. As they sleep on in their warm beds and covered blankets, wandering through eternal dreamscapes and nighthoods, they leave their trails of bread crumbs and broken stalks across the reflection worlds—these shadow lands, these glimpses of the yet-true. The snowflakes carry with them the thoughts, the memories, the hopes, and fears, of your world through mine. This is the Mambo. It is the fading ocean tides of life, where half-truths and half-realities transcend into forever dreams.

"It is hard to let go of youth, surely. Somewhere, a part of you doesn't want to. This is understandable. But the truth is, you have to move on. Just as the snow leaves a little of itself as it travels, so too do we leave impressions of ourselves with the people and the things we meet in our lives. Embrace this. Then say good-bye. Discard the loss of your innocence. It's time to let go. It's time to grow up."

The sky was beginning to lighten as the avalanche of upwards snowfall started to taper and disappear. A few lost flakes foolishly remained, floating despondently in the air, clinging and melting through the thinning atmosphere. The two girls didn't speak as they climbed their way down the great tree.

"And now, the end," said Dot, as their feet touched the ground.

With that, she leaned in and kissed Miranda. Before she could react, a soft heat passed through Miranda's lips. And then, she was on fire, the flickering flames engulfing the two young women. As Dot's kiss permeated throughout her body, Miranda felt her heart singing out its final moments of dreaming and waking, its voice filled with clarity and emotion, and of the deepening consequences of being disastrously mortal.

"Goodbye."

Miranda blinked. The familiar noises of early-morning traffic and passing pedestrians echoed along the common corridor. Around her, the pots of Madam Siri's cactuses sat neatly on their ceramic pedestals, solid, unbroken, and untouched.

For a second, she was breathless. And then she realized that she was still holding onto the bright orange ticket, one side torn away.

THE MOON AND THE STARS

Andrew Cheah

A typically foetid Saturday night. An apartment complex lit up yellow and blue by streetlamps and halogen-dappled swimming pool waves. Shifting veins crept up an elongated tower. Black figures floated up trees, behind mirrors, under carpets, watching and listening to university students frolic amongst themselves. Jokes and speeches echoed between walls and across rooms, broadcasting a muddy signal to anyone who would listen.

The party had moved on from introductions, and the students were somewhere between buzzed and drunk, playing truth-or-dare games, spending inordinate amounts of time in toilets, adjourning to bedrooms and kitchens, attempting to display knowledge of intricate international and domestic political situations, discussing naked pop stars and/or hot women, progressing on to toilet habits, cooking tips, the sexual experiences of friends of friends of friends, under dim lights, whirring fans, and buzzing air conditioners, light trails dragging pink raffia ribbons across the room.

"I'll never understand non-cat people," said Regina.

"You mean people that don't like cats or people who don't spend their free time dressing up as cats?" asked George, wearing a set of bunny ears he'd found sellotaped to a washing line.

"I mean people who don't like cats," said Regina, not getting the joke, "you know, like, the opposite of dog people."

"Bunny-eared dogs!" shouted George. He held back a joke about pronouncing Regina wrongly. He reached back to scratch his head and felt his rabbit ears being taken from him.

Boaz Lin, recent graduate in Business and Marketing, moonlighting as an insurance agent, half-drowned in tequila and smelling of chocolate cake, attempted to balance the rabbit ears on his left wrist, charting his way past a long-haired girl in a kimono, an idiot in a tank-top, a clique of 22- year-olds (probably a Christian cell group playing *tai tee*), and Serene, a lone dancer spinning and crashing into anyone close by.

"I suddenly have this massive craving for chocolate cake," Serene disclosed to Boaz, leaning into him for balance.

Boaz chuckled awkwardly.

"I need you to take me to the kitchen. To find the chocolate cake."

"I think it's finished." Voice low and hesitant.

"No. No no no no no no. It's not!" She grabbed his hand and dragged him to the kitchen, bunny ears attached.

In the kitchen stood a crew of three: Moses, Wei Ling, and Peterson Chan. Moses and Wei Ling were discussing their political manifestos and their subsequent feelings towards the coming National Day Parade. Peterson Chan was in the corner leaning against the fridge, sucking on a wedge of orange.

"I have to say, the fireworks I enjoy," Moses explained. "I like the fireworks. Very *shiok*."

Wei Ling replied, "But that's about all. They put on all these Mickey Mouse pieces. One time with soldier, another time with children, sometimes with adults, sometimes Malay and sometimes Indian and sometimes alien and sometimes gay."

Serene swiped her hand in the direction of a cluelessly cute Peterson, prompting him to move out of the way of the refrigerator door. She let go of Boaz and rummaged through the fridge, ass in the air, muttering about chocolate and how it could never be found.

"You know, since I was young, my sis always hid the chocolates in the house," she announced to no one in particular. "She claimed it was to stop me from having pimples. But *she* never had pimples!"

Boaz leaned against the doorway and shrugged at the ceiling.

Peterson Chan, born in Hong Kong, a migrant to Singapore at age six, currently studying geology, and now a smoker in remission, carefully retrieved the orange peel from his mouth and grinned at Boaz, revealing a set of surprisingly white teeth.

"With all the underground tunnelling going on, one day the grandstand is going to disappear in a gigantic sinkhole," continued Wei Ling.

Outside, through the window, a hanging bra spun in the breeze, providing a pair of outsized, compound, insectoid eyes that stared intently at the group of four in the kitchen, partially obscured by window grills. Lips moved to form words, and eyes shifted to betray emotions.

Peterson moved to the window, lit a cigarette, inhaled, and blew a cloud of smoke out to the bra. Serene emerged from the fridge with a plate of half-eaten chocolate cake, and began to devour. Boaz found a stool in the corner and sat, leaning against stucco blue-white tiles.

Wei Ling and Moses, noticing the cake, were distracted from their non-culinary conversation. They joined Serene in finishing off what was left, scooping out pieces of cake by the palmful. Peterson and Boaz watched the feeding session, one impassive, one amazed.

From his stool, Boaz stretched out his hand and introduced himself to Peterson, who manoeuvred past three chocolate-coated mouths to speak to his new friend. Squatting on the floor,

Peterson Chan, pantry handle digging into his neck, proceeded to talk.

Outside the kitchen, a curiously quiet girl, clad completely in a white dress, black hair done up in ponytail and chrysanthemum flower, leaned in to eavesdrop on the two. Hearing enough, she surreptitiously took the bunny ears, moved to the laptop, and changed the music track.

And as the compressed sounds of a synthesiser filled the room, as strangled beats fought to drown a thin, keening, high, wailing voice, Peterson and Boaz shifted closer to each other, and the girl moved towards front door. She picked up a pair of black converse sneakers with white soles, and put them on. The girl, saying goodbye to no one, left the party, to be claimed by the shivering shadows outside, never to be seen again.

A friendship formed that night between Peterson Chan and Boaz Lin. They exchanged phone numbers, later chatted online, hung out with friends, watched movies, ate dinners and lunches, and in general developed a kind of camaraderie.

Each knew specific things about the other that neither would dare tell anyone else.

Peterson knew about Boaz's love for bad American sitcoms. *Everybody Loves Raymond* being a prime example. He knew about how Boaz would even cry when watching some episodes; notably the ones where the Raymond's less loved older brother, Robert, would go out of his way to help Raymond.

Peterson knew about Boaz's paranoid mother, who had recently installed a wooden bar to his front door to prevent the *hantu* from coming in. He knew about how she would obsessively disinfect every chair, shoe, keyboard, and light switch in the house, in the fear of germs or fungus taking over. He also knew the reasons for her paranoia, fully admitting his possible inheritance of said psychosis, a family history of gangrene, and a childhood spent close to a sprawling banyan tree. Untouched, the tree had spread its mangled roots onto pavement, road and wall, and was rumoured to house a malevolent being: a floating woman dressed in white. And even then, just the week before, his mother had found white footprints, missing the big toe on the left foot, that had come from the staircase and followed the corridor, stopping mysteriously outside their flat.

When asked about the footprints, Boaz said, "We actually reported it to the police. The footprints were strange. Whoever they belonged to, the person had nine toes. According to the policeman, that someone also had flat feet. Not that it helps. My family has come up with a bunch of explanations. The simplest is that someone simply stepped on white paint and walked around the neighbourhood. But why the sudden stop outside our flat? Mum thinks that someone jumped the barrier and killed himself, but no one's killed himself in our area. And the idea of stepping in white paint before jumping makes no sense. My brother and I think it's some joke by the kids two doors down, playing with white paint and in their joke stopped outside our flat, probably because of the fifteen talismans my mum places on our front door. And I haven't even gotten to the nine toes. The kids don't have nine toes, and a missing big toe, although easy enough to fake, isn't easy enough to be worth the trouble. One day we'll probably leave a fake toe in the kitchen sink and make my mum cry."

Peterson had vegetarian tendencies. "Tendencies" because there was no underlying creed or philosophy behind his preference for vegetables. He simply liked the taste, even preferring the taste of fake meat to the taste of real meat. Fake *lap cheong*, fake chicken, fake *bak kua*, fake shark's fin, fake *hashima*, fake duck, fake innards, all made of mushrooms and tofu of varying species.

Peterson was also very passionate about tomatoes.

"They're not a vegetable. Tomatoes are technically fruits," he said, in a slightly Hong Kong-tinged accent, intonations rising and falling in a regular pattern. "You cannot say a tomato is a vegetable because the tomato, it has seeds. It reproduces itself, you know. The seeds germinate to become another tomato plant after the tomato is eaten by a bird or some other animal. They grow out of faeces of the animal."

Boaz liked the way Peterson pronounced "vegetable" as "veggie-table."

"I don't understand."

"But you must understand! Everyone gets it wrong! The tomato, it is not a veggie-table. A veggie-table is a plant. It's a leaf. Like *kai lan*, or spinach, or broccoli. Tomatoes are closer to fruits. Berries, in fact."

This conversation took place in Little India in front of a fruit stall. Flies buzzed in the sun, scavenging on mandarin orange peels, stray *kang kong* leaves, floating fish scales, mushroom heads, apple stalks, sweet wrappers, and water-soaked biscuits. The fruit stall uncle, his view of potential customers blocked by their form, yelled at Peterson and Boaz to move away and go disturb someone else.

They decided to leave the market, catching a glimpse of the legless, eye-patched man whom, minutes earlier, had harassed them for money. Catching sight of the pair, he let out a strangled scream and made a beeline towards the fruit stall at a terrifying speed. Efficiently nimble, he slid across the wet floor on fraying jeans, metal bowl clanging fiercely on the cement, forcing Peterson and Boaz to make a break for it, entering the crowds of Indians mingling on the roads and pavements outside.

And in the crowd, Peterson and Boaz squeezed together and became a part of the flow of people, pushing along the streets and spilling out onto the main road, some arcing back towards the pavement, some jaywalking to the other side. The Indian men and women around them were all smiling, happy in the afternoon sun. Some were holding hands, others were jumping about, hands in pockets, faces to the sky, feet to the road, completely ignoring the two Chinese boys being carried along with the current.

Peterson and Boaz exited Little India, chaos and beauty dripping from the sky. They headed towards the closest covered walkway, and decided to drift towards Newton, with the intention of picking up some *char siew baos* along the way.

Meanwhile, inside the *char siew bao* stall, Madam Lau awoke to the songs of Theresa Teng. The honey-coated voice wafted across steam and evening air, the ghosts of her childhood slipping up the walls into the cracks of the ceiling, the fragrant smell of *char siew* calling her out from a nameless dream. She joined her daughter at the counter, helping to top up the *char siew baos* inside the display case from a Tupperware bucket.

"It was very funny, you know," she would say later on. Madam Lau had had no recollection of making so many *baos*. Within the bucket there was a mix: chicken *baos*, labelled with a yellow dot, vegetable *baos*, with a green dot, mushroom *baos*, a brown dot, and of course, *char siew baos*, with a red dot. Right on top of the mass of *baos*, though, there was a new kind of *bao*, marked with a red circle surrounding a five-cornered star. Drifting in the saccharine sweet haze of nostalgia, Madam Lau didn't recognise the sign from anything related to church, or God, or Satan. She remembered the sign as a lingering memory of her neighbour, Choo Mei Ling, in the shadow of the second World War.

Choo Mei Ling, hair always tied in a ponytail, permanently decorated with a chrysanthemum flower. Madam Lau remembered waiting in the morning for the sound of her mother's sewing machine to start, to look out her window for Mei Ling to come skipping down the road. She would run out to join Mei Ling, to talk about school, about *char siew baos*, about parents, about the radio, dresses, dolls, syrups and shaved ice.

Madam Lau lost herself remembering her childhood best friend's sudden disappearance from her life. It had happened in the night time. Mei Ling, in a glowing white dress, chrysanthemum fixed to her hair, climbed into her room through the window. The young Madam Lau lay on the bed and looked up expectantly at her friend. Wordlessly, Mei Ling tip-toed to her side, knelt down, and kissed Madam Lau on the forehead. And as Madam Lau felt her eyelids begin to droop, Mei Ling smiled, backed away towards the window, and floated away into the night.

Madam Lau had dreamed of Mei Ling, just out of reach and hidden behind a yellow lotus-embroidered silk curtain. Oblivious, happy, laughing, sad, and crying. The dream ended with a bottom-up view from beneath the surface of a river, moon and stars dripping down from the sky, wild spiders floating aimlessly in a web of crests and arrows.

The following morning, Madam Lau had found the pale white outline of Mei Ling's footprints branded onto the wooden floor, missing the left big toe. She knew, without needing to look to the silent empty house next door, that she would never see Mei Ling again. Lost in her thoughts, she opened her bedroom door, intending to head into the kitchen for breakfast, when she bumped into her autistic brother in the middle of the front room, wearing a pair of bunny ears, holding a white chalk, and crying. He was sitting in the centre of a crudely drawn pentagram.

Boaz Lin, having eaten one of Madam Lau's badly cooked, satanic, *char siew baos*, was now crouched in the centre of a crudely constructed bathroom cubicle, relentlessly vomiting into the toilet. Outside, Peterson was sitting on a bench in the night air, trying to ignore the hoarse retching by listening to the sporadic car traffic, and the distant cheers coming from the Padang where the National Day Parade rehearsal was being held.

The rehearsal audience sang along to the songs about national unity and pride. The stage was packed with children in blue, each holding a piece to a larger work, the completed picture forming a human ocean carrying a junk, from which a *papier mâché* Merlion would emerge triumphant, lasers shooting out of its eyes into the rapt audience, flags and glowsticks shimmering in the stands. Those in attendance all anticipated the grand finale of the show: the extravagant fireworks display that Singaporeans had come to expect every 9th of August.

In the darkness to the south of the Padang, two Chinese boys walked beneath perfectly trimmed rain trees, admiring the reservoir, the sea, and the reflections of lights coming from the Singapore skyline. They marvelled silently at the city lit up red, yellow, and white against the night sky. A slight breeze rustled the leaves as Boaz, weak from his regurgitation, leaned against Peterson for support.

"It's not right. You're the one who always *kena* food poisoning, not me."

"I don't know. I think it's because I didn't eat the *char siew bao*. You should've eaten the veggie-table *bao*."

Behind them, a figure carrying a camera furtively traced their steps, taking care not to make too much noise or be seen. It had only a black fuzzy shadow for a head. Its breathing was slow, deep and soundless, and it glided from tree to tree, a silent spectre, taking shots of the pair as they wandered along the path.

"You and your veggie-table *bao*! The *char siew bao* must have been badly cooked!"

"I think it was a mistake. Maybe the star meant something was wrong with the *bao*."

"What star?"

Peterson knew about pentagrams, and the mark of Satan, but he didn't want to say so. Not just yet. It would be too ridiculous and Boaz wouldn't be able to handle it anyway. He decided to change the subject.

"Do you think we'll get arrested if we pee in the water?"

"My *char siew bao* tasted normal! I've even eaten there before. It's one of my favourite *bao* places…and why was there a star?"

Less than 500 metres away, jeeps for the National Day Parade rehearsal were circling the makeshift stadium at the Padang, each connected to balloons of smileys, parrots, stars, and flags. The Merlion was still on the stage, now spewing out a fabric-jet of water, simulated by children waving blue flags, into the fake sea.

"I don't think anyone is going to know if we pee in the water anyway."

"I'm going to merlion in the water."

The sound of a fly unzipping, and the groaning of a victim of food poisoning. Peterson, in a unique style particular to himself and all the males in his maternal family line, stood legs wide apart and head tilted upwards, and delivered a commanding stream of urine in the direction of the Benjamin Sheares Bridge. Boaz, in contrast, fell to his knees and retched at the breakwater, attempting to push out the remainder of the offending food matter in his stomach.

The spectre saw all of this, and stood up from its vantage point on a tree branch, causing it to lose its balance and fall ass-first onto the grass, consequently disturbing the tranquil illusion of zen that Peterson was creating in his own head.

Still peeing, Peterson half-turned his head back, catching in the corner of his eye the spectre rising up from behind a bush, eight feet tall, elongated arms, and glowing white insectoid eyes. The spectre took a giant step towards Peterson, causing him to panic, step to the left, and pull at Boaz's tee shirt.

"We have to go."

Slightly delirious and with tears in his eyes, Boaz turned to look at Peterson, wide-eyed and desperate. He staggered to his feet, turned to face the spectre, which was taking another picture, and fell backwards, pulling Peterson along with him.

The two boys rolled down the stones of the breakwater arm in arm, and stopped abruptly at the surface of the water with a hard splash. With his face half-submerged, breathing bubbles erratically into the water, Boaz tried to keep calm as his nerves, sensing a hairline fracture in his shin, sent throbbing pulses up to his brain. Peterson, still shocked and scared and with his fly undone, lay below Peterson and held him up to keep him from drowning.

Peterson regarded the spectre at the top of the breakwater with fear. It stood there motionless for a few minutes, and then floated away into the night. Breathing easier, Peterson slowly pulled Boaz from the water, not noticing the fireworks beginning at the National Day Parade rehearsal. Against the skyscraper backdrop of a lonely city-state, a single rocket sliced a clean line up into the night, ending triumphantly in a chrysanthemum-shaped burst of red, yellow, and white.

THE DISAPPEARANCE OF LISA ZHANG

Dave Chua

At times like these it is hard not to reach out and touch the screen. The other cubicles at the cybercafé are busy with maids chatting with their families on this Sunday; they are all sitting on blue vinyl chairs that appear to have been taken from a restaurant. There is the overly sweet smell of Fanta, the sound of laughter and occasionally, some sobbing. Annie has clumsily mastered Skype, and the signs at the shop indicate that there are no viruses on these computers.

She presses her arms to her body. Her daughter is herself in a run-down cybercafé back in the Philippines, and the boy in the seat next to her twitches and swings his head about as he plays some game. The monitor's settings are faulty, and her daughter is tinted green.

They go through the usual questions. Annie asks about her grades, any gossip regarding the relatives and family, and what is new in the village. She tries to control her voice. Her daughter is getting bored, but it is important that they talk every weekend, and she knows she only has this machine for 30 minutes. Her daughter's grades are in the B to B-plus range, there was an argument over some garbage thrown near their house, and an old Ford driven by the science teacher rammed into the side of a lorry carrying papayas. The teacher was found to be a bit drunk, she whispers, but no one was hurt.

Amid the conversation, she knows Emily is hiding something. Annie presses her. They talk about Grandmother, a subject that her daughter does not enjoy conversing about, and it succeeds in breaking down her defences.

Her daughter looks around her, sees that the boys next to her are too engrossed in their games, and whispers into the mike. She just used her first sanitary pad a few days ago. It was at home, and she did not know what to do but she stayed home and Grandma helped her. Annie is ashamed that she was not there. She tells her daughter that it is normal, and that she is now a woman. Annie tries to offer advice about using pads, but Emily sits back again, as if a spell has ended. They go back to talking about trivialities. She says Grandma is losing her sense of taste, and puts too much salt in her cooking. Annie says she will try to speak to her mother about it.

The call ends. The store owner, an Indian man with round glasses, is not the type who would charge if she were to exceed the time limit, but she does not want to stay on the machine for too long. She hands over the dollar bill and thanks the owner. He motions to the sleek black LCD screen in front of her.

"This is what happens when those monitors slim down," he says. It takes her a moment to realise he has made a joke, and tries to smile. She waves and tells him she will be back next week. He is already signalling to the next customer, mindful of not wasting time.

Annie turns to her handphone and finds that she has missed several calls from her employer, Mrs. Zhang. She immediately calls back and Mrs. Zhang screams at her. Lisa has gone missing. The tone is both accusing and desperate, but they both know that this is Sunday and Annie's obligatory day off to do as she wishes, even though she does not do much with the time.

~

Annie wants to go to church to pray for her family and herself, but she rushes home. It is a terrace house, wedged in with others of similar design. From certain angles it looks like the neighbours are squashing in on them. Compared to most Singaporeans, though, her employer is rich. The house is located on a slight incline in a country that is almost flat, and that equates to wealth.

The shouting begins when she steps into the house. There is a policeman present, but that does not stop Mrs. Zhang. Annie lets her employer scold, saying yes and no ma'am. Mrs. Zhang leans over her with her thin neck. Her face is puffy from crying, and Annie thinks that she must be hurting inside. Annie recites the Lord's Prayer in her heart, to get through the moment.

Annie says she has no idea where Lisa is. She can find out the number of her friends. The policeman, a Malay man with pale palms, constantly directs his eyes elsewhere around the house. The wooden horse in the living room, the modern painting of coloured blocks, the photos of Lisa at her 10th birthday party from last year, where they hired a magician who pulled a plush rabbit out of his jacket and twisted balloon animals.

The policeman makes a call, and stands close to Annie. She realises that she must be a suspect. Mrs. Zhang eyes her like a stranger does. "Where were you all day?" The tone carries an accusation.

Annie is brought into the kitchen and questioned by a female policeman, who sits down next to her on a bare wooden stool and nods her head. She asks a lot of questions, about where she last saw Lisa, whether she has mentioned anything about running away, and other questions. Annie tries to recall, and she senses Mrs. Zhang hovering in the background, moving around the house.

Annie recalls seeing Lisa in bed that morning before she stepped out of the house. No, she did not remember Lisa mentioning anything about going out of the house, much less running away. Annie does not remember any strangers around the neighbourhood.

The policewoman asks her where she went for the afternoon. Annie tells her about going to the cybercafé. The policewoman asks for the address of the café and the names of some of the other customers, and Annie gives the information without hesitation, adding that the owner knows her. She repeats the joke he said, and the police officer smiles.

She asks Annie if Lisa ever talked about running away, and Annie shakes her head. "She is a happy child," she says.

However, Annie recalls how Lisa slapped her with a ruler three days ago; she seemed to delight in the frantic, insect-like vibration of the ruler, slapping Annie again and again on the arms and the legs. The impacts were not strong enough to leave marks, but they still hurt. She decides not to tell the policewoman about this incident. When the policewoman is done, she thanks Annie for her answers.

Annie hears Mrs. Zhang telling the other policeman that Lisa always takes her mobile phone, but that it is still in the house. The policeman tries his best to reassure Mrs. Zhang.

Annie has never really spoken to Mrs. Zhang. From the onset, she was given orders. Her knowledge of Mrs. Zhang's life has come across from working for her. She is a servant, not a friend; that much has been made clear.

The door to Lisa's room is open and everything appears to have been overturned. Her toys are on the floor, her books are draped on the windowsill and even her compact discs have been taken out of the cases, as though they could provide a clue to her location. Books and papers are scattered. Annie is uneasy, but right now all she does is her duty. Mrs. Zhang is talking too loud, as she often does when she is distraught, complaining about her husband (who spends most of the year away in China), or

Annie's cooking (which is never good enough), or the neighbours (whose plants reach over the fence and throw shadows into her garden).

She searches the room, trying to remember where Lisa kept her contact list. Lisa's favourite bag, which resembles a huge puppy, has been turned inside-out and the papers within are spread all over. Annie has to be careful moving around the room. Pencils and pins hide in the carpet. There is a corkboard with pictures of Lisa and her friends, one of Mrs. Zhang, and even one of herself. Annie had felt uncomfortable when she pinned it up, but Lisa said that she deserved to be there. She has fetched Lisa home from school since she was five years old, ironed her clothes, made her meals and even carried her to the bed when she fell asleep watching television in the living room, taking each step on the stair slowly to ensure that she did not wake Lisa up.

"Annie! Have you found it?" Mrs. Zhang shouts.

"Not yet, ma'am," she says, just loud enough.

"Why don't you hurry?"

Annie crawls under the desk and finds a piece of paper folded so many times it is as thick as a slice of bread. She unfolds it and sees the list of numbers of Lisa's classmates. She brings it down, running.

"Here it is ma'am," she says. Mrs. Zhang grabs the piece of paper out of her hands. The policeman still has his hands folded.

"Do you want a cup of tea or coffee, sir?" Annie asks, but the man waves it away.

"This is two years old," Mrs. Zhang says.

"Yes, ma'am, but the friends and classmates are almost all the same," Annie says. Her tone is not defensive. She knows she needs to be calm. Annie goes over to the cordless phone and picks it up, delivering it to Mrs. Zhang's hands. She goes to the kitchen and prepares a cup of ginseng tea for Mrs. Zhang and coffee for the policeman anyway.

It was seven years ago when she signed up with the agency. Things at home had just soured, and the man she had married walked out of their house and never came back, supposedly flying off to Dubai. She gave birth to Emily and raised her for five years, but funds were running dry, and her mother had invested in a get-rich-quick scheme that left her even poorer. Annie signed on with an agency that sent her to Singapore. Hong Kong was preferred, as they paid more, but the agency had assured her Singapore was better. There were a series of fees to be paid, including training for work that she already knew how to do, like ironing and cooking, but there was no way to escape it. The head of the agency was a Singaporean who spoke good Tagalog, with a statuette of the Virgin Mary next to his fax machine, and seemed to be trustworthy.

When she arrived and cleared customs, they placed her in a dorm and made her wait with other maids-to-be, to be assigned and hired. She wore a red polo shirt with a blue collar, and the maids went silent whenever a potential customer walked in. She felt like a pet waiting to be adopted. The owner of the agency assured her that she would find an employer quickly. She was not "too pretty," and Annie wondered if that was ever an asset.

Mrs. Zhang walked in on the second week. Annie could hear Mrs. Zhang talking openly to the agency owner's wife, who pointed to the maids like they were chickens at a market. The business owner signalled her to come forward, and Annie felt relief. Every meal she'd eaten while waiting had counted toward the debt to be repaid. There would be forms to be filled in, and other matters to be settled, but Mrs. Zhang wanted her to start as soon as possible. There had been problems with the previous maid, Mrs. Zhang said. Annie started the next day even though the paperwork had not quite been cleared. Lisa was four at that point, a year younger than Emily. She was curious about Annie, and asked why the previous maid had been dismissed, but Mrs. Zhang told her to never bring that up.

Annie brings the drinks out. The policeman declines, smiles then stops himself. He says he has to be on his way and that they are investigating. They have questioned the neighbours, and there might be some leads.

Mrs. Zhang jumps at the news. She says she saw a man with a cap outside the house earlier today. The policeman writes the information down. It must be him, she says.

The policeman says that they will investigate. He turns to Annie and nods to her as he leaves. Mrs. Zhang resumes her calling, dialling some of the numbers a few times. Annie goes to prepare an early dinner: steamed fish and tofu. When she announces the dishes, there is no acknowledgement. Mrs. Zhang's makeup is faded and the worry on her is apparent. Annie wants to console her but cannot find a way to broach the line drawn across their relationship.

That night she guides Mrs. Zhang to bed, who has scrawled down notes and numbers all over the piece of paper, despite Annie placing a notepad next to her. She has called the police officer twice. She asks why there is nothing on the news about her daughter, and she has blamed Annie at least five times for her disappearance. The second time, she slapped at Annie but Annie dodged the blow. She left the room briefly before returning, and Mrs. Zhang returned to being civilized.

Mrs. Zhang gets out of bed and goes out to talk to the neighbours: the ones across the street who have been abusive to her, and even the ones who spend their weekends singing Cantonese karaoke until midnight. Annie wonders if Mrs. Zhang suspects them, but it is far-fetched to believe that the families would resort to kidnapping Lisa. The punishment for kidnapping is death. Annie goes to the balcony to keep track of Mrs. Zhang's movements. She finds Mrs. Zhang talking animatedly to most of those she speaks to. Undoubtedly they are sympathetic, and the thought of there being a kidnapper must be frightening to those in the neighbourhood.

Mrs. Zhang, still in her nightgown, returns home then takes the car out. Annie is secretly glad that she leaves the house. Annie stays awake, unsure of what to do. She has talked to the other maids on the street, but none have seen anything out of the ordinary. There are always cars cruising around the streets, examining various houses, but she thinks they must be estate agents assessing property or just aspirants who wish to purchase one of the houses for themselves one day to fulfil their own Singaporean dream.

At 2:45 a.m., Mrs. Zhang returns home, her phone clutched to her chest. She is haggard and goes to sleep without changing clothes. When her employer is asleep, Annie goes downstairs to her room. Even though there are two guest rooms, she sleeps in a spare room that has been converted from storage space. The bed just barely fits, and the door knocks against it when it opens. On warm nights, she has to leave it ajar in order for enough air to flow through.

Her clothes are kept under the bed, and there are plastic crates where she keeps the rest of her things. Wedged against the wall are framed posters from Mrs. Zhang's shop, which markets tours to Jerusalem and other holy sites. On the wall are photos of Annie's mother and daughter. She sees them once a year when she goes back home during Easter. Above the bed is a wooden carving of the Virgin Mary holding the baby Jesus. Annie prays that Lisa will be found soon. She, too, feels distraught, and can understand why Mrs. Zhang is behaving this way. If Emily disappeared, she would do all she could to find her too.

Annie thinks about the previous maid. How did Mrs. Zhang treat her? Were they happier then? Why was she dismissed? She remembers a conversation with the neighbour's maid, about how Mrs. Zhang screamed and shouted at her. The maid was often seen sobbing, and wore long-sleeved shirts to hide her scars. Mrs. Zhang occasionally scolds and hits her, but Annie bears with it. She thinks of the already fading photo of Emily, and their house, and the Virgin Mary.

There is a pile of newspapers at least three days old next to the bed. Annie occasionally tries to read them, particularly for news of home, although she is not allowed to take them away until they have been thoroughly handled, just in case Mrs. Zhang still needs to look through them. Unable to sleep, she turns on her bedside lamp and flips through a few pages. She sees a news story about a maid falling to her death after trying to wash a window in an upper-level flat. She must have been as disoriented as Annie was when she arrived, in a city full of buildings that were taller than anything she had ever seen, so unlike the villages that most of the maids in Singapore had come from. Do their employers ever know their stories? What happens after their deaths? Do they warn the new maids about the dangers? Annie has cleaned the outside window before until Mrs. Zhang screamed at her, though she thought she heard her saying something about losing her deposit if Annie died.

As she rubs her eyes, she thinks she sees something passing overhead quickly. She stares above but the ceiling is bare.

She passes into the realm of sleep and then dream. She is back at home in the Philippines. A rooster strides on the rooftop, passing tut-tuts snap, flowers bloom from vines, a breeze filled with the scent of fish blows through the window. Just like in real life, she rushes to Emily's room. She wants to hold her and tell her how much she misses her. But when she arrives, the room is empty, and there are blood stains on the bed and on the floor. She rips up the bedsheet and beneath it is her own mattress.

She charges out of the room, but she is back in Singapore, and she can hear Emily crying. On the day when she left the village, Emily refused to talk to her, unable to understand why her mother needed to go so far away. Annie continues to work, hanging out bedsheets, but every time she puts one on the clothesline and turns to the basket, there are still more.

There is a sound from the street, and the sky above has turned gray. The houses all look similar to that of the Zhangs; an infinite series of wedged houses, too thin and too tall. She notices a figure outside, and she hangs the bedsheet before approaching. Is it a delivery person again or the mailman? But there is something familiar about the person.

The gates open automatically, and the figure, a woman with long hair, stands there. Annie sees the polo shirt that she wore at the office when she first arrived in Singapore. She cannot bring herself to look at the woman's face, but she knows the jeans and the brown sandals are hers. When she is finally able to summon the strength to lift her head, she slips out of the dream. But as she wakes up, she is left with the startling vision of night-black eyes.

It has been a warm night, and she goes to bathe and wash off the smell of sweat. She looks at the clock; it is 6:24 a.m. She should have been awake half an hour earlier to help send Lisa to school. Annie rushes to the room, expecting to see Lisa there, but the floor is still a mess and the bed is quiet, and she remembers what has happened. She checks the bathroom but it is still unused. Annie is worried. Despite everything, the house had a rhythm that has now been disrupted.

She goes to Mrs. Zhang's bedroom. The door is open, letting out the cool air of the air conditioning. She sees Mrs. Zhang on the bed. Above her is a studio portrait of her and her husband. Mr. Zhang is riding a bicycle and she sits behind him, her hands around his waist. She wonders at the age of the photograph. There is a light smile on Mr. Zhang's face. Annie doubts if they were the kind of people who ever actually sat on a bicycle. From the two gleaming cars in the driveway that she has to alternately wash every other day, even though one of them does not have a certificate for usage, she thinks Mr. Zhang was amused that the photographer had asked them to pose this way.

Annie goes to prepare Mrs. Zhang's breakfast and busies herself. She takes clothes to wash, and cleans the living room even though she is only supposed to do so on Tuesdays. She reminds herself to call her mother later, to tell her not to skimp on money for Emily's sanitary pads. She must tell her how much is to be allocated, else she might buy the cheapest variety or even worse, not bother at all. She knows she should be there telling Emily how to use them, and at times like these, her absence from her daughter's life wrenches her heart. She recites the Lord's Prayer to calm herself, being careful to whisper so it cannot be heard.

While she is mopping, she hears her employer slowly waking. Her heart tightens. Mrs. Zhang has changed her tee shirt and there is an urgency in her features, but not the wild look that she possessed yesterday, which frightened Annie.

"Have there been any calls?" she asks.

"No, ma'am," Annie replies.

"Are you sure?"

"Yes, ma'am."

Annie does not know why this triggers Mrs. Zhang, but it does. She rushes down the stairs and slaps Annie, fast as the strike of a grasshopper. Annie reels from the blow, clutching her face. She trips over the bucket, which turns over and spills dirty water onto the floor.

"Look what you did! Look what you did!" Mrs. Zhang shouts, like a schoolyard bully. Annie tries to get up, spreading more water around. She slips on the soapy liquid as she tries to get up. Another blow comes down upon her, and her hair is being pulled. She shouts in pain, calling for mercy. She tries to grip Mrs. Zhang's hands.

Then a mobile phone rings and it breaks Mrs. Zhang's fever. She lets go of Annie's hair. Annie flops to the floor. Mrs. Zhang rushes to the phone, her feet skating over the wet floor.

Annie runs to the kitchen, examines her face against the cold metal of the basin. She sees a red welt, and tells herself to forgive. While gently washing her face she senses a shuddering in the space around her. She turns around, expecting Mrs. Zhang to be behind her, but there is no one there. She cannot escape the sense that she is being watched.

She spends the rest of the morning cleaning up the mess created by the spill. When Mrs. Zhang comes down, Annie cowers in a corner, but then, to her relief, Mrs. Zhang runs out of the house. Annie hopes that Lisa will turn up somehow. Even after the slap, she can understand Mrs. Zhang's state of mind.

She thinks that she should call Mrs. Zhang about lunch, but tells herself not to. As she starts tidying Mrs. Zhang's bedroom, she senses once again that she is not alone. She goes to the window and looks out, and sees some Indian workers cutting the branches off trees. The morning sun glints off the windscreens of cars.

When evening comes, Annie retreats to the maid's room. It is almost time to call. She is exhausted from the housework and the stress. She has wished Mrs. Zhang not to return, for her to be left alone, and for Lisa to be found.

Annie ventures into Lisa's bedroom. She thinks about cleaning up; since Mrs. Zhang was the one who made the mess, it would be all right to clear it. Leaving it like this in the house clouds Annie's mind. It lingers like an open wound. The sooner she tidies it up, the sooner she can continue to her other duties. She thinks that if it is tidy, something will turn up.

She takes the books and the pencils and puts them aside. The dolls she places on the floor. She removes the bedsheet to wash and replaces it with a fresh one of sky blue. As she works the room, she remembers that Lisa enjoyed keeping an online journal; she showed it to Annie a few times, asking her not to tell her mother. Annie read some of the entries, which mostly dealt with school and friends.

Annie turns on Lisa's computer, peeking her head out of the window to ensure that Mrs. Zhang has still not returned. She opens the browser and goes through the history. Her heart is thumping faster. Computers are items that are not normally to be touched.

She finds the web address for the journal. Lisa's password is still saved. The last entry is from two nights ago, at about 8:15 p.m. It starts about being bored with schoolwork, and wanting to finish so she can call her friends. There are pictures of flowers and shaggy cats. There is a rant against her science teacher. There is a YouTube link to a music video which starts playing, and Annie starts to panic. Annie scrolls down, reading even more quickly.

She feels a certain chill in the air. She wonders if the aircon has turned on by itself. She reads on. There must be answers here.

There is an entry about being in the house alone on Sunday, and wondering where Annie goes. Annie feels slightly perturbed. She does not want her life outside of work to be known. The entry reads about how stupid Annie is, and how she puts too much spice in the food and works too slowly.

She reads on and finds something about hearing somebody crying. Lisa thought it was her mom at first, but the voice was not familiar. She was "creeped out" but thought it might have been a dream. Annie hears a sound now, a sobbing, from what sounds like inside the bedroom wall. She calls out, "Hello?" but does not hear a response. She continues to read but a sound above her grabs her attention.

She looks up and gasps. Pressed against the ceiling is a creature that smells of the rawness of the jungle. Annie knows it is the creature of her dream, the one with the long hair that came through the gate.

As it skitters down the wall like a gecko, Annie backs away. She picks up a book and holds it in front of her.

The creature stares at Annie with dead, black eyes. It is dressed in a faded frock that appears to have been washed and rewashed. Its skin is chalk pale, and its breath old and nauseating, like prawns left out overnight. It is an old thing, and there is a patience about it, as if knowing it will outlast her.

Annie is frightened, but her hands touch the cross around her neck as she drops the book.

"Where did you take her?" Annie asks.

"Where do you think?" it says. Its voice carries the cries of insects and night birds. "I did it to protect you."

"Why do you protect me? Please, let her go," Annie says.

"You know I have done it for you," the spirit says. Annie fears staring into the black orbs; she whispers the Lord's Prayer again in her heart.

"She is only a child," Annie says.

"She *was* a child," it says. Annie knows why it says the words it does. "If this is what you want, then it shall be."

"She might have done some wrong things but she can learn from them," says Annie.

The creature smiles, knowing how false her answer is. Annie realises the nature of this spirit, how it is formed from the spirits of others like her, from their prayers and dreams.

"I command you to release her," Annie says, ready to shout at it, hoping to deceive it into thinking that she is brave.

"Very well," it says.

The creature bends down and skitters away, so quickly Annie is unable to see it disappear. A light breeze blows into the room, and the curtain ripples. Coins of light flit along the bedroom wall. Annie presses her hand to the illuminated spot, and it vibrates, the feeling radiating through her hand, hard enough to rattle her bones. Her crucifix tingles. She thinks her arm is about to shudder loose.

The wall irises open into a hole large enough for a child to step through. Annie sees Lisa within the concrete. She reaches in and pulls Lisa out. Lisa is asleep, with fine sand-like scratches all over, but otherwise unharmed.

Annie thanks the spirit in her mind but it is already gone. The gap in the wall closes, as if it has never been there. She takes small steps so as not to wake Lisa as she places her on the bed. She is reminded of how she did the same when Emily was young.

She phones Mrs. Zhang and tells her that Lisa is back home. She hangs up before she is asked to explain why. She takes a towel, dampens it, and carefully wipes the concrete dust away from the girl's skin. Lisa's eyes open weakly; she turns her head and looks at Annie.

"Where was I? Can you get me some Panadol?" Annie nods. "Please bring warm water this time, not cold," Lisa adds sharply. "You always get it mixed up."

As Annie steps out of the room and falls back into her maid's role, she is reminded of the fierceness within Lisa. She thinks about the incident with the ruler, and the cruel remarks on Lisa's online journal. Annie knows that she is Mrs. Zhang's daughter, after all.

She reminds herself of Emily as she returns to the room with a glass of water and two tablets of Panadol, and then continues to wipe off the scars and scratches, even as she hears Mrs. Zhang's car storm through the gates. Annie braces herself, remembering what she must do for her daughter's sake, ready to face her employer's rage.

OPEN

Tan Ming Tuan

"The story of life is quicker than the wink of an eye."
—Jimi Hendrix

This story begins with a thud. The driver brakes immediately but it is a little too late. Under a flickering street lamp, a figure staggers from the bumper to the passenger door. A face appears at the window. The driver is relieved that he hasn't killed anyone. He asks the most natural question that a man who has hit someone with his car should be asking.

Are you okay?

Yeah. No problem, kid, no worry. Just a scratch, says the stranger.

Under the dim light, the details come slowly. A foreigner's face. The stranger is dark-haired, with a tinge of brown. A generous stubble sheathes the lower half of his tanned face and he speaks in a slightly broken English with an accent that is probably south European, maybe Mediterranean. The kid guesses that he is about as old as he is.

Are you sure you're all right? I'm really sorry, man. I was turning the corner and didn't see you.

No worries, says the stranger, his hands dusting off his sleeves. There is indeed a scratch on his elbow from where he fell.

Do you need a ride anywhere?

The stranger is on a stretch of road that one might call *ulu*, not a place you would normally find yourself at this time of the night unless you had been working overtime in the nearby office buildings. Suddenly, he regrets asking, but the invitation has been offered.

Could you buy me a drink?

Pardon?

A drink. Alcohol, like a beer?

It is not the request that is strange, but the context in which it has been asked that makes the kid hesitate. He plays it cool; life has been a little dull recently anyway.

I know a place nearby.

The stranger gets in, and buckles his seatbelt. Don't want to get fined or something, he says. A little joke.

The kid nods. A typical stereotype of this island, the many fines. No chewing gum. Too many laws. He wants to say something about it, but decides it would be too tedious.

So, where you from?

Querétaro.

Oh, Europe?

No, Mexico.

Ah, Mexican. *Hola, señor.*

Oh, you speak some Spanish?

Only enough to make people ask that question.

Ah, you funny guy.

Ten minutes later they pull up at the side of a small lane somewhere in Clarke Quay. Broken glass crinkles under the Mexican's shoe as he steps out of the car. A half-working neon sign glows weakly at the entrance. The font is indecipherable and guessing the actual name of the joint has become some kind of drinking game for the patrons of this bar.

So that is all you want? A drink?

Sí. That would be enough. Maybe two.

The bar is empty save for a few lonely people who obviously have nowhere else to go tonight. They take their places and the kid raises his hand to catch the attention of the waitress, who leans on the wall outside the restroom, texting on her cell phone. The bartender spots the hand out of the corner of his eye but shrugs and continues to polish the glasses with a grimy-looking "good morning" cloth behind his counter.

You come here often? asks the Mexican, amused by the treatment.

Sometimes, with my colleagues. It's always like that, but the drinks are cheap.

He expects the Mexican to ask him about his job next, the most logical route to making small talk, but instead the man leans back onto the couch and starts to hum a tune with his eyes half-closed. Feeling obliged to break the silence, the kid speaks.

So, what are you doing in Singapore?

Just passing through. I'm taking a year to travel Asia. *Ay-zee-ah.* He says this with a grand sweep of his hand which just covers the vicinity of the bar.

That's cool.

It is. Very nice. But expensive, no?

Yes, it is a little expensive compared to the rest of Asia.

The waitress finally approaches and they order the beers. The kid asks for two Coronas but the Mexican asks for his to be a Heineken.

Why don't you tell me a story, he says. His arm makes a gesture towards the kid, as if he was introducing him on a stage.

What kind of story? You want to know about Singapore?

No, tell me your own story.

Sorry, I don't get what you mean. We've only just met.

Countries have no stories. It is the people who have stories, I like collecting stories. I think we know each other well. You knock me over with your car and I ask you for a drink and now we are here, having a drink. Yes, I think we know each other well enough.

My story? The kid drains the bottle of its last drop, trying to stall for time while thinking of some story he can tell this strange man, who was probably drunk already when he picked him up off the asphalt. The kid has many stories to tell, of course, just like everyone else, but he has one story which he has never told anybody, a story that has been solely festering in his mind alone. A story that is him.

Well, I have one story that I've never told.

Then it is not yet a story. How can it be a story if no one speaks it? The Mexican chuckles at this thought of his. Sorry, go on, he says.

The kid picks up the second capped bottle of Corona. Holding the neck in his left hand, he casually rests his right palm on the cap and exerts just the right amount of pressure while tilting his hand to the right and letting the tips of his index and middle finger find an angle under the crimp of the cap. The gas hisses for a moment, like it is trying to tell a secret. The cap snaps open and drops onto the glass table. He takes a long sip.

The Mexican looks curious, but unimpressed. In India, I saw a man on the street open a beer bottle with his teeth, he says. And in Bangkok, there are ladies who open the cap with their—

Yeah, I've heard of those shows. The thing is, I've been able to open just about anything with my hands for as long as I can remember.

Anything?

Things that have the potential to be opened. A tight lid, a locked door, a stuck zipper. All kinds of things. My mother mentioned to me once that somehow I could open bottles and boxes lying around the house before I could walk, but she never talked much about it. In my school days, I would wander the corridors and stairwells, looking for rooms and storage closets to hide in. They were always open to me.

Open? Even if locked?

Yes. It is difficult to explain. Something like a special touch. It just happens.

But what's the use?

Use? The kid took another swig of the golden liquid. To me, it was my freedom. I could go anywhere. As a child I did not know what a locked door felt like. I went anywhere as I pleased, as long as nobody stopped me. I would go into buildings and take the lifts to the highest floors and tug at the padlocks, feeling the springs line up perfectly, the bolts release. Click. The rooftops were the best places to go. It's amazing how they are just there, you know? On top of almost every building, and yet few are lucky enough to find their way up there, unless there is a gate that the maintenance people forget to lock. Whenever my father came to visit I would run up the stairs and hide on the rooftop where no one could come after me, where I couldn't hear them shouting downstairs. I would lie on the edge and try to look for the stars. You don't see many stars at night in this city.

Your father, he leave your family?

I don't know what to call it. He just wasn't around. He came by once in awhile to leave some money. Every few months. As if trying to compensate for some mistake he made. I don't know what he did, didn't need to know. On the rooftops, I was free from all of that. None of that past could be imposed on me, and I am sure my mother wanted it that way too. I would come back a few hours later and the door would be locked. Mother usually left it locked so that father could not come barging in again. But she knew I'd find my way in somehow.

Locks. Do you believe in destiny, friend? asks the Mexican.

I don't know.

Well, it doesn't matter. Here, I have a thing you can help me with. The Mexican puts a hand into the pocket of his jeans and produces a small padlock that was once silver, now caked with rust, no bigger than a watch. There are some inscriptions on its face, and two diamonds linked together by a bold line.

The kid takes the padlock, turning it over and over a few times in his own palm and feeling its weight. He grips the shackle between his thumb and index and pulls sharply. There is a satisfyingly crusty click.

Found it on a beach in Vietnam, says the Mexican. Hit my toe when I walk on the sand. I thought it make a good souvenir and so I keep it in my pocket until now. Dong Chau beach. A little padlock travels from Dong Chau beach in this Mexican man's pocket to Singapore to be unlocked by this Chinese man in a bar on a Monday night. I wonder what other adventures this little lock had before I found it! Maybe one day I will find its key. Or maybe you are already the key. He seems amused by the thought.

The kid lays the padlock on the table. He was humming along to Santana's "Europa" in his car right before he turned the corner and nearly ran this man over.

Maybe we just like to attach meaning to everything that happens to us, says the kid.

Meaning, eh?

Our meeting is nothing more than a coincidence, and the padlock is merely convenience, maybe luck, if that is what you believe.

Then your gift, power—whatever it is called—is coincidence?

It is just something I happen to do, nothing more.

Do you believe in God?

Maybe.

Ah, but how do you think you have this power?

So you think God exists?

I know God exists, but now, which one? That is the problem. Your story, if it is true, just imagine what you could do.

It is true. You've seen enough to know.

Maybe, but I dare not hope for much. Things change for you, I can tell.

If you'll let me finish my story.

Please, go on.

As I grew older, I realised that there were other things that could be opened. Not just doors and tight lids. I caught only glimpses at first. It would happen if I let my gaze linger on someone for too long. It was like opening a gap in a window. A breeze would flutter through, and I would be looking at a person. A human being.

Otra vez, por favor, says the Mexican man to the waitress. She glares at him. He makes a circular motion with his finger around the empty bottles on the table. Excuse me, go on.

When you think of a person, someone you've known, the first thing you think of is usually the face, am I right?

Unless I am blind.

And when you stare at a face for too long, sometimes they start to look unfamiliar, their eyes and nose and mouth don't make sense, do you ever get that feeling?

Sí, sí. I know what you mean.

It started slowly at first. I learned that every person had a different scent, a sort of colour. Their faces seemed to fall apart to me, as if it was no longer important. No longer needed. I could see people for something else besides their faces.

You talk about scent. Like a smell?

No, it was more of a feeling. Instinct, something basic. The more I tried it, the better I got at it. I didn't understand it at first, I could not understand what it was supposed to mean. Or if it was meant to have meaning any more than the spaces between our two eyes are supposed to have a meaning. We were in

263

difficult times, me and my mother. She lost her job and father was the only reason we could still live in that flat. One day, as she was sitting by the kitchen window, where she liked to get lost in her thoughts and daydream about the past, I saw it, the whole window of her was wide open.

Saw what?

Soul. Spirit. Heart. Whatever you called it. The raw essence of a person.

Ah, the soul maybe. What was it like?

A mess. A real mess. Just one huge, tangled mess of experiences and emotions and motivations and dreams and nostalgia. Too much going on. I felt nauseated. I couldn't make sense of everything but what I could make sense of, that was enough.

What scared me the most was the uncertainty, the uncertainty that was in the soul. I always thought that my mother knew everything, and when I realised that she didn't, that's when I understood I couldn't be a child anymore.

After that, I had trouble unlearning what I had learned. I stumbled around for weeks, months, gazing into every person I saw, opening every window, trying to find some kind of meaning to it all. I even walked into temples, churches, mosques, trying to look for a God in the worshippers. I didn't find much.

Maybe you were looking in the wrong place.

Maybe. Anyway, this spark, this thing that made us who we were, I was searching for some noble purpose behind its existence. Perhaps you could even say that I was trying to find the meaning of life when I was fourteen years old. I was hungry and I could not stop even if I wanted to.

How did you stop, then?

I just got tired. One evening I gazed into a mirror, into myself for the first time. You cannot imagine how much courage it took, to bare my soul to myself. I was afraid of what I would find. Afraid of finding a stranger in myself.

But what I saw was everything I knew myself to be, and a little extra. It was like re-reading a book. A sense of familiarity along with some things you didn't really notice the first time. That was when I realised, people are who they are. It didn't matter really matter what was inside me. People say that it is what's on the inside that counts, but what is the use if it stays inside forever? Like this story that has not been told.

How could I be any much more than what people saw of me, what they expected of me? The soul defines the person and the person defines the soul. And our existence is defined by the existence of others. Like crisscrossing threads. A single thread holds little meaning but add a few more and it is part of a pattern. After I understood that, my gift became less special to me. Perhaps I had seen all that I had needed to see. That is my story.

Interesante. You do me the favour?

The kid opens another bottle for the Mexican.

Never seen anything like it. Maybe I tell you some of my story, in exchange.

Sure.

The Mexican talks about his own life on the ranch in Querétaro, and the smell of fresh tortillas on cast iron by the family cook who was hired because he had experience working for the drug lords. That's how they knew he was good cook: he still lived.

He talks about moving to the city to study, and how he would skip all his classes and lie in the grass outside the cafeteria all day, waiting for dinner time. Sometimes the mariachi would pass by and he would ask them for a song. He still got his degree.

He talks about an uncle who liked to sit on the porch of his cabin on the ranch after dinner and watch the horses trot in the light of dusk. His uncle would ask him, with tears in his eyes: Where have all the owls gone? *¡Los búhos!* The Mexican always wanted to know what his uncle meant but it was too late now. Maybe you are right, he said. There is no need for meaning in everything.

The kid sees that the Mexican is getting tired. The stories start to slow down. The kid has work the next day. He can't spend the whole night listening to stories, but he has told his own and that is enough.

It's late. I have to get some sleep.

The Mexican sits and stares at the ceiling, perhaps not knowing what to say next, or not having the courage to say it.

Could you...open me?

I thought you might ask that, the kid says. I'd rather not; it might be too much for you.

Why is that?

You see, when I open people, they are usually unaware of what is happening to them, that I am looking straight into their being. How do I explain it? To open you now, with your full knowledge, would be like putting you through an operation without anaesthetic.

Painful?

Not physically of course, I don't know, I've never really done it before this way.

Then how would you know?

I just...know.

Do me a favour, do it if your story is true.

The kid is uncomfortable with the proposition, but what the heck, he thinks. He takes a deep breath, and closes his eyes. It has always felt like untangling a knot, a simple knot, that's all.

The Mexican feels a strange twisting sensation in his gut. It is over in a second, the longest second of his life. This must be what people mean when they say that life flashes before their eyes, he thinks. In that second, he feels naked, his whole self exposed and laid bare for the scrutiny of the world.

But there is only the kid. There is nowhere to hide, suddenly the Mexican is back in the desert where he used to follow his father on camping trips. He sees a million versions of himself, strung up on clotheslines stretching into the horizon under the searing brightness of two white hot suns. Not a single shadow is cast. He opens his mouth, and so do the million others, each telling a different story, a different secret, talking about all these things which he has lived through, but now he hears them as if for the first time. The noise is deafening, he finds himself speaking and telling every single truth about himself to the sky, his hopes and fears and every good and bad thing he ever did because the soul is made up of these things and but also more, much more.

Suddenly, he is back in the bar. The ceiling fan still spins noisily above, its motor clogged by years of dust built up in its cogs. The world goes by as if nothing has happened.

Don't try to tell me what you saw, just don't, he says to the kid. The kid was right, it was maybe too much.

Like I said, there is nothing in you that you don't already know.

The Mexican tries to think about what he saw in that moment, but realises he can barely remember it, like a dream slipping out of his mind.

Yes, I understand, I understand now. Thank you. Well don't worry about me, my room is not far from here, I can walk. Goodbye, kid.

They part at the entrance of the bar. The Mexican doesn't look back; he strolls down the dimly lit street whistling a tune. For a while, the kid watches him, listening to the tune. He thinks it is "Europa," but the whistling isn't very good and maybe it is not. The worldly man walking the world, meeting the world, carrying his world in a backpack, he thinks. The kid tried it once, but reality was always the stronger force. He tries to open his car door but it remains locked. He shrugs and takes out his car keys.

Somehow the kid has always known that this would be how it ends. The story is the power, and as he told it to the Mexican, he felt the world closing in on him, this special freedom of his dissipating. Strangely, it feels good to be in a world now where boundaries exist for a change, where locks need keys and some things are just meant to stay unopened.

The Mexican continues to wander through the region, collecting many more stories from locals and travellers, but none are as strange as the one told to him by the man who almost ran him over. That kid. The opener.

One day he decides that it is time to head home, and he has also run out of money. The padlock is still in his jeans; he has not taken it out of his pocket since he left that bar in Singapore. As he sits in an airport watching the planes take off one by one, wondering which one is his, he toys with the lock in his pocket. He clicks it shut, and tries to open it again. The shackle hesitates at first, then it opens, and so does everything else for the rest of his life.

Many years later, when the Mexican has his own family and enjoys sitting on the porch overlooking what was once his uncle's ranch, he thinks of buying a ticket to Singapore, to find the kid who told him the story. Then he realises there would be no meaning in it; he has misplaced the padlock he found on that Vietnamese beach many years ago, and that story is now his to tell and that is all.

ZERO HOUR

Cyril Wong

Aishah could not wait to get out of bed. She rushed through her morning shower, but did not forget to take the required amount of time to condition her hair. She liked it that her hair was soft and fragrant after every shower. The conditioner she applied, before she washed it off, filled the bathroom with the smell of fresh flowers. After she came out from the bathroom, she picked out a white blouse from her cupboard and decided to couple this with a pair of black jeans. Then after blow-drying her hair, which had grown too long and was slowly becoming unmanageable, she tucked it all back with a dark hair band, and delicately put on her *tudung*—pale blue, her favourite colour. It was a Saturday and she had planned to meet her friends at Bugis Junction for breakfast. They would then shop until lunch, and after that she would meet Khairul—it would be their fourth date today—for a movie. They had not yet agreed on whether they would watch the latest Bollywood romance, or some Hollywood film about Greek gods and hunky mortal-heroes at war with each other; they would probably argue a little about it before he would give in to her preference for American movies and even offer to pay for the tickets. He was sweet like that. She met him in her second year of university, during which they had both decided to major in political science after taking a few modules together. She knew he found her attractive, and was intrigued by the seeming contradictions in her personality, such as the contrast between her argumentative nature during tutorials, and her pious, religious self outside of school. She just thought he was hot. The fact that he was gentlemanly, kind, and a smooth-talker, merely added to his appeal.

Just as she stepped out of her flat and walked to the lift, she wondered if perhaps the jeans she had chosen were too tight for her waistline, or too uncomfortably snug around her butt; she really had to watch her weight if she wanted to keep herself attractive for Khairul. When the lift door opened, a sudden sense of foreboding crept into her, followed by an unexpected chill. It was a bright morning in Bedok North and the air was predictably humid; there was no reason for such a chill to enter her body. The empty lift stayed open, waiting. *What was that about?* Shrugging off any lingering sense of unease, she rode the lift all the way down to the ground floor. When she arrived at the void deck downstairs, the feelings of uneasiness returned. She looked around the neighbourhood and wondered where everybody was. There were similarly tall flats on either side of her but nobody was hanging out in the void decks or heading out. Even the nearby streets were empty of vehicles. It was a clear day and she was the only one here—not that this was really anything in particular to be worried about. Maybe everyone was still asleep. It was a weekend morning, after all.

As she walked to the Bedok train station, her uncomfortable feelings became harder to suppress. It was not possible that nobody else was up at this time of the day! That playground where annoying children would play, while their maids or grandparents watched, was deserted. The two familiar swings were not even moving, even though she distinctly felt a mild breeze. She looked up at the flats in the distance, and saw no one standing at the windows, hanging laundry or just peering blankly out into the sky. There was not even the faint sound of children laughing, crying or being reprimanded by their parents. It was all very still and way too quiet. Judging from the slight perspiration gathering at the edge of her forehead, made warm by the *tudung* hanging slightly over her eyes, Aishah decided that this could not be a dream. Surely one did not perspire in dreams, right? She kept on walking, but a little faster this time. It was not that she was in any hurry, yet instinct buoyed her along.

She walked and walked until the train station came into view. It crouched like a frightened animal astride a twin pair of roads leading in opposite directions; a mall squatted impassively beside it. The closer she walked to the station, the more she knew that something was not right. Usually, from where she stood now, she would be able to see commuters waiting for the train on the elevated, open-air platforms. But nobody was in the station. She turned to look in another direction, whirling a little too violently, in an attempt to affirm an earlier subconscious thought that had been born secretly within her. People were also shockingly absent from inside the bus interchange across the street. This helped explain why the white noise of buses leaving or coming did not penetrate her ears, the grind of their engines that would normally add to a general buzz of activity from commuters restless in their organised queues. The only buses that she saw were all parked in an orderly fashion, without any intention to drive off anywhere. The whole place was impossibly quiet. *Ghostly*, she thought, hating the word instantly.

But how could this be? At the same time, Aishah could not stop herself from walking to what she was now certain to be a deserted station. She stepped tentatively into the station, rode the escalators—even with nobody else riding them along with her, they seemed to be operating just fine—then she moved past the turnstiles, which stood curiously open, and paused, at last, on a deserted platform. She noted that there was no sign of any train arriving or departing. She gazed out and squinted into the distance, hoping that if she stared hard enough, a train would appear. Soon a childhood fantasy—a slightly sick and disturbing one—replayed itself in her mind, about what it would be like to jump off from the platform and play along the railway tracks, even touching the track itself, electricity jumping all the way into her. It would be the best time to play out this fantasy for real, as nobody would see her. Was this some half-buried suicidal tendency that had lingered within her since she was five? Or just a universally-acknowledged, morbid curiosity; one shared by all but denied, or repressed, by everyone? Aishah instinctively folded her arms. She decided to wander up and down along the quiet platform, her body sliding through the heavy stillness like a knife.

Call Nora! a small voice at the back of her mind shouted. She stopped. She had forgotten that she had a mobile phone in her pocket. Nora was one of the friends that she had planned to meet today. She reached into the front pocket of her jeans, which was difficult since her jeans had become too tight for her, and yanked out her iPhone. She touched the numbers on the screen, and placed the phone against her ear, waiting for a ringing tone, instead receiving only a numb silence. She looked at her phone. There was not even any reception. She waved the phone up in the air, half-believing that this might help in catching some phantom wave of connectivity. She brought the phone back down to her face so that she could see the screen again—there was still no reception. "Fuck," she uttered, out loud this time, and before she could stop herself. She seldom used such language, especially not when there were other people watching her. "But there's no one here!" she shouted. Her voice had a strident ring to it. And why shouldn't she shout? Who would care or hear her anyway?

But still she turned around to look, just to make sure no one was there. A frightening thought came, that perhaps there was someone, after all; somewhere in her peripheral vision, hiding perhaps under the bench, watching and waiting. Was she afraid of being heard to swear? Or was it something else altogether that scared her? An image from a movie popped into her head in that instant, a man in a mask crouching under one of the nearby benches; a mask with huge goggles, behind which the man's face would be green, slightly decomposed, or maybe there would be no face at all— *Stop it! How childish and stupid!* Maybe this was an elaborate prank or something. Or had everyone left the country in a state of emergency and all without telling her? But how? And why? Had something happened last night? Why was she utterly unaware? Had there been an announcement on the evening news? And what about her parents? Were they at work or had they left too, leaving their only child behind? She could not call them on her mobile; that was surely out of the question now. But how about a public telephone? They still had those around in the station, right? She always saw Bangladeshi construction workers making overseas calls on those phones, or Burmese and Filipino maids, during the weekends.

Aishah could feel her heart running a little faster. She dug into one of the pockets of her jeans to see if she had any coins. She always left crap in her pockets, sometimes torn movie tickets or leftover scraps of tissue paper. She found a ten-cent coin and immediately ran from the platform area, racing down the escalators, which moved at an eerily steady speed. She quickly found a row of pay phones just to the right of the bottom of the escalators. At the corner of her eye, she noticed that nothing had changed; there was still nobody entering the station, and nobody loitering outside in the brightening sunlight. The morning was already coming to an end and afternoon was slowly closing in. Was there a chance that Nora and the others were still waiting at

Bugis Junction for her to show up? Were they going through what she was going through at this present moment? Or had they vanished too? Was she the only one left in this godforsaken country?

But first things first: she picked up the pay phone, pushed in her coin, and dialled her mother's number at the travel agency where she had worked for twenty years. At first she heard a sustained ringing tone, but then the line went swiftly dead. "What the—!" she exclaimed uncontrollably. The same happened with each pay phone on either side of the middle one that she had used. On the left phone, she pressed the number for her father's school where he taught Malay studies, and then on the right phone, she dialled Nora's mobile number again. All the phones refused to work. Still gripping the handset in her fist, Aishah let it rip from inside of her: "What the fuck is going on— you motherfucking *bastards!*"

She was stunned by her outburst. Who was she cursing at anyway? A part of her felt relieved at having shouted, and only for a moment. Another more distant part of her noticed that her voice had echoed from the corners of the empty station in an unsettling way. She let the handset drop from her hand. It swung uselessly on its cord. Aishah took a breath, followed by another. Without knowing why, she peered up at the ceiling. There was no sky above, only the train station ceiling. She started to pray. In her mind, she composed the words haphazardly, "Please help me find my parents! I love them and if they find me missing, they'll be worried sick. Please help me find my friends. And Khairul...*won't you stop fucking with me so I can go on my date with Khairul!*"

Not surprisingly, there was no reply. In the past, when she used to pray at the mosque or at home, she would imagine that a deep baritone voice—full of love and warmth—would answer her with reassuring platitudes whenever she was stressed at school or after a fight with her parents. Perhaps that voice was silent because she was too pissed off, even if she was only angry in her own mind, an anger now wildly projected to that anonymous entity which had made this universe, the same entity that was allowing this madness to continue around her. She looked back down from the ceiling, and realized that she had put on the wrong pair of shoes by mistake when she stepped out of her flat this morning. She had wanted to wear the black ones, not this orange pair that clashed with the colour of her head scarf. What would Khairul think if he saw that her clothes and shoes did not match? She closed her eyes and squeezed them shut for as long as she could. Then she opened them again. She looked around—there was still no one around. She sighed. Her heart was no longer beating as quickly as before. What was she to do now? She looked out at the sunlight streaming into the train station entrance, and decided she would wander back out of the station. She stopped when her shoes landed dully on the warm pavement outside. "This is the worst day of my life," she lamented, softly under her breath.

Maybe the whole country's population had been abducted by ugly, green-faced aliens. Or crazier still: maybe she was dead, and the reason she could see nobody else was that, as a ghost, she was simply not able to? Maybe the dead wandered the planet alone because they were detached from the living and had no more part to play in daily life. Maybe the living were around her now, just that she could not see them, and she could only move through them as though *she* were the only one here. If this was true, then where were the other ghosts? Wouldn't there be others that she would encounter along the way? Or were ghosts destined to drift in complete solitude, in some sadistically-arranged, purgatorial state? Was there some lesson she was supposed to learn by being alone in this phase of her supernatural journey? And then what would happen after this momentary hell (if it was at all momentary)? Heaven? Rebirth? Or just a gnawing, soul-sucking void? No god or even a minor deity to greet her with open, loving arms. Just a relentless fade to black, an endless falling into an infinite nothingness...

As these fragmented thoughts wafted in and out of her mind, another angrier and more urgent thought pushed through: if she were dead, why was she still perspiring? She touched her forehead, and her fingers made contact with sweat. In an uncontrollable fit of rage, she grabbed her *tudung* and tore it off her head. Clutching it for a moment in her fist, she flung it to the ground, and as she stormed away, she made sure that her wrongfully-chosen shoes crushed it further in passing. She also pulled off her hair band and threw it away as she continued to walk on without any direction in mind. Then she began to cry. The tears came forcefully and seemed to have burst through a thick dam that had been built up inside her. With hair falling over her face, she wiped the tears away with the back of both hands, and kept on walking. She was slowly making her way out of Bedok now and entering a different neighbourhood; not that this neighbourhood looked any different from hers. The surrounding flats appeared the same as the flats she had passed before; dull-coloured, with the jarring picture of some national flower half-heartedly painted onto one side. Another identical train station loomed in the distance. As usual, nobody watched her approach from the elevated platforms. No trains arrived or left to break the silence. But Aishah noticed none of these things. She just kept striding forward, crying unstoppably.

Finally, the midday sun wore her down. She had to stop and catch her breath. A low steady hum entered her ears. Her tears subsided. Curiosity made her gaze back up at the sky. What was that sound? Where was it coming from? The hum started from an exceedingly low pitch, then rose ever so slightly, and settled on an even tone. Swelling in volume, the humming seemed to rise out from the very ground beneath her. She even felt it vibrating in her chest. It felt peculiar, but not necessarily discomforting. She turned in a frantic circle and looked around the deserted neighbourhood. There was nothing that alerted her to the potential source of the sound. The hum was growing even louder now; soon it would be deafening. She looked up again. An unexpected breeze caressed her hair. But there was nothing in the sky, even though she half-expected to see something—maybe a plane or a helicopter, even a flying saucer or some crazy shit like that.

Instead, the cloudless sky was brightening. The entire canvas of sky arching above her was turning from blue to white. Yet there was no real change in the level of heat pressing against her face. Maybe whatever had come to claim everyone else was coming back now for her, realising that by some bizarre error during their epic calculations, they had forgotten all about Aishah, the girl who was supposed to grow up to be a schoolteacher like her father, to get married to a handsome and kindly man and have four children with him, to live with her family in one of the newly constructed flats in Tampines, to retire by fifty-five and watch her own children grow up to be lawyers, bankers, even politicians. What else could they do in this country? How else would they be able to support themselves—*and* their aged parents? The light continued to burn up the sky and seemed to erase her surroundings with every second. Although she was becoming blind from all the light, Aishah refused to close her eyes; she wanted them pulled wide open. She wanted to be ready for whatever it was that would take her away from here. The humming sound was truly deafening now. She tossed her head back and flung her arms wide open, without hope—and resolutely without fear. She was not even aware that she was crying again. She had never before felt this alive, or so unspeakably light and free.

CONTRIBUTORS

Carrick Ang is currently training to be a professional film animator. Besides prose writing, he also dabbles in graphic design and illustration, as well as other forms of storytelling. He believes fantasy stories are true and slightly slanted reflections of reality-at-large. If you were to offer him a mojito, he would probably not refuse you.

Ivan Ang's writing has appeared in *Ceriph* vol. 1 and 2, *MAGE*, and *Mobtoon Magazine*, and was one of the winners of the microfiction competition at the 2007 Singapore Writers Festival. He was a webcomic artist until 2008, and designed the merchandise and clothing catalogue for Disney/Pixar's *The Incredibles* for Walt Disney Singapore in 2004. He is currently the Deputy Head of General Paper at Anderson Junior College. You can follow him on Twitter at @Agonized_Writer. "The Digits" is his second published piece of speculative fiction.

Shelly Bryant divides her year between Shanghai and Singapore, working as a teacher, writer, and translator. She is the author of two volumes of poetry, *Cyborg Chimera* and *Under the Ash*, and travel guides to the cities of Suzhou and Shanghai. Her third volume of poetry, *Voices of the Elders*, is slated for release in 2012. Her most recent projects include translating Sheng Keyi's novel *Northern Girls* for Penguin Books. Shelly's poetry has appeared in journals, magazines, and websites around the world, as well as in several art exhibitions. You can visit her website at shellybryant.com.

The Centipede Collective was formed when the Pen and the Eye decided that dreaming of alternative realities was far more weird and wonderful than being stuck in the current one. The Collective deals with all things irrelevant and irreverent in a closed-loop of creativity. The Pen (Brandon Chew, writer) thinks in black ink and white space, and the Eye (Olivia Lee, designer) prises the whimsical out of the banal. Together, they create the concepts that redefine the universe. Bring ramen.

Andrew Cheah writes short stories when he feels a single sentence is not enough. He has been published in *GASPP: A Gay Anthology of Singapore Prose and Poetry*. Other stories can be found at andrewcheah22.wordpress.com.

Dave Chua's first novel, *Gone Case*, received a Singapore Literature Prize Commendation Award in 1996, and was recently adapted into a two-volume graphic novel with artist Koh Hong Teng. Chua's latest book, *The Beating and Other Stories*, was longlisted for the 2012 Frank O'Connor International Short Story Award. His speculative fiction has appeared in publications such as *ChiZine* (where it won second prize in their 2010 short story contest) and *Innsmouth Free Press*.

Marc de Faoite is a semi-fictional character who occasionally appears through wormholes in the space-time continuum to feature in the ongoing drama known as life. He was born, bred and buttered in Ireland, but has spent more than half his life living in England, Belgium, France, India and currently Malaysia, where he lives a quiet, reclusive life on Langkawi island. In 2011 he had two stories featured in *Sini Sana: Travels in Malaysia* and one in *The Irish Times*. Besides writing short stories, he likes to drink tea and listen to the frogs singing in the paddy fields at night.

Noelle de Jesus has an MFA in Creative Writing from Bowling Green State University in Ohio, and has won a Carlos Palanca Memorial Award for her short fiction. She has published short stories in the region and in the US, a children's book and a chick lit novel. She is wife to a banker who writes as well, and mother to two teenage budding writers who are writing better than she did at that age. To make a living, she is a freelance editor, journalist and copywriter. She has lived in Singapore since 2000. "Mirage" is her first piece of speculative fiction.

Isa Kamari graduated with B.Arch. (Hons) from the National University of Singapore in 1988. He obtained an M.Phil in Malay Letters at the Universiti Kebangsaan Malaysia in 2008. He has written eight novels in Malay, three of which have been translated into English. He has also produced two collections of poetry and written song lyrics, scripts for theatre and television drama serials and documentaries. In 2006, Isa was conferred the S.E.A. Write Award in Bangkok. He is a recipient of the Cultural Medallion and the *Anugerah Tun Seri Lanang* Malay literary award.

Justin Ker is a doctor in the Department of Neurosurgery at Tan Tock Seng Hospital. He won the 2nd prize for fiction in the 2011 Golden Point Award contest.

Grace Chia Kraković is the author of two poetry collections, *womango* (Rank, 1998) and *Cordelia* (Ethos, 2012), and served as the 2011-12 Writer-in-Residence at Singapore's Nanyang Technological University. Her poetry and short stories have been published in *Singapore Literature in English: An Anthology*, *Mining for Meaning*, *The Straits Times*, *SilverKris*, *Awareness*, *WOW*, *Di-Verse-City* (US) and online journals *HOW2* (US), *Stylus Poetry Journal* (Australia), Walleah Press online and *Flying Inkpot*.

Wei Fen Lee is the co-editor of *Ceriph*, a literary print journal based in Singapore that promotes the work of emerging writers and artists. She is also a freelance writer and researcher of South Asian diasporic literature in Southeast Asia. She recently co-edited *Coast* (2011), a mono-titular anthology of poetry and fiction by three generations of writers from Singapore.

Archaeologists first discovered **Jeffrey Lim** in 1999, where digging on a book named *Faith & Lies* (Ethos, 1999) unearthed 17 stories containing speculative fiction, and stories of hope and despair. Further work into this obscure personality, yielded little in further artefacts until a collection called *The Coffin That Wouldn't Bury* (Ethos, 2008) provided 20 more pieces described as an "assault on reality, blurring the distinction between insanity and imagination." Little else is known, but rumours of this once-extant civilisation are scattered across the roughly grown weed field of Singapore literature. Further discoveries await.

Jason Erik Lundberg (editor) is the author of several books, most recently *The Alchemy of Happiness* (2012) and *Red Dot Irreal* (2011), as well as the founding editor of *LONTAR: The Journal of Southeast Asian Speculative Fiction*, and co-editor of *A Field Guide to Surreal Botany* (2008) and *Scattered, Covered, Smothered* (2005). His writing has appeared in over 50 publications in five countries, and he has lived in Singapore since 2007. You can find him online at jasonlundberg.net.

Ng Yi-Sheng has published four books, including *last boy* (which won the 2008 Singapore Literature Prize), and a novelisation of the award-winning movie *Eating Air*. His shorter stories have been published in *Crime Scene Singapore* and *GASPP: a Gay Anthology of Singapore Poetry and Prose*. He currently teaches creative writing at NTU, reports for the queer website *Fridae* and the kids' newspaper *What's Up*, and co-organizes the monthly performance event SPORE Art Salon. He's also co-editing a collection of stories based on Asian folktales, titled *Eastern Heathens*. He blogs at lastboy.blogspot.com and tweets at @yishkabob.

Victor R. Ocampo lives on a diet of science fiction, fantasy and postmodern literature to counteract the reality of living in clean, clinical Singapore. He credits his wife, Patricia, for planting the seed of writing fiction in his techno-organic soul, for being both his muse, as well as his (merciless) editor. Victor is also father to two lovely daughters, Isabella and Sophia, as well as master and psychiatrist to Prince Zardos, their neurotic, time-displaced dog. "Big Enough for the Entire Universe" is his first published short story in Singapore; his fiction has previously appeared in the anthology series *Philippine Speculative Fiction*.

Ben Slater has been living in Singapore for over a decade. He's the author of *Kinda Hot: The Making of Saint Jack in Singapore* and his writings on film have been published internationally. He has script-edited several feature films including *Helen*, *HERE*, *Endless Day*, and *Mister John*, and is co-writer of the sci-fi thriller *Camera*. To read more, visit gonetopersia.com. "Punggol" is adapted from the audio journey *Punggol 2021*, which can be downloaded and listened to at Ghostwalking.sg.

Born in 1989, **Tan Ming Tuan** is a student of Communications and New Media at the National University of Singapore. In his free time, he is a hobby writer and guitarist for local band Strait Groove. "Open" is his first published work.

Cyril Wong is the Singapore Literature Prize-winning author of *Unmarked Treasure* (Firstfruits, 2004), *Tilting Our Plates to Catch the Light* (Firstfruits, 2007), *Let Me Tell You Something About That Night: Strange Tales* (Transit Lounge, 2009), and *Satori Blues* (Softblow Press, 2011).

Jason Erik Lundberg

Daryl Yam is currently reading English Literature and Creative Writing at the University of Warwick. His work has been published in literary journals *Ceriph*, *Quarterly Literary Review Singapore*, and *Cha: An Asian Literary Journal*, and has contributed writing to *The New Paper* and AWARE. He was also a mentee in the Ceriph Mentorship Programme's prose category. He blogs at yamscribbly.wordpress.com and tweets via @yammonation.

JY Yang is a scientist-turned-writer-turned-journalist who gets the odd SF/F short story published every now and then. She likes chicken rice and furry hats. She blogs at misshallelujah.net and has lived in Singapore all her life, in the company of the occasional Pomeranian and an overactive imagination.

Yuen Kit Mun is a freelance writer, photographer, and hopeless movie buff. He has tried to write, and then abandoned, at least four science fiction novels. A post-zombie-apocalypse novel set in Singapore is his latest futile attempt. Influences include Joss Whedon, J.J. Abrams, Michael Crichton, Neal Stephenson, William Gibson, George R.R. Martin, David Eddings, Michael Mann, Shane Black, Steven de Souza, Brian Helgeland, Lawrence Kasdan, Akiva Goldsman, Mamoru Oshii and Matthew Vaughn.

MORE FROM INFINITY PLUS

Strange Mammals
by Jason Erik Lundberg

"Jason Erik Lundberg's stories, launched from the real world on a trajectory to the surreal, fuse the idle daydream with the desperate heart. You should read them." —John Kessel, author of *The Baum Plan for Financial Independence and Other Stories*

Strange superheroes and the magic of the quotidian; stories of piercing darkness and quirky, surreal humor; writing from the heart and soul; phantasmagorical journeys into what it means to be human.

Strange Mammals collects together stylish and elegant short fiction that knows no boundaries. Stories that are by turns fantastical, realist and strange, but which always move and surprise.

A breathtaking collection from an author whose writing "explores the randomness of magical occurrences" (*Green Man Review*) and "teems with imagination, location, originality, and fine writing" (Jeffrey Ford).

**For full details of infinity plus books
see www.infinityplus.co.uk**

The Fabulous Beast
by Garry Kilworth

A set of beautifully crafted tales of the imagination by a writer who was smitten by the magic of the speculative short story at the age of twelve and has remained under its spell ever since.

These few stories cover three closely related sub-genres: science fiction, fantasy and horror. In the White Garden murders are taking place nightly, but who is leaving the deep foot-prints in the flower beds? Twelve men are locked in the jury room, but thirteen emerge after their deliberations are over. In a call centre serving several worlds, the staff are less than helpful when things go wrong with a body-change holiday.

Three of the stories form a set piece under the sub-sub-genre title of 'Anglo-Saxon Tales'. This trilogy takes the reader back to a time when strange gods ruled the lives of men and elves were invisible creatures who caused mayhem among mortals.

Garry Kilworth has created a set of stories that lift readers out of their ordinary lives and place them in situations of nightmare and wonder, or out among far distant suns. Come inside and meet vampires, dragons, ghosts, aliens, weremen, people who walk on water, clones, ghouls and marvellous wolves with the secret of life written beneath their eyelids.

"Kilworth is a master of his trade." —*Punch*

"Garry Kilworth is arguably the finest writer of short fiction today, in any genre. " —*New Scientist*

"Kilworth is one of the most significant writers in the English language. " —*Fear*

**For full details of infinity plus books
see www.infinityplus.co.uk**

Ghostwriting
by Eric Brown

Over the course of a career spanning twenty five years, Eric Brown has written just a handful of horror and ghost stories – and all of them are collected here.

They range from the gentle, psychological chiller "The House" to the more overtly fantastical horror of "Li Ketsuwan", from the contemporary science fiction of "The Memory of Joy" to the almost-mainstream of "The Man Who Never Read Novels". What they have in common is a concern for character and gripping story-telling.

Ghostwriting is Eric Brown at his humane and compelling best.

"Brown is a terrific storyteller as the present collection effectively proves...All in all an excellent collection of entertaining and well written dark fiction." —*Hellnotes*

"Eric Brown joins the ranks of Graham Joyce, Christopher Priest and Robert Holdstock as a master fabulist" —Paul di Filippo

**For full details of infinity plus books
see www.infinityplus.co.uk**

Genetopia
by Keith Brooke

Searching for his missing sister, Flint encounters a world where illness is to be feared, where genes mutate and migrate between species through plague and fever. This is the story of the struggles between those who want to defend their heritage and those who choose to embrace the new.

"A minor masterpiece that should usher Brooke at last into the recognized front ranks of SF writers" —*Locus*

"I am so here! *Genetopia* is a meditation on identity – what it means to be human and what it means to be you – and the necessity of change. It's also one heck of an adventure story. Snatch it up!" —Michael Swanwick, Hugo award-winning author of *Bones of the Earth*

"Keith Brooke's *Genetopia* is a biotech fever dream. In mood it recalls Brian Aldis's *Hothouse*, but is a projection of twenty-first century fears and longings into an exotic far future where the meaning of humanity is overwhelmed by change. Masterfully written, this is a parable of difference that demands to be read, and read again." —Stephen Baxter, Philip K Dick award-winning author of *Evolution* and *Transcendent*

**For full details of infinity plus books
see www.infinityplus.co.uk**